The Other World's Books Depend on the Bean Counter

Bean Counter

Depend on the Bean Counter

MAGIC RESEARCH EXCHANGE PLAN

3

YATSUKI WAKATSU

ILLUSTRATION BY
KIKKA OHASHI

YEN ON
New York

The Other World's Books Depend on the Bean Counter

3 YATSUKI WAKATSU

Translation by Kim Morrissy
Cover art by Kikka Ohashi

ISEKAI NO SATA WA SHACHIKU SHIDAI Vol. 3
MAHO GAIKO SEIJOKA KEIKAKU
©Yatsuki Wakatsu 2021
First published in Japan in 2021 by
KADOKAWA CORPORATION, Tokyo.
English translation rights arranged with
KADOKAWA CORPORATION, Tokyo through
TUTTLE-MORI AGENCY, INC., Tokyo.

Yen On
150 West 30th Street, 6th Floor
New York, NY 10001

Visit us at yenpress.com
facebook.com/yenpress • twitter.com/yenpress
yenpress.tumblr.com • instagram.com/yenpress

First Yen On Edition: March 2025
Edited by Yen On Editorial: Leilah Labossiere
Designed by Yen Press Design: Liz Parlett

Yen On is an imprint of Yen Press, LLC.
The Yen On name and logo are trademarks of Yen Press, LLC.

The publisher is not responsible for websites (or their content) that are not owned by the publisher.

Library of Congress Cataloging-in-Publication Data
Names: Wakatsu, Yatsuki, author. | Ohashi, Kikka, illustrator. | Murphy, Jenny (Translator), translator.
Title: The other world's books depend on the bean counter / Yatsuki Wakatsu ; illustration by Kikka Ohashi ; translation by Jenny Murphy.
Other titles: Isekai no sata wa shachiku shidai. English
Description: First Yen On edition. | New York : Yen On, 2024. | Contents: v. 1: Holy maiden summoning improvement plan
Identifiers: LCCN 2023047036 | ISBN 9781975364342 (v. 1 ; trade paperback) |
    ISBN 9781975373733 (v. 2 ; trade paperback) | ISBN 9781975389208 (v. 3 ; trade paperback)
Subjects: CYAC: Fantasy. | LCGFT: Light novels.
Classification: LCC PZ7.1.W3466 Ot 2024 | DDC [Fic]—dc23
LC record available at https://lccn.loc.gov/2023047036

ISBNs: 978-1-9753-8920-8 (paperback)
        978-1-9753-8921-5 (ebook)

10 9 8 7 6 5 4 3 2 1

LSC-C

Printed in the United States of America

The Other World's Books Depend on the Bean Counter

CONTENTS

CHARACTER INTRODUCTIONS

SEIICHIROU KONDOU

A workaholic who got caught up in the Holy Maiden Summoning and transported to another world, Seiichirou proved his skills when he started working for the Accounting Department. However, his body reacts badly to the magic that permeates the other world, and he falls sick easily, so his lover Aresh always protects and takes care of him.

ARESH INDOLARK

Commander of the Third Royal Order and the son of a marquess, sometimes called the "Ice Nobleman." When he meets Seiichirou, he falls in love and gradually becomes more expressive, inspiring others to look upon him fondly.

LARS ERIC EGOROVA

Third-born prince of the northern kingdom of Egorova. Has a beautiful, doll-like face. He visits the Romany Kingdom as a diplomat for cultural exchange purposes. He is interested in Seiichirou.

CAMILE KARVADA

The levelheaded, shrewd, and capable prime minister, said to be the most powerful person in the Romany Kingdom. He has a high opinion of Seiichirou's abilities and is pretty much guaranteed to involve him in vital tasks.

YUA SHIRAISHI

A high school girl who was summoned as the Romany Kingdom's Holy Maiden. Although she was initially taken advantage of for her ignorance, she has now adapted more to her surroundings and works to support the church, among other things.

YURIUS ROMANY KASLOVÁ

The firstborn prince of the Romany Kingdom and first in line to the throne. Although he initially coddled the Holy Maiden out of his infatuation for her, she remains clueless to his feelings, and he is now pestering others with his love problems.

Prologue

Back when he lived in Japan, his mornings followed a routine: His alarm would ring, he would bury his head in his soft pillow and, after lingering for a short while, get up, and wash his face. Then he would put on the kettle, have some instant soup and salad for breakfast, then some coffee. He didn't really get hungry in the mornings, but since people were always telling him that skipping breakfast was a terrible idea, he always tried to put *something* in his stomach. After that, he got dressed, left the house, and got on the train, making sure he got to the station a little early to avoid the dreaded packed train cars. This meant he got to work much quicker, although he never bothered to stamp his time card then. He just got started ahead of everyone else and stamped when they came in.

Such was his life.

"Is there something you want to say?" a handsome black-haired young man demanded from across the table. He was known as the "Ice Nobleman" in high society and the "Black Beast" to the kingdom's knights and foreign armies. Aresh Indolark, commander of the Third Royal Order, inspired that kind of trepidation.

"Oh, nothing," said the assistant director of the Royal Accounting Department, who was on the other side of the table, separated from Aresh by a white tablecloth. He had black hair and eyes, and his features didn't particularly stand out except for the bags under his eyes. His name was Seiichirou Kondou, and he was summoned from Japan to the Romany Kingdom alongside the Holy Maiden.

Ten months ago, he had been on his way home from work (even though technically it was his day off) when a girl named Yua Shiraishi—the aforementioned Holy Maiden—screamed. He rushed to assist her... and wound up getting dragged with her to another world.

The kingdom only needed the Holy Maiden. Seiichirou, the tagalong, was just a nuisance. Yet they couldn't leave him to rot, so they came up with a plan to keep him around and support him with a basic stipend. This all changed when they asked him what he wanted. He answered, "A job," and went on to show his talents at the Accounting Department.

The situation became even more complicated when Seiichirou became ill from the magicules permeating the air. Since his body had no tolerance for the magic of this world, he developed acute poisoning and collapsed. It was Aresh who came to his rescue. He refused to stand by and let Seiichirou's workaholic nature exacerbate his frailty.

Aresh's protective instincts only grew as he looked after Seiichirou. Eventually, he became convinced that only *he* could tend to the otherworlder, and he insisted on buying a house and living together.

Seiichirou, for his part, felt smothered by Aresh's overprotective behavior, but he owed his life to the man. Besides, Aresh was the only person in the world to demonstrate true, genuine concern for his well-being. Sometimes, he revealed a childish side that belied his appearance, which Seiichirou found very endearing. And so, after many twists and turns, they became romantic partners.

"I doubt it's *nothing*. There's always something you're upset about whenever you go into a long spiel," Aresh declared, as if nothing could be more obvious.

Seiichirou grimaced in embarrassment. Their romantic relationship was still in its early days, but here Aresh was, seeing right through him. Even before, he'd always had a keen grasp of the fluctuations in Seiichirou's expressions. People always said that Seiichirou was a hard fellow to read, but Aresh had been carefully observing his physical condition for quite a while.

"Are you unsatisfied with your life here?" Aresh asked, lowering his tone slightly.

Seiichirou promptly shook his head.

"How could I be? You and so many others have been treating me well."

This was the truth. Valtom, the butler who had cared for Aresh since his infancy, was genuinely considerate toward Seiichirou, as was Milan the maid and Pavel the chef. They meticulously prepared meals light on magicules, which meant that Seiichirou could build enough of a tolerance to eat most foods without trouble. Just having people around who cared about his lifestyle was a massive improvement over his days spent in Japan as a salaryman.

"What is it, then? Say it."

Aresh must have figured out from the way the conversation was going that *he* was the source of the other man's discontent. Seiichirou knew it, too. *Now what?* he asked himself.

His partner got unexpectedly hung up on small things—so much so that he was still insecure about something Seiichirou had once said to get people off his back about his relationship with the Holy Maiden: *"I'm not romantically interested in younger people."* Seiichirou intended that to mean that he was never going to see Yua in that light, nor was he into children with no experience in adult society.

Seiichirou wasn't planning on mentioning what was currently on his mind. It wasn't such a serious topic that it deserved an early morning discussion. But the mood was bound to turn sour if he insisted on staying silent. Seiichirou sighed, and then took another breath.

"I'd like to stop sleeping on your arm."

Aresh's estate was situated in a corner of the nobles' district, not terribly far from the royal palace. But that still meant walking some distance compared to the nonexistent commute time from the residence hall, where Seiichirou had once stayed. Not that many people in the nobles' district actually walked—Seiichirou normally commuted by carriage, and he shared a ride with Aresh if their work happened to start around the same time. Going home together, however, was mandatory as long as Aresh didn't have any pressing business. Nevertheless, knights and civil officials lived in different worlds. Couple this with the lack of fixed working hours within the palace, and that meant Seiichirou and Aresh rarely showed up together. Seiichirou preferred it that way, since the two of them were bound to draw attention if they suddenly made a habit of it.

Today was no different in that respect. Aresh was off duty, so Seiichirou headed to the palace by himself. The whole business about arm pillows remained up in the air; Seiichirou expected a rehash when he got home. Before they became partners, Aresh would forcibly ensure that Seiichirou stayed in bed instead of slipping off to work, but now that they were officially in a relationship, Seiichirou had no qualms about sleeping in the same bed. After some discussion, they settled on making love twice a week, although Aresh insisted on sleeping together every night. Seiichirou had no problems with that either. Aresh wanted to touch Seiichirou whenever he had the opportunity, and their intimacy improved Seiichirou's constitution.

The problem was that it was rather uncomfortable to sleep on a person's arm. Nothing more or less.

Although the well-toned Aresh said he had no problem offering his arm to sleep on, that didn't make it a comfy pillow. It was a human arm, and a muscly one at that. If pressed, Seiichirou would admit a preference for soft pillows over hard ones. Besides, an arm couldn't compare to a tool specifically made to aid sleep. Now that he was over thirty, Seiichirou's body ached the next day whenever he slept uncomfortably. Being a young and fit man in his early twenties, Aresh found it difficult to wrap his head around this, Seiichirou knew, but it really was a strain on his neck and shoulders. When

Seiichirou said as much, Aresh made his usual suggestion to cast a healing spell and do some you-know-what to acclimatize him to the magic. Seiichirou brushed that off and left for work—and that about recapped his morning.

As convenient as magic was, and despite Aresh's immense talent and capacity for it, it was still an imposition on the younger man.

Seiichirou really didn't want Aresh casting magic on him outside of life-threatening situations. His attitude was rooted in his upbringing in a world without magic. The road to mutual understanding was long and steep.

"You're early, Kondo," a well-built man called out to him when Seiichirou stepped off his carriage.

"Good morning, Commander Radim."

It was Radim Makovska, commander of the Second Royal Order, who was charged with protecting royalty and other key figures. Seiichirou often saw him serving as Crown Prince Yurius's bodyguard. They first became acquainted after members of the Second Royal Order assaulted Seiichirou, so Radim was often extra considerate whenever they interacted.

"You don't look too good. Did something happen?" Radim asked, examining Seiichirou's face.

"No, just an ache in my neck from sleeping at a funny angle."

If anything, Seiichirou's overall condition had never been better. Thanks to the efforts of Aresh, Pavel, and the others, his health was much improved, but he still looked sickly in Radim's opinion, apparently.

"His Highness wishes to ask you something about the private school at the relief house," Radim said.

"I have a meeting with the Sorcery Department today. Would His Highness be open to discussing the matter tomorrow or later?"

"...I'm sure you have things to do, but...you know he's the crown prince, right? Oh well, I don't think it's urgent. I'll pass on your message."

Given that Radim wouldn't have popped the request if they hadn't bumped into each other, Seiichirou figured that he could put it off for another day. Judging by Radim's attitude, Seiichirou was probably right.

"Please submit a request for an appointment time and place to the Accounting Department."

"Fine."

Seiichirou was the first to arrive at the Accounting Department. On the insistence of others, he was taking some steps toward delegating his work, but this was the one habit he couldn't shake. He found it easiest to relax and focus in the mornings, when nobody else was around.

In the past, the Royal Accounting Department merely existed to affix seals to whatever inflated budget requests came their way, but after Seiichirou reformed the budgeting system, new tasks came flooding in. The previously laid-back office, once derided as "the Funnel Department," was now treated as a respectable department in its own right and had expanded accordingly.

In this way, Seiichirou's life in the other world could largely be described as peaceful.

CHAPTER ONE

Appointed

About once every one hundred years, miasma would appear in the Romany Kingdom, and a Holy Maiden would show up to reverse the damage. The current Holy Maiden was Yua Shiraishi, Seiichirou's fellow Japanese. With training, she was able to purify the Demon Forest of its miasma. It was Seiichirou's idea to seal off the forest altogether.

Although many attempts had been made over the years to fell the trees, the ones that produced miasma were invulnerable to physical attacks. Striking them simply made them spew more poison.

Given that only the Holy Maiden's purification proved effective against the miasma, Seiichirou's suggested alternative was to seal off the entire area and monitor it, but it was an ambitious plan that required both facilities and manpower. Specifically, it required people who could create magical barriers while also being highly resistant to magicules. On top of this, Seiichirou was also involved in a plan to develop summon reversal magic, along with educating the children in the relief house and other impoverished children. The latter was partly about fulfilling Yua's wishes, although Seiichirou also saw it as a way of headhunting for his other projects. This meant an ever-increasing workload, which his overprotective knight commander wasn't too happy about, but Seiichirou believed that it was all necessary to achieve his goals.

"Wow, Sei. Your workload is still insane," said Norbert, who had recently taken up teaching arithmetic to the children at the relief house school.

Norbert Blanc was Seiichirou's frivolous young subordinate, complete with a magnificent crop of golden hair. It was an open secret that he was the king's bastard child, though neither he nor the company he kept seemed to care. He lived comfortably with Count Blanc, his adoptive father, and seemed relatively content with his circumstances.

"I handed off the private school work to you, and we've got more staff now covering other areas," Seiichirou pointed out.

"But there's still the stuff that only you can do, which is like three times more than what a regular person does."

Three times was an exaggeration in Seiichirou's opinion, but judging by all the fervent nodding from other Accounting Department members, that seemed to be their standard.

Seiichirou did not pay this any mind. Although he had been covertly bringing some of his work home, he was at least taking his regularly scheduled days off.

"It might be 'overwork' to moonlight in other departments or go on expeditions, but what I'm doing now is manageable enough."

"Yeah, back in the old days you used to come waltzing into work on your days off... But you've still got bags under your eyes."

That was because he was getting old—although even Seiichirou had enough dignity not to say this aloud.

In any case, Seiichirou found satisfaction in ticking straight-forward tasks off a list. He was in good health, and his work proceeded at a comfortable pace.

"Sorry for summoning you while you're at work."

An antique table and a perfectly firm sofa. An indigo-blue curtain with golden embroidery. And a fine-looking man with pink-blond hair. It was Camile Karvada, prime minister of the nation.

I'm getting major déjà vu here...

It was not Seiichirou's first time in Camile's office. In fact, they saw each other quite frequently. Camile was essential for Seiichirou—a humble civil servant—to get things done.

But such meetings were scheduled in advance as part of Seiichirou's regular workflow. It had been quite a while since the last impromptu summoning... The last was when he'd been sent to investigate the church.

Seiichirou was about to stifle the alarm bells ringing in his head and give a polite greeting when he noticed the smile in Camile's eyes. The other man appreciated Seiichirou's good instincts.

Camile's blue-gray eyes twinkled in amusement. "I'll get to the point. A foreign delegation will be coming to the palace."

"A foreign delegation...?"

Needless to say, the Romany Kingdom wasn't the only country in this world. Seiichirou had studied the global geographical layout before, though it was easy enough to be convinced that Romany was the center of the world. Its land was vast, and it was blessed with a good climate aside from the miasma. It was an economic and agricultural powerhouse, notable for the divine blessings it received from God and the Holy Maiden.

"Have you heard of Egorova?" asked Camile.

"I believe it's a cold country to the north? It has many mines, allowing for the robust production of magic stones. The study of magic and magic tools is quite advanced there..."

"You've certainly done your homework."

Being a southern country, Romany's climate was mild. It hardly snowed outside the mountainous areas, even in winter, nor were the summers humid like they were in Japan—instead, they were dry and crisp.

By contrast, Egorova was very snowy. Seiichirou had read in a book that snow covered the ground there for half the year. There were plenty of mountains to extract magic stones from, and apparently quite a lot of research went into developing tools to counteract the cold. It sounded like their people enjoyed a high quality of life, but Seiichirou was personally glad that he had not been summoned there. He had never liked the cold.

"Egorova, you see, has asked to do a cultural exchange with our country," Camile said.

Egorova was a magic-driven nation, and conducted its research separately from other countries. Much of its "culture" in that regard was highly confidential. In other words, Egorova wasn't inclined to share its technology.

So if it was proposing a cultural exchange, then...

"They're interested in our movement spell research," Seiichirou said.

The corners of Camile's lips turned up—a silent yes.

Movement spells were Seiichirou's ticket home, hence why he devised a plan to invest in further developing its techniques. More to the point, it would invalidate the need for a Holy Maiden to seal the Demon Forest. This meant that Romany would sacrifice its unique reputation as a country blessed by the Holy Maiden to pursue the path of magical technology.

The fact that Romany was advancing its magic, from movement spells to barriers, must have leaked to other countries.

"And you spearheaded the project," Camile said.

When he put it that way, then...yes. But Seiichirou was just acting out of self-interest. Besides, he didn't possess a lick of magical knowledge. In fact, the stuff was poison to his body. One could easily say that he was the *least* magical person in the entire world. Moreover, Norbert's adoptive father—Count Blanc—was the one who had officially taken credit for coming up with the idea, which would technically make Camile the ringleader.

"Count Blanc would of course have participated in the exchange, but he is currently occupied in the hinterlands and can't make it," said Camile.

Seiichirou mulled this over. "So the Egorovan delegation will be here within the next few days."

"Yes. They'll arrive in five days."

"Five days?!"

Seiichirou's eyes went wide in a rare display of emotion. He expected it would be soon, but not *that* soon. If the envoys were coming in five days, it meant they'd already departed from Egorova, and it was impossible to delay. In other words, Seiichirou's fate was set in stone.

"I would have appreciated it…if you had told me sooner," Seiichirou said curtly, his mind whirling. How was he supposed to juggle these envoys with his regular work?

"Sorry," said Camile, not sounding very sorry at all. "This was the only day I could tell you without your black guard dog around."

"Oh…"

Seiichirou pictured the beautiful face of the man he'd bickered with that morning.

He'd be mad. Definitely.

He was already saying that Seiichirou's normal workload was too much. And given the dangerous pickle Seiichirou had ended up in last time when he was dispatched to the church, Aresh was especially keen not to let Seiichirou out of his sight. Although that wasn't *supposed* to be the case, seeing as Seiichirou was a grown, working adult and all, he couldn't exactly ignore Aresh after he had saved him on many previous occasions. More to the point, he didn't *want* to ignore his partner.

So, he had to figure out how he was going to spin this to Aresh.

Camile gazed at Seiichirou's meditative expression in amusement. Soon enough, though, his eyes flickered to the door.

"Rest assured that you won't be tackling this alone," he said, turning back to Seiichirou. "I've assigned a specialist to accompany you."

Seiichirou looked up at the same time a knock sounded at the door.

"My apologies. There is a visitor," an attendant reported.

"Good. Let him through." Camile nodded leisurely.

The specialist was…another co-conspirator in the project.

Realizing this, Seiichirou promptly stood from his spot in the middle of the sofa and shuffled over to the edge to make room.

The attendant opened the door, and the visitor strode in. His brown hair was parted directly down the middle of his head, and he sported an impressive beard. His clothing choices indicated his status as a nobleman, from the frills in his shirt cuffs to his upright collar. He had the girthy waistline of a man past his prime.

And finally...there was a long purple cloak running down his back.

Every department in the Romany royal palace had its own color. Royalty wore white. Prime Minister Camile and the other members of the Legal Department wore blue. Aresh and the Third Royal Order wore black, while the first and second orders wore red and green respectively. The Accounting Department, which Seiichirou belonged to, wore a nondescript brown.

The cloaks also indicated who was in charge. The department manager would wear a long cloak covering both their shoulders, while an assistant manager would wear a shorter cut over one shoulder.

Which meant that this portly, unassuming-looking man with the long purple cloak across both his shoulders was Zoltan Barre, head of the Royal Sorcery Department.

This was not Seiichirou's first time meeting Zoltan. They'd met at the dinner party held before the Holy Maiden went on her expedition to dispel the miasma. They also saw each other quite often at official meetings, although Seiichirou discussed most matters concerning the project with the assistant director, Ist. As a result, Seiichirou did not have much contact with Zoltan.

For his part, Zoltan probably wasn't a fan of how Seiichirou, a wet-behind-the-ears otherworlder, had landed a civil servant job— and a management role at that—not to mention how he kept bypassing Zoltan to talk to Ist. Right at this very minute, he was frowning up a thunderstorm after greeting Camile and noticing Seiichirou in the room. His expression all but said, "What are *you* doing here?"

Seiichirou did a polite bow and pretended not to notice the hostility.

"Thank you for coming, Director Zoltan. Why don't you take a seat?" Camile suggested.

"Yes, Your Excellency!" Zoltan didn't look too happy, but he responded crisply nonetheless and sat a short distance away from Seiichirou. The sofa was of high enough quality that it didn't sink at all under his weight.

"As I explained earlier, I would like you to escort the Egorovan delegation around. You'll be working with Kondo, the assistant director of the Accounting Department."

So Zoltan got a heads-up? Seiichirou's eyes flickered in Zoltan's direction—the man looked *very* displeased.

"That is a great honor indeed, although I was not aware that I would be accompanied by another person. And, well…"

He trailed off there, likely because he did not want to outright call Seiichirou's loyalties into question. Seiichirou kept his mouth shut; he knew perfectly well that he was an otherworlder who had never sworn his fealty to the country he now lived in.

Camile didn't say anything about it, either. "They're interested in our magic techniques," he said, changing the subject, "but they're also keen to see how our nation implements them. Director Zoltan, I can't think of anyone more reliable than you on the technical side."

"Yes, of course!" Zoltan replied promptly.

This exchange reaffirmed to Seiichirou why he had been called here, along with the immense scale of the task.

Basically, the envoys weren't just coming to observe the movement and barrier magic. They were also going to see the facilities around the barrier, the movement spell research, and so on. These visits required budgets and publicizing, which meant collating paperwork not just from the Accounting Department, but also the construction and PR-related departments.

There were five days to do this, including today.

Even if Seiichirou did the bulk of the work, he would have to leave the specialized sections to their respective managers. Although Seiichirou could handle the financial side of the equation, like hiring people for the barrier or calculating their salaries, he certainly couldn't explain the unique structures of the buildings. Likewise, he could estimate the economic effects of the movement spells, but he had very little understanding of what the research entailed.

"So which individuals from that nation will be coming to our doorstep?"

Zoltan's words snapped Seiichirou out of his reverie. Apparently, not even Zoltan knew much about the envoys. Camile was certainly not the forgetful type, so either he deliberately didn't mention it, or Zoltan failed to ask. Judging by the smile on the kingdom's wiliest man, Seiichirou strongly suspected the former.

"Ah, yes. The group will be led by Egorova's third prince."

∨∨∨

"Ugh, why do I have to work with an otherworlder?" Zoltan huffed once he was out of the Prime Minister's office.

Seiichirou said nothing in reply. He merely announced his schedule and left.

Mentally, he went over what he knew about Zoltan: director of the Royal Sorcery Department, portly, had a beard, a suck-up to his superiors. Although his magic techniques weren't anything special, he got the director's seat thanks to his family name. His attitude toward Seiichirou was unsurprising, though Seiichirou didn't take it personally. If anything, he would say that he respected Zoltan— because he was *Ist's* boss.

Everyone in the palace would agree that Assistant Director Ist— the man with frizzy pink and orange hair and eternally drowsy-looking peridot eyes—was the most knowledgeable person about magic in the entire Romany Kingdom. His zeal for magic research was unmatched, and he was the kingdom's foremost sorcerer in terms of controlling magical energy.

On the flip side, he was totally uninterested in anything unrelated to magic. His social skills were terrible. He didn't abide by rules—they probably didn't even register in his brain. Although he would talk animatedly about magic, barely even pausing to take breaths, asking him about anything else would only ever result in vague, noncommittal answers. His grasp on polite language was debatable.

But he was an exceptional mage and researcher. In just three days, he created a tool that could accurately measure magical energy. His talent could not be overlooked, and so he was given an official position, but naturally, that didn't change his ways. It was inevitably up to his boss, Zoltan, to clean up his messes.

Zoltan had probably never imagined that this would be the reality of his job, but he had no choice but to cover for Ist, given his incontrovertible successes. The fact that he never lost his dignity throughout all of this was, in itself, worthy of respect.

Between his mountain of tasks, Seiichirou somehow managed to make his requests to the other departments and report to the Accounting Department. Norbert offered to prepare the documentation, so Seiichirou let him. This meant that he could swiftly pick out which documents to take home and look through.

Five days... He finished all the tasks he needed to do before he met up with Zoltan in three days. First, he compiled the labor costs of those involved in casting the barrier around the Demon Forest, the construction fees for the facilities, and the maintenance costs. This was easy to accomplish. Although Zoltan's work was centered around the movement spells, the paperwork was originally created with the idea of persuading the country to act. The other departments covered the finer details, so Seiichirou just needed to collect their documents.

Yes, some things were higher priority than others, but the trick to multitasking was focusing on the easier goals first. At the very least, this lessened the overall number of tasks. Seiichirou found it easy to deal with straightforward numbers, and it was good to feel like he was accomplishing something. Adding the movement spells to the equation meant that he would have to deal with a lot of finicky paperwork related to the Holy Maiden.

And so, even though he left work on time, there was still a veritable mountain of things to do at home...but none were *the most* important task.

The carriage dropped Seiichirou off right at the mansion's door, which meant that he got home before dark. It had been chilly, but now the days were getting longer and warmer. If the seasons were anything like Japan's, then it was probably spring at the moment, which suited Seiichirou just fine. Romany's climate was milder than Japan's and the temperatures didn't fluctuate much throughout the year, but he still preferred warm over cold. As he passed through the garden, which was diligently maintained by a gardener who commuted from outside the mansion, Seiichirou also noted the increased presence of bright and colorful flowers.

Finally, he reached the mansion door, which someone had left open for him.

"Welcome home, Mr. Kondo." Somehow or other, Valtom the butler must have known exactly when Seiichirou would return, because he bowed elegantly as Seiichirou walked in.

Seiichirou was still not used to this sight, though he mustered a bow in return. "Thank you for the warm welcome."

Although Valtom and the other servants in the house treated Seiichirou and Aresh equally as their masters, Seiichirou felt too indebted to them to drop his polite speech. Having been a commoner for most of his life, he struggled to adjust to other people waiting on him hand and foot.

"Where is Aresh?" he asked.

"I have informed him of your return. He is presently in his study."

Aresh got grumpy whenever Seiichirou returned late. Apparently, Aresh's servants were in the habit of reporting to him whenever Seiichirou approached the house.

"All right," said Seiichirou. "Thank you."

He made a beeline for the study. Although he figured it was best for them to have a nice and calm chat after dinner or something, he wanted to use that time to get deep into work if he could. Besides, they'd had a bit of an argument that morning. He didn't want any lingering awkwardness.

Knock, knock, knock.

"Come in," a deep, hushed voice responded.

Seiichirou turned the bronze doorknob and went in. On the other side of a stately table sat a handsome, black-haired man—looking exactly as he had that morning.

"I'm home." Seiichirou gave his usual greeting. Although they were romantic partners, he figured that Aresh deserved to be informed as the owner of the house.

Aresh's brow twitched in surprise. Although Seiichirou was rarely inclined to speak his mind, he did address the little things once they'd been verbalized, but there was nothing in his tone that betrayed concern about their morning spat. Still, he had made good on his promise to Aresh to leave work at a reasonable time.

Aresh reached out for him and asked, "Are you over what happened this morning?" as he took Seiichirou's hand, pulling the other man a little closer.

Seiichirou did not resist. He took a step forward and rested his other hand on Aresh's shoulder. Aresh was taller by about ten centimeters, but since he was still seated, Seiichirou was looking down on him for once. There was something amusing about that. When Seiichirou idly ran his fingers through the younger man's hair, Aresh decided to put a stop to it by wrapping his powerful arms around his lover's waist and pulling him close. Before long, Seiichirou ended up sitting on Aresh's lap.

"Gosh, Aresh..."

"You're fine as long as your head isn't on my arm, yes?"

"What?"

Aresh must have been stewing on this the whole time Seiichirou had been at work. Although Seiichirou had said he had nothing against sleeping together, Aresh—the same man people called the Ice Nobleman—had been restless and fidgety for over half a day.

Seiichirou felt a pang in his heart. Affectionately, he pressed his lips against Aresh's temple. Purple, almond-shaped eyes met his. Then Seiichirou found his lips being pulled toward Aresh's.

"Mmf...Aresh?!"

Kissing on Aresh's lap was a precarious balancing act to begin with, but Aresh took the opportunity to slip his hand between them and undo Seiichirou's belt. Being more familiar with this world's clothing than Seiichirou, Aresh's hand removed the intricate, bulky belt with ease. Then he started peeling off Seiichirou's knee-length jacket.

"What? We're doing it here? I just got back from work..."

Seiichirou tried to pull away. He hadn't taken a bath, and he had no idea when Valtom or Milan the maid would call them for dinner, but Aresh's large hand yanked him right back in. There was enough force in the gesture that Seiichirou's feet no longer touched the floor, and he collapsed on Aresh's lap.

This was the most awkward position for him. Seiichirou hurriedly tried to regain his footing, only for one of Aresh's hands to stubbornly keep him in place. The other hand latched onto Seiichirou's shoulder, preventing him from moving his upper body around. In terms of physical brawn, there was a world of difference between them.

Finally, it bore mentioning that Aresh's lips hovered at Seiichirou's ear.

"Don't worry. Valtom and the others know when to be discreet."

His deep, husky voice sent shivers down Seiichirou's spine. Aresh was under the impression that Seiichirou's ears were sensitive, but the truth was that it was Aresh's *voice* that made him weak in the knees. Seiichirou tried vainly to withstand the sensation, sensing that things would only escalate if Aresh found out what he was feeling.

But then Aresh kissed and nuzzled the tip of his lover's ear, before adding his tongue to the equation. With Aresh's breath blowing directly into his ear, Seiichirou could do nothing to hide his trembling shoulders.

"Mmm… Ahhh…"

Seiichirou's shirt was already long gone. Aresh's large hands stroked his naked back.

With their bodies pushed together, Seiichirou could feel the telltale sign of Aresh's arousal through their clothes. His legs trembled; he couldn't stand up.

"Oh…geez…" He exhaled heavily.

"Hm?"

Resigning himself to what was to come, Seiichirou relaxed his body and entrusted his weight to Aresh. Begrudgingly, he wrapped his arms around the other man's neck and drew his lips to Aresh's ears.

"I have work tomorrow, so let's be reasonable about this, please."

"All right. I'll cast a healing spell."

Then their lips met once more.

∀∀∀

When he woke, he was in bed.

His body felt clean, and there was no hint of aches or pain. He did feel slightly dazed, though, which indicated that Aresh had cast a healing spell.

His head was resting not on Aresh's solid arms but his muscly shoulders. Aresh, still half-asleep himself, noticed Seiichirou stir and opened his eyes.

"...So you're awake."

Illuminated by the dim light, Aresh's naked body looked more erotic but also somehow more youthful than when it was covered by his black uniform. This was Aresh's unvarnished self, the side he only ever showed to Seiichirou.

Seiichirou searched his mind for what to say, before finally settling on: "...I told you to be reasonable."

"I cast a healing spell." They hadn't agreed on *that*; it was something he'd added after the fact. "Are you hungry? I can arrange something for you."

Glancing at the clock in the dimly lit room, Seiichirou realized that it was less than three hours before he normally went to bed.

He shook his head slowly. He wasn't that hungry, and he certainly didn't want to create extra work for Milan and Pavel at such a late hour.

Bringing his head from Aresh's shoulder to his chest, Seiichirou realized that it was much more comfortable and soothing to rest on than Aresh's arms. Perhaps it had something to do with the amount of muscle, or how it was more relaxed. As Seiichirou snuggled against Aresh's chest again, Aresh kissed his hair with relish.

Seiichirou decided that now was as good a time as ever to say his piece.

"By the way, Aresh, I'll be coming home late for a while. I've been ordered to guide the Egorovan diplomats around when they arrive in four days."

".........Excuse me?"

Ah, but still, Seiichirou was thinking all the while, *cotton pillows are better.*

∀∀∀

The royal palace had a main building where the bulk of administration took place. Since it was also where foreign visitors were received, it was both heavily guarded and resplendent in design, featuring lavish carpets that absorbed footsteps and sounds. But even those carpets groaned underneath the furious steps of a pair of black boots.

"C-Commander Indolark! You need an appointme—"

"No, I don't. Out of the way."

Aresh brushed aside the knight from the Second Royal Order and flung open the office door.

"Well, if it isn't Commander Indolark. May I ask what urgent matter brought you here without an appointment?"

The man on the other side of the desk must have guessed what the commotion outside was all about, or perhaps he had anticipated that this would happen. Camile, the office's occupant, leisurely took off his glasses.

The Romany Kingdom's strongest knight did not relax his glare.

"You know what this is about."

Even this blunt declaration did nothing to chip away at Camile's smile. Only his blue-gray eyes flitted away—to look at the man behind the fuming knight.

"Sorry, I couldn't restrain him," said Seiichirou, not sounding terribly apologetic as he poked his head out from behind Aresh's black cloak.

"That's no good, Seiichirou. You need a proper hand on the reins." With that mild declaration of exasperation, Camile stood up from his seat.

Seeing this, an attendant ushered Seiichirou and Aresh to the sofa.

"I did try…" Seiichirou said.

"Ugh… Just when I thought you were staying put, you pull this on me! You sly fellow!" Aresh said to Seiichirou.

"Isn't that slyness his strong suit? Oh, and I'd love to hear about what he did to placate you." Camile sent an amused yet undeniably lascivious gaze in Seiichirou's direction.

Aresh's mouth drew into a tight line, and he put Seiichirou

behind him. As Camile's shoulders shook with uncontainable laughter, he bid the two to sit down once more.

Once they were reluctantly seated, an attendant put tea in front of them. Aresh grabbed Seiichirou's hand just as he was about to take the cup. Only after Aresh had sniffed the tea and taken a sip did he say, "You can drink it."

"It's like you're testing for poison," Camile remarked.

"The tea here has made him ill before."

"Really? Sorry about that, Seiichirou."

"Oh no, it was quite a while ago," said Seiichirou, feeling sheepish about the belated apology, "and I was careless at the time."

It had happened over half a year ago, back when he'd had barely any magicule tolerance to speak of. Now that he'd built up a fair amount of resistance, he was fine with anything barring magicule-heavy indulgences like alcohol and tobacco.

"But, well, I hope you can refrain from such behavior while the visitors are around. It could cause diplomatic issues," Camile said, steering the conversation back on topic.

Aresh's eyes reignited with fury. "Does our country possess such a shortage of civil officials that it must dispatch a man with no magic resistance to guide foreign envoys around on a *magic* observation tour? Bearing in mind that his constitution is so delicate that even his tea drinking must be monitored."

"Ha-ha-ha, have your dalliances with Seiichirou made you chattier?"

The old Aresh disliked small talk and only engaged in the bare minimum of conversation. Although one could say he lacked the social acumen of a nobleman, he more than made up for it with his martial and magical talents.

"Don't change the topic. I'm asking why you picked *him*." Despite his coarse manner of speaking to a man with an equivalent rank to Japan's prime minister, their standings were more or less the same in a country where the government and military hierarchies were independent of each other.

"Well, now… I'm sure *you* understand Seiichirou's work better than anyone, yes?"

It was all thanks to Seiichirou that the kingdom had started research on movement spells and a system for funding it. In terms of pure credentials, nobody was more suitable for the task. Frankly, if Seiichirou had been in Camile's position, he would have made the same call.

"I…do understand. Yes." Aresh shot a glance at Seiichirou.

When Seiichirou gave him a little nod, Aresh was relieved and the tension on his face eased. He understood that Aresh wasn't trying to slight or underestimate his work. Yes, Seiichirou was the most knowledgeable about the subject at hand, but the issue was about his status as an otherworlder and his incompatibility with magic.

A diplomat—and a prince, no less—had to be met with someone of equal standing. It was strange for the role to be filled by an Accounting Department middle manager with no claim to nobility.

"It doesn't take much to kill him," Aresh commented. "Remember that he almost died in that church incident."

"He'll have a proper guard this time around," Camile said.

"I was not aware of that."

This comment came from Seiichirou.

He had assumed that Zoltan and some assistants from the Sorcery Department would be tagging along, and that was about it. But a guard meant someone from the Second Royal Order, and Seiichirou did not mesh well with that group.

He'd had a nasty run-in with them before, when some of the members exacted their vigilante justice on him for perceived rudeness toward the Holy Maiden. The only positive things to come out of that experience were the damages paid and the political leverage he got out of it. Between that and Commander Radim trying to rope him into supporting a romantic relationship between the prince and Holy Maiden, Seiichirou was much happier staying as far away from them as possible.

"Then I'll be his guard."

What on earth was Aresh saying? Seiichirou inadvertently squinted at the man next to him.

Aresh belonged to the Third Royal Order—and he was the commander, no less. Being well-versed in magic, the Third Royal Order occupied a special place among the knighthood. They mainly existed to defend the kingdom against the external threat of magical beasts.

They were frontliners, basically. Not bodyguards for random civil officials.

"You? The commander of the Third Royal Order?" Camile was wide-eyed, too.

"This is a vital matter for the future of our kingdom." Was Aresh trying to claim that his involvement was justified here?

"Yes, I know that you and the Third Royal Order are magic experts, but you've got too many frontline duties to tackle matters inside the palace, too."

"This tour will have a major effect not just on our kingdom's plan to develop magic but also our diplomatic relations going forward. The Third Royal Order is indispensable to such important matters of the state."

"Oh my, and so that's why you're offering the Third Royal Order's full support on this occasion?"

Uh-oh! This is—

Seiichirou tried to grab Aresh's arm, but the other man answered quicker.

"Of course."

Oh nooooo...

The curl in Camile's lips was not lost on Seiichirou.

The man had successfully baited them.

"I won't accept anything else!" Aresh growled under his breath, his hand on the table clenched tightly into a fist.

Seiichirou could only sigh. In retrospect, Camile had them dancing on his palm the whole time. It didn't matter whether he handed the role to Seiichirou on Aresh's day off, because Seiichirou was bound to tell Aresh anyway. It was clear that nothing Seiichirou could have said would mollify the young man.

The job itself was of national importance, and Seiichirou's necessity was an undisputable fact. Aresh wasn't so foolish as to argue blindly against that. And so Camile had stoked Aresh's protective instincts—to manipulate the kingdom's elite magic knights into taking on a duty outside the frontlines.

Third Royal Order Vice Commander Orjef Rhoda raised his hand. "Nah, I'd say I'm the one who's unhappiest about this," he declared as he observed his dejected commander and the sighing Accounting Department official.

They were in Aresh's office.

"I heard there were Egorovan envoys coming. And I knew that the otherworlder—Kondo—was involved." Orjef paused there, glancing up again at his cousin and senior officer. "But why do *I* have to be a guide?"

Come to think of it, the last time Seiichirou had been in Aresh's office was when everyone apologized for that assault incident. Each commander of the knight order had their own office outside the knights' station. Aresh's wasn't as big as Camile's, which was devoted to office work, but it still had an impressive-looking desk, bookshelf, and a space for visitors to make themselves comfortable. It was similar to Aresh's personal room in the sense that it was filled with simple yet high-quality items and decorative swords.

In contrast to such luxury, however, the room's inhabitant still had his head in his hands. His fists were clenched, and his gaze was downcast. He wasn't saying a word.

"So...what's going on here?"

It was fair to say that only Vice Commander Orjef, who had been summoned to the office without warning, had his head held high.

The very fact that Orjef Rhoda was the vice commander of the elite Third Royal Order was a testament to his talents as a knight. He was also capable of handling clerical matters, as evidenced by how he used to take care of the paperwork and odd jobs that Aresh had avoided before he met Seiichirou. Finally, being one of Aresh's blood relatives, he was the only member of the knights who could speak frankly to the commander. He was an invaluable man indeed.

"The prime minister has ordered that you serve as a guide for the Egorovan envoys who will be arriving in four days," Seiichirou answered for the still-dejected Aresh.

Orjef turned his auburn and blue eyes in Seiichirou's direction. "That sounds backward. Wasn't it that *you* were supposed to be the guide and I was supposed to be the guard?"

"Given my involvement in the movement spell project, I expect that I will be tasked with explaining the logistics to the diplomats. However, we are dealing with a large nation, and apparently the main diplomat will be the third-born prince of Egorova himself."

"Say what?!" Orjef blanched—he'd only heard that the diplomats would be from Egorova, not that they were royals. After a pause, he said, "...Okay, now I get it. So I'll be the one in the line of fire *and* I have to protect you."

"I'm glad you're quick on the uptake."

Orjef was right.

Although Seiichirou was unusual in the sense that he was from another world, he was no Holy Maiden. At the end of the day, he was just a civil official. He was not a good fit for guiding the prince of a foreign nation around. At worst, it might be interpreted as a slight.

And so Orjef, the vice commander of the elite magic knights and the son of a count, would ostensibly serve as the guide, while Seiichirou would offer supplementary explanations...but the reality was the opposite. Seiichirou was the guide, and Orjef was his guard.

This way, Seiichirou would be squeezed for all he was worth while Romany's two most powerful magic organizations would equally shoulder the burden. And hierarchy would be observed as well, which would keep Egorova happy.

"All right, I get the Prime Minister's thinking. But why me and not Aresh? Isn't the Sorcery Department's director showing up personally?" Orjef asked bluntly.

Aresh's head sprang up. "Exactly!" was practically written across his face.

"Don't be like that, Aresh. Remember what you were told?" Seiichirou reprimanded him softly.

"......" Aresh said nothing. He looked away again, his brows knitted in consternation.

"What was he told?" Orjef posed the obvious question.

After a short silence, Seiichirou answered:

"Aresh and I are too close."

Camile's reasoning was more or less the same as when he assigned Seiichirou to the church investigation.

"You see what I mean?" the prime minister had said in the office. "I've told you before that your *closeness* to Seiichirou, an otherworlder, could be seen as a political bias. And that would be a problem, wouldn't it?"

It could cause needless misunderstandings and interfere with the project. As someone who prized efficiency, Seiichirou felt tempted to apologize for the trouble.

"Besides, this job is going to affect future international relations. We wouldn't want to expose the weakness of one of our most valuable players to a foreign country, now would we?"

"Good point..."

"I have to admit..."

It bore mentioning that Seiichirou assumed that the "player" was referring to Aresh, the young and brilliant commander of the Third Royal Order. Meanwhile, Aresh assumed that this was about Seiichirou, whose wit and ability to get things done had sparked a revolution in the kingdom.

For just a moment, Camile's face flickered with an indescribable expression—he had an inkling of what the insufferable duo was thinking.

He sighed, and his next words made the two men stiffen.

"If you're going to be like that, you might as well get married and make your partnership official."

"…………"

"…………"

Both Seiichirou and Aresh fell silent after giving Orjef a very brief summary of that conversation as explanation. Orjef eyed them suspiciously as they looked away, but that perspective had quickly made sense to him.

It's clear as day that Seiichirou's completely under Aresh's protection, he thought, *so of course a lot of people would get the wrong idea.*

He understood that high society was full of people who would nitpick others and make up stories to drag them down. Aresh was impervious to such talk, but the frail otherworlder was bound to attract negative attention. To be fair, it was too late to backtrack given that people had seen them eating together in the dining hall every day. Nor was it a secret among their acquaintances that they lived together. But if the story got out in a more public way, then yes, there could be trouble.

"In any case, let's find somewhere to talk. There are a lot of things I ought to tell you, Vice Commander Orjef," Seiichirou said more stiffly than usual, in an attempt to dispel the slightly awkward atmosphere.

Instead of the man who was being addressed, Aresh reacted first.

"Hang on. This is a fine enough place for a meeting. Why do you have to leave?"

"This is *your* office, Aresh. I'm sure you have work to do, so I ought to take my leave."

"It's fine. You can stay."

Seiichirou took a deep breath. "……No. I need to check some documents which I don't have on hand. My apologies to Mr. Orjef," he said, turning to the man, "but we must go to the Accounting Department…"

"R-right…"

A fresh recruit would have flinched under the pressure of Aresh's foreboding silence, but Seiichirou did not budge an inch. Orjef was the one getting secondhand psychic damage from this exchange.

"Uh, isn't this office fine?" he blurted out, cracking under the pressure. "Aresh said as much."

But the frail-looking otherworlder curtly dismissed him. "No. There would most definitely be interference. Let us go."

Interference? He had to be talking about Aresh, no two ways about it.

Orjef was baffled. He had never seen anyone treat Aresh like *that*.

"I have four days," said Seiichirou, before correcting himself. "No, I must assemble all the paperwork for the meeting with the Royal Sorcery Department by tomorrow. I'll need to brief you as well, if only on the basics."

Even if Orjef was only there for appearances, he'd embarrass the Romany Kingdom if he couldn't answer simple questions.

In any case, time was of the essence. Seiichirou had to focus on the job.

Orjef left the room, glancing at Aresh's sour expression as he went. Then, as he made for the Accounting Department, he looked down at the man walking beside him.

He had a plain face and an unremarkable hair color. He was a fragile man whose fatigue was evident in the permanent bags under his eyes. Just by looking at him, it was impossible to imagine that he had been chosen to represent the kingdom in an interaction with a foreign power.

But...

"Vice Commander Orjef, as I mentioned to you before, I will be meeting with Director Zoltan of the Royal Sorcery Department in two days. I ask that you attend."

"Er, um, sure."

"I have until tomorrow to hand in all the documents. Today, I'll be compiling information about the movement spell's efficacy and the research and labor costs."

"......" Orjef said nothing. He was starting to truly understand this man's brilliance.

"Is something the matter? Would you like to drop out as my guard?" Seiichirou asked smoothly, as if he thought nothing of it.

Something clenched in Orjef's heart.

"No. Why would you even think that? And hey, even if I wanted to drop out, who would replace me?" he asked, knowing full well that they needed someone who excelled in magic, came from a good family, and was strong enough to protect Seiichirou. There weren't too many people around who fit the bill. "Aresh can't do it."

"I have been told that the Third Royal Order has many knights from reputable families," Seiichirou replied nonchalantly, his eyes betraying no hint of emotion. "Any one of them would suffice. Yes, how about, say, Harvey or Matthew?"

"What?!"

It was only natural that Orjef's breath caught in his throat.

Harvey and Matthew were young knights who had once assaulted Seiichirou because of a personal grudge. Although it was Seiichirou's own decision to let them return to the Third Royal Order after a short suspension and a hefty fine, he had to possess unbelievable nerves to elect people who had *attacked* him as his bodyguards.

"Of all the...! What the hell goes through your head?"

"I get that a lot. I believe it is what makes me suitable for my job."

"Damn... For a guy who looks so meek, you sure have a mouth on you..."

"Is that what you think?" Seiichirou's expression was as blank as ever.

Orjef would have to spend at least a week with this man. Just the thought of what he'd have to put up with made him sigh in earnest.

CHAPTER TWO

Dressed Up Again

The royal palace had multiple conference rooms. The room they were currently in was on the small and simple end of the spectrum, though one could still lay twenty tatami mats across it. Four chairs surrounded the table.

"My goodness, what a surprise that you were selected for this task, Vice Commander Rhoda! It's an honor, I must say! We don't get many opportunities to meet."

"Yes, the Third Royal Order is often away on duty."

"Though I suppose we could meet at parties...?"

Zoltan, ever the brown-noser, was in high spirits. He seemed unaware that Seiichirou was in charge and that Orjef was actually just a cover. It would have been a hassle to correct him, and the misunderstanding meant less friction with his elitist attitude anyway, so Seiichirou just kept quiet and turned to the other person in the room.

It was a Sorcery Department civil official who served as Zoltan's aide. A calm-looking man in his mid-thirties, his name was Qusta. Judging by his demeanor and the fact that Zoltan had chosen him for the task, he was of noble standing.

"It is nice to see you again," Seiichirou said.

"Yes, it has been a while, Mr. Kondo."

Seiichirou often saw the man when his work took him to the Sorcery Department.

"By the way," said Seiichirou, "may I ask about *him*...?"

"He's doing fine. He's been absorbed in researching that magic stone he received not long ago. The other day, he said he'd found a new application for it, and he's been holing himself up in the lab ever since."

"Well, that's good to hear."

Orjef eyed Qusta and Seiichirou as they nodded to each other. "Who are you referring to?" he cut in.

At this point, Zoltan noticed the change in topic.

"Oh…that would be the assistant director," he replied, scowling.

"The assistant director, hm? Now that you mention it, I realize that the assistant director is not your aide."

Zoltan was the director of the Sorcery Department. Orjef was the vice commander of the Third Royal Order. Seiichirou was the assistant director of the Accounting Department. It stood to reason that Zoltan's aide would be the assistant director, but…

"Absolutely not! He's not fit to be out in public!"

"Indeed. His talents lie elsewhere, I am afraid."

The two representatives of the Sorcery Department promptly shook their heads. Having only ever seen the man in question from afar at public junctions, Orjef turned to Seiichirou. "Is that talented sorcerer really such a character?" his gaze asked.

"In the worst-case scenario, he could cause a diplomatic incident," Seiichirou responded with uncharacteristic graveness.

Orjef decided not to pursue the matter any further.

"I decided to feed him some bait so that he won't come out of his hole for a while," Seiichirou added.

"You're a big help as always, Mr. Kondo," said Qusta.

Orjef pretended not to hear that, either.

Seiichirou led the entire conference…which perhaps only made sense given the sheer number and variety of documents that needed explanation. Although Qusta presented documents of his own from the Sorcery Department about spells and research methods, the jargon was too specialized for Seiichirou to understand.

From Orjef's perspective, the explanations were a little *too* dumbed down, but this made sense—they didn't need to show their entire hand to a country they didn't have formal relations with. Camile and the other members of the Legal Department planned to trickle out more information if this tour went well.

It was also reaffirmed at the meeting that while Zoltan and Orjef would serve as the figureheads, Qusta and Seiichirou would provide more detailed explanations as their aides. At the Egorovans' request, the tour itself would take place in the tower where the Holy Maiden had been summoned, which was also where the Sorcery Department was located. *He* would have to stay thoroughly contained until it was over.

"The first thing to worry about is the dinner party to welcome them," Orjef remarked.

"Yes. If they're bringing a prince, then our royalty will have to meet them," said Zoltan. "I believe Prince Yurius has it under control."

Seiichirou was reassembling the stack of documents when he processed that statement.

"………Excuse me?" he interjected dumbly.

"What's got you so shocked? Prince Yurius is going to be our next king. Of course he'll entertain foreign guests," Zoltan said, as if it were obvious.

But that wasn't the point.

"A visit from foreign royalty means there's going to be a party, right?" Orjef guessed.

For Seiichirou, these words dredged up flashbacks of presentations with other companies back in Japan. Despair flooded his entire being.

"Do I...really have to participate?" he asked.

"Well, obviously."

∀∀∀

"What a pickle..." Seiichirou muttered to himself.

After the conference, he had finished his regular work and gone home. He'd exchanged some cursory words with Milan the maid, then went into his room and sat on his bed.

Who knew there would be a party on the first day?

It made sense that foreign royalty wouldn't immediately get to work after a long journey, but it hadn't occurred to Seiichirou that there would be a dinner party. The word "party" didn't exist in a modern Japanese salaryman's dictionary.

He had to redo his presentation documents...but no, the bigger problem was that he had to attend the party. What was the dress code? The etiquette?

It had been ten months since he'd arrived in this country. It wasn't like he hadn't been to *any* parties. Maybe he could use the same outfit from that one time... Would Norbert still be up for helping? Or maybe it was better to wear his work clothes since he was a civil official and all? No, that didn't sound right...

Seiichirou was still wallowing when the owner of the house returned.

"Are you home, Seiichirou?" Aresh emerged from the adjoining bedroom, already changed into more comfortable indoor clothes.

Upon noticing this, Seiichirou lifted his head. "Oh... I bid you welcome, Mr. Aresh."

"Get out of work mode."

"Oh, sorry, Aresh."

Aresh hated it when Seiichirou addressed him formally, but a mere civil official from another world couldn't speak to a nobleman and a knight commander like an equal, so Seiichirou was only barred from such language while at home. Aresh was always saying that Seiichirou could stand to speak even more casually, but that would take time.

"Having a problem?" Aresh asked, surmising that work was causing Seiichirou's unusual attitude.

"Not a problem, per se," Seiichirou answered with a rueful smile, "but there is a dinner party..."

"Oh, yes. I've already got an outfit ready for you," Aresh said casually.

"You do?" Seiichirou's eyes widened.

It was rare to see that look on his face; there was something guileless about it. Aresh's lips curled into a smile.

"Your formal clothes and accessories. They're already prepared. I figured you'd be working right up until the day, so I got someone in the palace to arrange it for you."

Aresh had read him like a book.

"That...is a big help. Thank you...but how did you know that there would be a dinner party?"

"It's a diplomatic visit with royalty involved. Of course there'll be a dinner party."

Seiichirou couldn't even muster a groan at this no-nonsense demonstration of nobleman logic.

"More importantly..." Aresh sat next to him on the bed, causing the high-quality mattress to sink slightly under his weight.

A large hand cupped Seiichirou's cheek, followed seamlessly by a kiss.

"Mm... Aresh?"

Aresh tilted his head and dove in for a second kiss. Feeling the warmth of Aresh's lips and the arms wrapped around his back, Seiichirou's eyes flickered open.

"The envoys will be here tomorrow, yes? I need to cast a barrier on you."

Barrier spells worked as a safeguard against the magic that permeated the world. Although they defended Seiichirou from the poisonous magicules outside his body, it did nothing about the things he ingested. But still, the spell was a great boon for someone like him, whose tolerance for magic was far too meager for a world in which magic was ubiquitous.

But since barrier spells were themselves a form of magic—and a powerful one at that—magic-sickness was assured.

"It's in two days, actually..." Seiichirou retorted. He'd been thinking of meekly asking for a barrier the day before the arrival, but he didn't expect Aresh to offer it to him today.

Aresh kept his expression cool; only his purple eyes were clouded with desire. "This one will be extra thick as a precaution. Would you prefer me to wear you down in one night, or would you rather take it slower over two days?" he asked.

Seiichirou mentally weighed his work, the remaining time, and the limits of his stamina.

"The latter, please," he said with a grimace, after much deliberation.

Aresh grinned.

∀∀∀

It took quite a bit of courage to tread on the magnificent carpets, with their red and gold embroidery set against a white background. Why on earth did they pick white, the easiest of colors to stain? Maybe it was a flex of wealth to keep the white pristine.

Though Seiichirou knew very little about art or interior design, just treading through the opulent waiting room was giving him the jitters.

He was at the welcome party for the Egorovan delegation.

The last party Seiichirou had attended was meant to show off the Holy Maiden before she went on her purifying expedition, and it was an opportunity for the distant nobles to make connections. In that sense, it was a relatively simple affair. Not that a former middle manager salaryman like Seiichirou was in a position to make accurate comparisons, but at that party, at least, he'd been able to move around freely and help himself to the buffet. It also felt like an extension of work because he'd worn his work cloak over his formal clothes.

This time, with a foreign member of royalty as the guest of honor, everything felt completely different. For one thing, the attendees waited in a fancy room. After enough time had passed, they would move to a hall where the function would begin. It was a classic dinner party in the sense that everyone had designated seats.

As a side note, neither the hosts—the Romany royalty—nor the Egorovan guests of honor were present in the waiting room. The main characters had a separate waiting area and were scheduled to appear later, but even Seiichirou's current waiting room was filled with people in flashier clothes than at the last party. Although there weren't many people in total, most of them were strangers.

"Hi there, Seiichirou."

Seiichirou turned around in response to the husky, melodic voice. He would never admit that he felt slightly relieved to see a familiar face.

Camile was wearing a somewhat gaudier outfit than his usual neat and prim uniform. Although the blue cloak that identified him as the director of the Legal Department was made of noticeably high-quality fabric, the sleeves on this outfit had finely embroidered green parts and tasteful accessories hung from his arms. What really stood out was his rose-gold blond hair—normally, he kept it slicked back, but today some of it hung onto his forehead. It was impressive how much a change in hairstyle could affect a person's entire appearance.

"What's with that look? It's rich coming from you." Camile sighed as his gaze swept over Seiichirou.

Although Seiichirou wasn't ugly, fatigue typically exuded from his features. He looked "wiped," to use common parlance. Even his neat civil official uniform did nothing to dispel that impression.

For the previous party, Norbert got expert beauticians to cover up the bags under Seiichirou's eyes, but this time Milan the maid went the extra mile to bathe and massage him, so his skin glowed more than usual. Moreover, Aresh had spent two days diligently applying barrier and healing spells. The lovemaking had rendered Seiichirou mentally exhausted but physically pristine. He was amazed that, at the ripe old age of thirty, he could inspire such passion from a romantic partner.

Finally, the outfit Aresh had arranged for him was more of a simple suit than an extravagant display, but the feel of the fabric was on a different level. Though the cuffs weren't large, they were studded with quality gems. The flap of his collar featured a silver flower lapel pin with a purple gem casually embedded in the middle.

Camile's eyes took all this in. For a moment, a grimace came over his face.

"Geez," he sighed.

"Is something the matter?" Seiichirou asked, not understanding the meaning behind the sigh. He knew very little about the formal dress code in Japan, let alone this world, so he figured he'd better check before the dinner party began.

Camile shook his head, smiling sheepishly. "If I didn't give *him* this much leeway, he would have demanded he show up to the party, too."

In other words, there was some trace of Aresh in Seiichirou's appearance. The collar was completely done up, hiding the marks on his neck, so maybe it was something about the outfit? He knew he shouldn't have left everything to others out of his own ignorance.

Just as Seiichirou was contemplating going home to check, Norbert showed up and snorted in laughter. Understanding soon dawned on Seiichirou, accompanied by horrible embarrassment.

"In Romany, wearing an accessory on your chest means you've got a partner," Norbert explained. "And that there's a mias flower, which symbolizes eternity. You use it to signify that you're married or betrothed. Oh, and the silver ones are super expensive, and the gem in the middle usually represents your partner."

Norbert's gaze drifted to Seiichirou's cuffs.

"And the cuffs are purple, too," he said with a carefree smile. "He sure was thorough!"

Basically, Seiichirou's outfit screamed: "I have a rich and possessive spouse/betrothed whose signature color is purple."

......*Damn it! It's my fault for leaving the whole thing to Aresh!!*

As he trembled with a flood of different emotions, embarrassment chief among them, Seiichirou vowed to confront his partner as soon as he got home.

What was Aresh thinking? There weren't too many people in this country with purple eyes. This rendered the whole "don't approach Seiichirou in front of the foreigners" thing moot. Weren't they supposed to be keeping their relationship on the down low?

"Aww, he loves you, Sei!" Norbert said with a snicker.

Seiichirou decided to ignore that. "Anyway, why are you here?" he asked, turning back to Norbert.

"Didn't I tell you before? I'm technically royalty and I was raised to be a retainer. I get called to these kinds of public events pretty often so that I can learn what my role is as a retainer."

"Ah, yes, you did mention that..."

"Plus, my adoptive father's away on an inspection in the boonies, so I'm here in his place."

"You? What about Count Blanc's biological children?"

"There's a limit on guests. They wanted to keep this party low-key, apparently."

Indeed, there were about twenty people at the event. Countless nobles wanted to participate, seeing as it was an inaugural cultural exchange with a powerful nation, but the envoys preferred something less conspicuous.

Norbert's inclusion here probably isn't just about "learning his role" as a retainer, but a precautionary measure in case the duties of royalty ever called him, thought Seiichirou. From what he had seen after over half a year of living there, the crown prince Yurius was all but guaranteed to become the next king. As for Norbert, Count Blanc's family raised him as if he were their real child, and he adored his adoptive parents. There was no need to stir the pot.

Talking with Norbert eased a lot of his tension. Seiichirou met up with Orjef and Zoltan next.

"Whoa."

Orjef's face scrunched up when he caught sight of Seiichirou. Seiichirou didn't want to ask why. Keeping his expression deliberately blank, he greeted Zoltan. The man normally arranged the sleeves and color of his work uniform to accentuate his noble standing, so his formal clothes were predictably even flashier and frillier than ever. Although Seiichirou knew that frills were a common fixture on formal clothing, an overweight, fifty-something-year-old bearded guy in frills was a strange sight to behold.

"What? I didn't know you had a betrothed. Some people have unusual tastes."

Hearing *Zoltan* of all people point this out made Seiichirou want to crawl into a hole, but it was Qusta, who was standing next to Zoltan in much humbler clothes, who delivered the crippling blow.

"Oh, so you finally got engaged. Congratulations."

"...?!"

He dispensed well wishes without a second thought.

How on earth did he know? Well, it wasn't as if Seiichirou was hiding it...

It was an open secret within the palace that Aresh was passionately devoted to Seiichirou's care. People also knew that they were living together because he'd told Seiichirou to move into his new house when they were standing right in front of his previous lodgings.

From how Aresh's servants had reacted, Seiichirou had gotten the vague impression that this country was tolerant of same-sex relationships. The nobility allowed for common-law marriages. Although the large houses demanded an opposite-sex marriage to secure an heir, everyone else in the same family was allowed to adopt children.

The "finally" in Qusta's statement piqued Seiichirou's interest. Did the entire Sorcery Department happen to know...?

"Huh? Well, Mr. Kondo, you're always cloaked in that man's magic, you know?"

Apparently, someone with high sensitivity and a decent knowledge of magic could see that it went beyond mere healing and barrier spells. Combine that with the rumors of Aresh's overprotective behavior, and even the research-obsessed nerds of the Sorcery Department could tell that Aresh was more than just "the other-worlder's guardian."

Hearing this spelled out to his face, Seiichirou felt just about ready to collapse on the spot. He made a mental note never to approach the Sorcery Department the day after "acclimatizing" to magic.

The next moment, the waiting room door opened, and firstborn prince Yurius Romany Kaslová strode in. All eyes in the room turned to him, but Yurius showed no sign of diffidence. His attendants and bodyguards filed in behind him, including Radim Makovska, commander of the Second Royal Order.

It was exactly the sort of majestic display one would expect from a future king, but just as Seiichirou got sucked into the moment, he sensed Yurius's gaze on him. For a second, the other man's eyes glimmered.

Seiichirou got a vague, slightly bad feeling about this, but the prince's entourage merely passed him.

"As you may already know, Lars Eric Egorova, third prince of Egorova, has come to our nation for a cultural exchange." The crown prince's voice boomed throughout the waiting room. Nobody dared interrupt him. "Their tour will have a great impact on Romany's future culture and trade. Tonight's dinner party holds great significance. As representatives of the Romany Kingdom, I ask all of you to conduct yourselves in a manner that upholds the dignity of our nation."

The nobles' eyes brimmed with their sense of duty.

The door to the hall opened, revealing an even more extravagant and refined vista than the waiting room. The beautiful, perfectly cut chandeliers shone just the right amount of light, and pure white tablecloths stretched out across a cavernous table. A pale yellow cloth was spread directly in the middle, not drawing too much attention to itself, with a magnificent candle stand and array of flowers as centerpiece.

The napkins and cutlery were already lined up across the table. The servants began ushering the guests to their seats—Seiichirou's was the furthest from the guest of honor, and he was also quite some distance away from Orjef and Zoltan. Qusta sat across from him diagonally.

He was surprised when Norbert got the seat next to him, though Norbert was even more surprised.

"Huh?! But you're my boss, Sei! And wait, aren't you supposed to be the guide? How come you're so far from the important people?!"

"I'm guessing they're prioritizing nobility over the work hierarchy?" Seiichirou figured that today was simply about getting people familiar with each other, hence why the nobles got dibs. The real work would begin tomorrow.

"Gee, sounds unfair."

"Why are *you* complaining?" Seiichirou thought that the bigger issue was putting a member of royalty next to the least important seat, but Norbert himself didn't seem to mind. Perhaps it was the prudent thing to do in terms of instilling his place as a retainer. It was the furthest one could get from life as a salaryman in a democratic country.

Anyway, with everyone in their correct spots, Yurius looked over the crowd from the head of the table. After exchanging a look with his attendant, his voice boomed out once more:

"Now then, we extend our welcome to the diplomats of Egorova, who have come to our kingdom from afar to share their culture with us."

Yurius turned his palm toward a different door than the one Seiichirou and the others had used. All eyes watched as two Romany soldiers slowly opened the door.

A tall, silver-haired man stood at the fore. Compared to the Romany nobility, there was a slightly different look about him. He had green, almond-shaped eyes, pale skin, and a perfectly composed, doll-like face. In addition, a dignified aura exuded from his person. This was without a doubt the third prince.

Two men who looked like knights came in behind him, followed by two other men who appeared to be civil officials. Their ages appeared to range from mid-thirties to about fifty or so.

And they were all tall, which made it rather difficult to see the short person who came in last. He was a head—no, three heads shorter than the other men. Even from a distance, his youth was plain to see.

Judging by the order of seating, the young boy ranked higher than the civil officials. He sat directly next to the prince of Egorova.

Lars and Yurius shook hands.

"As you may know, this is Prince Lars, the leader of this diplomatic mission." Yurius introduced him.

Lars accepted this with a greeting of his own.

"A pleasure to make your acquaintance. I am Lars Eric Egorova, from Egorova. I thank you for your warm welcome today."

Lars, who looked like a bisque doll Seiichirou had seen a long time ago on TV, smiled. It made Seiichirou a little uncomfortable— it was *too* composed, almost phony. Aresh had a nice face, too, but since he wore a permanent scowl, it was hard to liken him to a doll.

"Our nation of Egorova is cold and mountainous. Thus, we specialize in researching magic and magic tools. However, there is a limit to what we can achieve alone. Tales of the Romany Kingdom's eye-opening advances have reached even our mountain-locked land. I hope that today's cultural exchange can be fruitful for both our nations. As a member of the royal family, I came here because I thought it would be best to learn from you myself. Were I to gain even a fraction of your knowledge, I would consider it a great boon. Let us work together for our mutual benefit."

Although he downplayed his own nation in favor of uplifting Romany, one could see his pride in Egorova between the lines. *He's good at this,* Seiichirou thought.

Lars then introduced the two civil officials and the boy beside him. "This is Georgi Lepkin, our nation's foremost magic tool expert. And this is Donato Abayev, a sorcerer."

The brawny-looking official in his fifties was a technician, while the nervous-looking man next to him was apparently a sorcerer.

The crowd's eyes then turned to the boy.

"This is Luciano Delidov, a distant relative of mine. Despite his youth, his knowledge of magic and magic tools is already exemplary.

I brought him on this trip because I believe that he will be a key figure in our kingdom's next generation. Please give him a warm welcome."

"Thank you for having me," the boy—Luciano—intoned. His voice was high-pitched; it had not yet broken. He did not bow.

When Lars mentioned that they were related, Seiichirou thought that he could see the resemblance. Although Luciano had neatly trimmed black hair, they shared the same green eyes and pale skin. Even the shape of their noses seemed quite similar. But it was the aura around him that evoked the strongest resemblance. If Luciano was a relative to royalty, he was probably the son of a distinguished member of the nobility.

He's probably around the same age as Sigma, thought Seiichirou as he peered at the group from the farthest seat. Sigma, a boy whom Seiichirou had met downtown, was currently on a scholarship so he could one day join the Sorcery Department. He was twelve, if Seiichirou's memory served him correctly.

Seiichirou was struck by how Luciano's gaze swept over the people at the table, as if he was trying to categorize them. Seiichirou looked away, figuring that he would be introducing himself tomorrow.

Things followed a predictable flow after that. The food was brought in, and the conversations started. The upper-ranked people spoke only to their immediate neighbors. This was not the kind of party where people were free to move seats and mingle with whoever. Everyone stayed in their lane. Seiichirou, for one, was glad to be near Norbert and Qusta. It went without saying that Camile was in one of the better seats.

But there was a bigger problem...

"Hey, Sei. You good with the food? You know you can give me anything you can't eat," Norbert whispered into his ear.

Indeed, that was Seiichirou's biggest problem. Although he had now built up a great deal of tolerance for this world's food—or, more precisely, the magicules in them—thanks to the combined efforts of

Aresh and his chef Pavel, that wasn't exactly the case for the palace food.

The density of magicules in food dishes depended on how the ingredients were grown and prepared. A full course of rare and expensive cuisines made with the kingdom's finest techniques was many times denser than the usual fare. For Seiichirou, it was outright dangerous.

Seiichirou restrained the urge to cradle his head in his hands.

"It's not rude to leave food on my plate, right?"

"Uh, I think you should be fine...wait." Norbert tilted his head as he peered at the appetizers. "Isn't there something different about *your* food, specifically?" he said quietly.

Seiichirou looked carefully at his plate for the first time. Right there in the middle of the white and gold-patterned plate was a beautiful array of red-brown mushrooms and vegetables, with green sauce on top. Norbert's plate had mushrooms, vegetables, and sauce as well, but of a different variety.

Seiichirou whipped his head around to look at the person who had just served him—a muscle-bound man in a black waiter uniform. He was on his way back to the kitchen, but just before he left, he turned around, smiled, and gave a thumbs-up.

"P-Pavel..."

The sight of those all-too-familiar muscles and that cheerful smile made Seiichirou feel like collapsing again, but fortunately, he was seated. Although he had no idea how Pavel had managed to worm his way into the function, it looked like Seiichirou would get through this dinner party intact.

This meant that there was nothing else tonight that he had to push through. Apparently, people would usually move to the salon next door to mingle after they had finished eating in the main hall, but out of consideration for the Egorovans who were tired from their journey, it wasn't mandatory. The third prince and the young sorcerer seemed inclined to stick around, though.

"Are you okay to leave early, Sei?"

"I'm sure there are plenty of other people who'd like to make introductions. I'll be seeing them tomorrow, anyway." Not to mention that Seiichirou doubted that anyone would be calling for the guy in the lowest-ranked seat.

The nobles who were keen on making some sort of connection turned their attention toward the Egorovans, but Seiichirou's job would begin the next day. Apologizing for his early departure, he stood from his seat.

"Are you leaving, too, Mr. Kondo?"

"Oh, Qusta."

Qusta, who sat across from him diagonally, was also making motions to leave.

"I have things to prepare for tomorrow," Seiichirou explained.

"Still planning on working, hm? Oh no, Mr. Kondo, you'll get wrinkles if you work too hard," said Qusta.

"No overdoing it, Sei!" Norbert piped up.

The documents for the tour were already in perfect order, so all Seiichirou really needed to do was interrogate Aresh about his accessories.

"It won't take long," Seiichirou insisted, looking back over his shoulder at Norbert.

It was then that he noticed an individual who *should* have been over by the upper-ranked seats standing directly behind Norbert. He froze on the spot.

"Sei?" Puzzled by Seiichirou's gaze, Norbert looked back over his shoulder, too, only to jump at what he saw. "Whoa!"

"Ah...you must be Lord Luciano. To what do we owe this pleasure?" Qusta spoke for them as the highest-ranked person in their immediate circle.

The individual in question was Luciano, the young boy who was a relative of the Egorovan royalty.

Seeing him close up, his perfectly proportional features looked even more like a doll. Selio from the church was quite a good-looking youth, but Luciano exuded refinement. It had to come from the royal blood. He could not have looked more different from Romany's lowest-ranked royalty, however, when he fixed Qusta with a haughty glare.

"I heard that you're the guide for the Sorcery Department. Am I wrong?"

"You are quite correct. I am Qusta Rein of the Royal Sorcery Department, and I will be your guide tomorrow. A pleasure to make your acquaintance," said Qusta, not batting an eye at the boy's precocious attitude.

But Luciano's immaculate eyebrows knitted into a frown.

"Why—?"

"Master Luciano, let us go."

A bodyguard knight appeared seemingly out of nowhere just as the boy opened his mouth. Gently, he pushed Luciano's back, prompting the boy to shuffle reluctantly out of the room.

"What was that all about?" Seiichirou cocked his head, mystified.

For his part, Qusta seemed to have an inkling, because he just shook his head slightly with a sheepish smile. He did not explain the reason behind the encounter.

∀∀∀

"Welcome back."

Lars's eyes widened slightly when he entered the room. "You're still awake?"

Luciano was relaxing on the sofa of Lars's assigned room, already dressed in indoor clothes.

"You just had your first long journey. I told you to rest." Though Lars's words were reprimanding, his tone was gentle.

"I'm fine. Anyway, it looks like our guide from the Sorcery Department is just a regular sorcerer, just as I suspected."

"Oh, really? He didn't come to the salon. I suppose he was in the hall?"

"Yeah, it was the brown-haired man in one of the lower-ranked seats. His name was Qusta or something."

"A lower-ranked seat? So did you meet *him*, too?"

"Who?" Eager to call out the sorcerer for his mediocrity, Luciano responded to this sudden change in topic with surprise.

"The young man with blond hair and blue eyes. He was there, yes?"

Almost everyone who had been allowed into the party was a powerful noble, which meant that there were hardly any young people present.

"Oh...yeah. There was a blond guy."

"Interesting. He's a member of the Romany royal family."

Luciano's eyes went wide at this nonchalant statement.

"What? But he was in one of the lowest-ranked seats."

Lars smiled fondly at Luciano's rapid change of expression. At the same time, he stifled a different kind of smile.

"Yes, he was born from a mistress and adopted into a retainer's family. I hear he's working in the palace as a retainer himself."

Luciano paled. "How foolish... They need talent more than lineage to support the country." The blond youth's capabilities were unknown, but the young sorcerer thought it distasteful that the kingdom would go out of its way to invite him to the dinner party and then put him in the lowest seat.

"There's no real succession drama in this kingdom, it seems. Prince Yurius, whom we met today, appears to be the surefire candidate for the throne."

"Prince Yurius, huh? Well, he seems okay, but he *is* just getting things handed to him on a platter."

"Ha-ha, you certainly have a competitive spirit, Luciano." Lars chuckled at Luciano's petulance.

"The top seat should go to the person with the most merit!" Luciano retorted. "Obviously! Just like how *you* ought to be king, Elder Brother!"

"Shush now. You mustn't call me that here," Lars said with a forced smile.

"Oh, sorry, Your Highness..." Luciano went quiet. "But...I really..."

"Yes, I know. Thank you." Lars stroked and kissed the luscious black hair on the top of the dejected Luciano's head. "Now go to sleep. Tomorrow's a big day."

"Okay..." Luciano nodded without retort, knowing that Lars was in no mood for further conversation. Above all, Lars was tired after his first dinner party in a foreign land.

But then another thought seemed to occur to Luciano.

"If that fellow was royalty, who was the other man with him?" the young sorcerer said, turning around at the door.

"Which man?" Lars had not been observing that part of the table so closely.

"Oh, there was a fellow with black hair and eyes in the lowest seat next to him. He had this sort of listless look about him."

"I suppose he's a sorcerer?" Lars suggested, for that was what the word "listless" brought to mind.

But Luciano looked puzzled. "I wonder. He did seem friendly with Qusta, the court sorcerer, but..." The young sorcerer tried to summon every recollection about the listless man who sat next to Norbert...but nothing really came to mind. He *had* been some distance away.

"Hm... Well, I'll keep an eye out for him. Now sleep, Lufi."

"Have a good night...Elder Brother."

Even after the door closed, Lars remained alone in his room, sorting through the information he'd gleaned from the dinner party.

∨∨∨

The dinner party ended early, likely because one of the main guests was a boy not yet of age. By the time Seiichirou got home, it was still only Wood Hour (before 9 PM).

"Welcome home, Mr. Kondo." Valtom greeted him at the door.

"Yes, I'm back. Now, about Aresh..." Seiichirou began to ask, though he quickly noticed the smile in Valtom's eyes.

No, it's not what you think. Seiichirou did not say this aloud, however, and simply went straight for Aresh's room.

Although their rooms were connected, only Aresh had the key to his personal room. *Fair enough,* Seiichirou thought. It *was* Aresh's house, after all.

Just as Seiichirou was about to knock on the door, he remembered that he was still in his dinner clothes. He contemplated going back to his room to change, but then decided that having the formal outfit on would help him demonstrate his point quicker. Gingerly, he knocked on the ornate, wooden door.

"Excuse me," he said when there was no response.

There, he found Aresh sleeping, sprawled on the sofa. Maybe it was because he was a knight, but he rarely showed his sleeping face to anyone.

The sofa's cabriole legs looked too dainty to support Aresh's frame, but it was made of sturdy stuff, and the cushioned section was as vast as a couch. It was probably custom-made.

Seiichirou had been ready to march right in and give his partner a piece of his mind, but the other man's snoozing face quashed his momentum. Aresh had such long eyelashes.

Then it occurred to Seiichirou that it was inefficient to stay in his current outfit. It would be best to change before it got dirty. Just as he turned around, he sensed a powerful weight on his back.

"Whoa."

He'd been prepared for the impact, but it was lighter than he'd expected. Maybe magic was involved. The next thing he knew, Aresh was straddling him on the sofa.

"You're back," Aresh said.

"Indeed I am." Seiichirou couldn't help but smile at the traces of sleepiness still evident on Aresh's face, but the bigger issue here was their compromising position. "Please get off me, Aresh. My clothes will get wrinkled."

"Who cares?"

"I care. They're expensive, and I can't compensate you for them."

Even Seiichirou could tell that his clothes were made with high-quality fabric and embroidery. Even an optimistic estimate of its price looked like well over a month's worth of Seiichirou's income. This was no meager sum, given that he received both a stipend from the kingdom and a salary as the assistant director of the Accounting Department.

Although he handed the whole stipend over to Valtom to pay for his rent and living expenses, he certainly wasn't poor based on his managerial-level salary alone. But the nobility had a *very* different idea of money. Seiichirou couldn't buy a house at the drop of a hat like Aresh could, nor could he afford to whip jewel-studded dinner clothes out of nowhere.

This thought made him remember why he had come to Aresh's room in the first place.

"They're yours now, so you can do what you please with them," said Aresh, which prompted Seiichirou to exert his barely existent stomach muscles and try to sit up.

"Yes, and that's what I'm here to talk to you about. Anyway, could you get off me, please?" Seiichirou asked, again trying to sit up. Aresh, however, refused to budge an inch. "Please, Aresh. It's important."

"Say it, then," Aresh urged him with his eyes, still not shifting his position.

Seiichirou gave the matter some thought. Deciding that it was best to rip off the band-aid, he gave up and got to the point.

"It's...about the lapel pin," he said. He peered at Aresh's eyes, the same color as the jewel embedded in the silver flower pin on his collar. Aresh said nothing. He waited for Seiichirou to speak. "I heard about what it means... I can't excuse myself for my ignorance, but when it comes to things like this, you really should have—"

"Would you have worn it if you knew?" Aresh cut off Seiichirou before he could finish.

"Huh...?"

"I'm asking if you would have refused to wear it if you knew beforehand," Aresh repeated himself.

Seiichirou's thought process screeched to a halt.

Wait... Wait, wait, wait. His mind quickly kicked back into gear. Inwardly, he shook his head. *That's not what this is about.*

The problem was that Aresh had sent him off to a public venue wearing a symbol declaring their engagement without him being any the wiser. Whether he would have worn it knowingly was a whole different question.

"Let's not change the topic."

"People from another country were there. You'll forgive me for wanting to deter any strange bugs from approaching you."

Seiichirou had no idea what Aresh was so worried about. He didn't say a single word to an Egorovan at the party—they barely made eye contact.

"That's not the issue here. I'm talking about your deceptive actions." Today, at least, he got strange looks from people he knew, which was very embarrassing.

"But you wouldn't have worn it if you knew."

Darn it all. They were going in circles. Seiichirou consciously breathed in, and then out. *I have to be the mature one,* he told himself.

As far as Seiichirou was concerned, Aresh's willful statement was very much the kind of thing a younger man would say to his romantic partner. It was cute, in a way, but it was still moving the goalposts. It was unwise to mix public and personal matters.

"Listen, Aresh. This is not about whether I would wear the lapel pin. It's about me unknowingly spreading a message in public."

The people in the Sorcery Department had mistaken it to mean "you're finally engaged."

"In other words, you don't want to be with me," Aresh said in a low voice.

"What?" Seiichirou looked up again. This time, he did not see

the pouting face of a younger man, but a look of composed serious-
ness. Seiichirou's words died in his throat.

As he'd said a thousand times already, that wasn't what this was
about. But he was powerless to change the conversation.

Was Aresh really saying that Seiichirou didn't want them to be
together?

"It's only been a month since we began this relationship," was
what he mustered.

Indeed. A mere month had passed since Seiichirou and Aresh
officially became romantic partners. They first met ten months ago.
One could easily argue that this was moving much too fast.

Aresh had different ideas, however. His hands pressed into Seiichirou's shoulders, making Seiichirou sink further into the sofa.

"You'll go back to your homeland if I take my time."

Seiichirou blinked.

Not wanting to hurt Seiichirou, Aresh pulled his hands away
from his shoulders, gripping only air.

Seiichirou was not from this world. He had proposed research
into movement spells so that he could return home.

But Seiichirou couldn't turn a blind eye to Aresh's dogged emotions. It wasn't as if he'd deliberately avoided thinking about their
eventual parting. The spell to send him home was not a simple one to
complete, and he figured that there was still plenty of time.

But Aresh thought differently.

"I have no intention of letting you go, Seiichirou." Aresh rested
his head against Seiichirou's shoulder so that the other man would
not see his deeply furrowed brows. Seiichirou could feel the ripples
of Aresh's voice against his body, perhaps because they were so close.
"I want to bind us together before you can leave."

There was nothing Seiichirou could say to that.

When, after some time passed, Aresh told him to leave his room,
all Seiichirou could do was nod. He couldn't even express his thanks
to Pavel.

The door to Aresh's room stayed locked from that day forth.

[CHAPTER THREE]

Crossed Paths

After a poor night's sleep—which should have been better given that he was alone and had a pillow—Seiichirou woke up the next morning, washed his face, got changed, and exited into the hallway. He looked at the neighboring room, but heard nothing beyond the closed door. He went down to the dining room, but didn't find Aresh there, either.

"Good morning, Mr. Seiichirou," said Milan, the plump and hearty maid.

He could only muster a half-hearted greeting in response.

"Um... Where is Aresh...?"

"He went to work early today."

"I see..."

It seemed Aresh was genuinely upset.

Seiichirou sat down and took a bite of his breakfast, courtesy of Pavel's cooking. Not even the fluffy soufflé omelets or Seiichirou's favorite soup tasted like much of anything today.

Seiichirou and Aresh literally came from different worlds. It was why Aresh took steps to stave off their eventual parting.

Come to think of it, they should have discussed this issue when Seiichirou first decided to accept Aresh's feelings, but it was hard for Seiichirou to imagine himself turning his back entirely on the friends and family he'd made over his first twenty-nine years of life.

Not to mention that the idea of rushing straight into marriage after just a month of being in a relationship was ludicrous to him.

Crunch. He stabbed his fork into his salad with more force than necessary.

Oh yeah, he didn't even apologize to me for the deception, did he?! He had plenty of time to tell me. It wasn't right of him to keep me in the dark!

Seiichirou owed the world to Aresh. And there were romantic feelings on his end, too.

But that was beside the point here. No, trust was more important than anything in a relationship, in Seiichirou's opinion.

That's all I wanted to say. And how does he react? He locks me out of his room and doesn't even show his face at breakfast... What is he, a child?!

This was starting to tick Seiichirou off. He decided not to say anything until Aresh broke the silence first.

Besides, he had to guide the Egorovan envoys around today. This was an important job with international ramifications—there was no room for error, and it certainly wasn't the time or place to get mopey about his love life.

Seiichirou forced the last of his soup down his throat.

∀∀∀

I told him I had nothing...

"You see, I was thinking of giving Yua a gift, so I'd like to pick your brain," said a handsome silver-haired young man in a tremulous voice, "as someone who came from the same world..."

Seiichirou could only look at him with a gaze that expressed that he felt dead on the inside. A knight from the Second Royal Order had accosted him the moment he arrived at the palace, and now here he was, languishing in a reception room.

It went without saying that the silver-haired man was Prince Yurius, first in line for the throne.

"Kondo, you ought to adjust your expression a little..." Commander Radim of the Second Royal Order warned in a whisper.

"I stopped trying for the impossible," Seiichirou answered flatly. His range of expressions lacked the capacity to respond to the prince's pining for the Holy Maiden. "I would like to mention that I came to the palace today to serve as a guide for the Egorovan diplomats."

"How dare the prince of the nation get in the way of an important job," is what Seiichirou was trying to say.

Yurius appeared to have heard his grumbling, because he lifted his head.

"Ah, worry not. The tour has been rescheduled to the Water Hour (2 PM) today. Some of the diplomats were up late at the dinner party last night, and they are also, of course, fatigued from their journey."

It was still only Wood Hour (9 AM). The Light Hour (11 AM) was already a late start, but now the tour had been postponed further.

"Is that so? In that case, I have some things to do at the Accounting Department," Seiichirou said as he tried to stand.

Naturally, Radim stopped him and forced him back onto the sofa. The sickly Seiichirou could never have hoped to overpower a distinguished military commander. It was the same song and dance as the day before.

The memory of it ticked Seiichirou off all over again.

Alas, he was in the presence of a prince. He couldn't worm his way out of this one.

"I called on you because I thought your perspective would be useful. You and Yua are compatriots and have been in a similar position romantically," said Yurius.

"........." Seiichirou said nothing.

By "similar position romantically," was he talking about being proposed to by a member of this kingdom?

Wait. There was a more fundamental issue here.

Yua Shiraishi, who had been summoned alongside Seiichirou to this world (well, technically, *she* was summoned as the Holy Maiden and Seiichirou just happened to get caught up in it) did indeed get along with Yurius. But as far as Seiichirou was aware...that was about the extent of their relationship.

"Have you and Shiraishi started courting yet, Your Highness?"

"—!"

"—!"

Both Yurius and Radim froze.

No way...

"You do not have a romantic relationship, and yet you are planning on proposing to her...?"

The incredulousness must have shown on his face. Radim shook his head, his face deathly pale.

"He has not...confirmed Yua's feelings exactly, but she surely feels the same way!" he insisted as his eyes flashed in warning. "And so the gift is to propose both marriage and courtship at the same time..."

"Yikes, that's a big ask," Seiichirou blurted out.

"—?!" Yurius's eyes went wide.

"Kondo! Watch your tongue!" Radim barked.

"Oh, my apologies. I couldn't help but say what I was thinking..."

"That's not an apology, Kondo!" yelled Radim. "That's not an apology at all!"

"I-is it my imagination, or have you been rather passive-aggressive toward me lately...?" said Yurius.

They could complain all they liked, but of course Seiichirou was going to be passive-aggressive when he'd been abducted to give dating advice right before an important job.

But still, between Yurius, who was trying to propose to a woman he wasn't even dating, and Aresh, who declared that he and his partner were engaged without asking how his partner felt about it, who was being more ridiculous?

Maybe the prince was more put-together...for at least asking the other person's consent.

"Firstly, I should mention that in our home country, sixteen is considered very early for a woman to get married."

Yurius blinked. "...Truly?!"

Although it was legal to get married at that age, most sixteen-year-olds in Japan were high school students.

"In Japan, the majority attend school until they are eighteen. Furthermore, many affluent or passionate students choose to further their education until they are twenty or even twenty-two." From what Seiichirou could tell, Yua came from a privileged household, so she would probably go on to college. "Many people only get married after they have joined the workforce and settled into their careers."

He decided not to mention how women these days were putting off marriage for later due to advancements in women's rights.

"Is...that so?" Yurius said shakily.

Seiichirou abruptly remembered that the prince was twenty years old. Given the similarities between the Romany Kingdom and medieval Europe, Seiichirou expected that the nobility would get engaged at a young age. His assumption seemed to be correct.

Sadly for Yurius, Yua was very much a modern Japanese girl.

"Honestly," said Seiichirou, "I do not think she will take well to an abrupt marriage proposal..."

"But a member of royalty cannot frivolously initiate relations with a Holy Maiden," Radim pointed out.

Seiichirou nodded, understanding the logic. It was a big deal for a prince to court a Holy Maiden—and not to mention that the two of them were of marriageable age in this country. Casual dating wouldn't fly here.

"Well, just try to keep Shiraishi's perspective in mind, I suppose."

The rest was their problem to deal with. Seiichirou did not want to be dragged into it right before work.

"Did you accept Aresh's proposal because of your age?"

Oof.

This time, it was Seiichirou's turn to freeze.

There was silence after that, a very long silence indeed.

"...............I have no recollection of accepting a proposal," Seiichirou answered finally.

Radim seemed to have figured something out, while Yurius cocked his head in puzzlement.

"What are you saying? Were you not wearing a sign of your engagement at the dinner party? I thought it was a deliberate signal to the foreign guests."

Seiichirou was silent for a while again before saying, "...............I did wear that, but I did not accept a proposal."

"What? Then how...?" Yurius frowned in puzzlement. "Oh, don't tell me."

Being the crown prince, he was by no means a dim fellow. As it dawned on him, his expression became one of comprehension. He shot a look over his shoulder at Radim, who nodded.

Yurius turned back to Seiichirou with a sympathetic gaze.

"So you didn't know."

"........." Seiichirou's silence was answer enough.

Although he was a grown man, he had been in this world for less than a year. Yurius did not seem inclined to ridicule him for his ignorance.

But...

"Well...somehow, I can understand Aresh's feelings."

"...On what basis?" Seiichirou asked, glowering.

"Don't give me that look. I'm the crown prince." Yurius waved a hand to ward off Seiichirou's baleful expression. "You and Yua are from another world. I suspect he fears that you will slip beyond his grasp if he does not latch onto you quickly."

Seiichirou's mouth drew into a tight line.

"Yua has declared publicly that she wishes to return to her world, and you are the very man who kickstarted research into movement spells for returning people to their worlds... You must wish to go back one day, yes?"

Yes. Yua and Seiichirou had both been dragged forcibly into this world. If they could return, they would. It was what they were working toward.

"………I do not have it in me to cast my homeland aside so easily," Seiichirou said after a pause.

"Understandable. I owe you an apology for putting you in this situation." Seiichirou's eyes widened. It was expressed as an afterthought, but it was the first time one of the kingdom's top brass had ever apologized to him. "What are you surprised about? I always... Well, not always. But I do recognize that I have done you and Yua wrong."

But he did not regret it, because he had done it to save his kingdom. For all his youth, he was very much a future king in that sense.

"Although it was our wrongdoing that brought you and Yua to this country, you have formed bonds here. Aresh and I are afraid of losing those bonds." And so they wanted to secure the one they loved before it was too late, even if it meant using force. "You might think it unreasonable, but that's how desperate Aresh must be. And I, too. I hope you can see that."

Seiichirou could not find the words to answer the prince, a young man in love. He could only respond with silence.

∀∀∀

"You had all this extra time before the meeting and you're still late! What in the blazes were you doing?" Zoltan barked at him.

After that conversation with Yurius, the prince kept pressing Seiichirou for advice about proposing to Yua all the way until lunch. By the time Seiichirou met up with Orjef and the other tour guides, everyone else was already there waiting for him. Since he couldn't very well say that His Highness had accosted him for dating advice, he simply apologized. He said sorry to Qusta as well, who was trying to placate Zoltan.

Zoltan's breath was ragged; he was probably on edge right before an important job. He was the one in charge, after all.

When Seiichirou turned his head to apologize to Orjef, he noticed the man looked worn out before the job had even started. He must have stayed late at last night's dinner party.

"Are you all right?" Seiichirou asked.

"Yeah, but no thanks to a certain somebody."

Orjef glared at him. Strange. Seiichirou had no idea what he did wrong, but if it had something to do with him, then Aresh was their point of commonality.

"Let's have a chat later," Orjef said.

"......Okay." Seiichirou nodded after a pause. He knew this was throwing his work schedule increasingly out of whack, but it was best to own up to whatever his mistake was. Plus, he was curious about how Aresh was doing.

"Oh dear, have you been waiting long?" A scant few minutes after the tour guides had assembled in the room, the Egorovan envoys made their appearance.

Lars led the group, dressed in a plain black outfit that could not have been more different from the formal clothes he wore the day before. Simple though it was, the quality of the fabric was plain to see. It suited the stylish and regal Lars very well.

The other members of the group, save for the bodyguard knights, wore matching cloaks—likely a uniform of sorts.

"Oh no, you have nothing to worry about. Now then, make yourselves at home." As Zoltan ushered the group to their seats, everyone on the Romany side stood up. They only sat back down again after the Egorovans were seated.

"Thank you for preparing such magnificent seats for us yesterday," Lars said.

"By all means! I am glad that you feel welcome in our country."

As Lars and Zoltan were talking, the other members of the Egorovan delegation looked around without much interest. They all seemed to be scholarly types.

"Allow me to reintroduce myself. I am Lars Eric Egorova, and I am participating in this tour as a representative of Egorova. A pleasure to make your acquaintance."

The Egorovans had already said their hellos the day before, but the other three members reluctantly reintroduced themselves with Lars's urging. Zoltan and Orjef responded politely in turn.

Zoltan introduced Qusta and Seiichirou next.

"This is Qusta Rein, my subordinate and a highly skilled sorcerer. I hope that his insights will be useful to you all." Then he glanced at Seiichirou before turning back to the Egorovans. "This is Kondo from the Accounting Department. He will be assisting in miscellaneous matters, so feel free to ask him anything."

So that was how he chose to spin it.

Seiichirou did not meet the eyes of the worried-looking Qusta or Orjef, who was glancing at him for his reaction. He merely kept his gaze ahead, unruffled.

Zoltan must *really* not have liked that Camile reached out to Seiichirou directly. Even though Seiichirou had created eighty percent of the paperwork for this job, he was relegated to "miscellaneous matters."

"Has he no family name?" the nervous-looking sorcerer— Donato, if Seiichirou recalled correctly—asked the obvious question.

It had been a deliberate move not to introduce Seiichirou by his full name. Although Kondo—well, Kondou, to be specific—was his family name, anyone who was introduced by first name alone was practically guaranteed to be seen as a commoner.

But Seiichirou was fine with that.

"My name is Kondou. I hope that I can be of some assistance to you on this tour. Pleased to make your acquaintance."

The name "Seiichirou" had an unfamiliar ring to the people of this world. Although the neighboring countries were aware that Romany had summoned its Holy Maiden from another world, it was a secret that another person was summoned along with her. It would be a bad look if it came to light that a random person got involved through no volition of his own—hence why the kingdom's initial plan was to keep Seiichirou confined as a pet of sorts. It was only because he had asked for a job and achieved stellar results that Prime Minister Camile increasingly trusted him with more work.

But Camile was still worried about how other countries would perceive it. It was his *job* to worry about that—especially when Seiichirou's existence was hardly known in other countries. If Seiichirou introduced himself as an otherworlder to these foreigners when they had come to observe the kingdom's movement spells, it would inevitably cause a major hassle. Zoltan's idea to downplay him was for the best.

Donato's eyes flickered with disdain, although Lars and Luciano looked at Seiichirou with interest.

"Can commoners rise to an administrative position in Romany?" asked Lars.

"Um, not really... I mean, well, yes, I suppose so." Zoltan was about to deny it until he remembered that his own department's assistant director was himself a commoner. With painfully gritted teeth, he answered in the affirmative.

"Ah, please don't take my question as an expression of offense. I was simply impressed."

True to Lars's words, nobody besides Donato looked displeased. Although perhaps it was more accurate to say that Georgi, the magic tool expert, was disinterested in the conversation altogether.

So the members of the royal family and their inner circle aren't elitists? No, maybe it's just those two.

Although Seiichirou knew nothing about Egorova's political circumstances, he felt the need to understand what the other side was thinking, if only for the sake of making this tour run smoothly. Hopefully, it would improve diplomatic relations, which would make it easier to import magic stones.

With the introductions out of the way, the meeting began in earnest.

Because this was the diplomats' first day of being shown around, the idea was to answer their questions in the reception room. Seiichirou had prepared a whole stack of documents for this purpose, and Qusta had done the same.

However, before they had gotten through even half the pile, Georgi began to tap his thick fingers against the table impatiently.

"How long do you plan to dawdle? I'd rather take a look around than waste time on endless papers."

The delegation would be staying for just seven days. Given that they had arrived yesterday, that left six days—today included.

So yes, Georgi was right in saying that their time was limited, although Seiichirou thought that he was rather quick to jump the gun given that the entire itinerary of the trip was currently being explained to him. But the other members seemed to share Geogi's opinion.

"Yeah!" Luciano chimed in agreement. "We came here to learn about movement spells!"

"Quite so," said Donato. "We don't need this much detail about numbers and logistics."

This was apparently a boring topic for magic scholars.

"My apologies, everyone," Lars said politely before turning to his own people. "Would you cut it out, you lot? They put in a lot of work to plan this visit."

Only Lars pushed back against the rising tide of impatience, although the others were not inclined to listen.

"But, Your Highness! Was it not the opportunity to study magic techniques that made us go to such pains to come here?! We learn nothing from being in a room without a single magic tool!"

"I agree. Magic is not something you learn from abstract textbook theories. You learn by seeing and doing."

"The Sorcery Department! I demand to see the Royal Sorcery Department!"

Uh-oh.

The same word bounded through Seiichirou, Zoltan, and

Qusta's minds. The three of them exchanged looks. There was no spell or magic tool for communicating telepathically, but in that moment, their thoughts were indeed aligned.

Zoltan coughed. "W-well then, shall I show you around the Royal Sorcery Department?"

"Are you sure that's okay?" Lars asked worriedly.

"Oh, yes! Perfectly! You all made such a long trek to be here, and His Highness the Crown Prince has asked that we accommodate your needs as much as possible." Zoltan was sweating, but he did a good job of hiding it as he gave a dignified response. One had to hand it to the nobility on occasion.

"Excellent. Then I shall go on ahead and prepare the venue for your arriva—"

Qusta tried to stand up, only for Luciano to stop him. "Oh, I have a question about one of those papers you showed earlier. Can I ask about it while I walk with you?"

Uh-oh.

Sadly, they couldn't refuse the boy. He was a relative to royalty and a formal member of the delegation.

Seiichirou stood up after Qusta threw a look in his direction. "Please accompany the group, Qusta. I will handle the communication."

"What's the hurry?" asked Donato. "You can ask an attendant to pass on the message."

Seiichirou, Zoltan, and Qusta froze for several fractions of a second.

The Royal Sorcery Department performed the kingdom's most cutting-edge magic research. There were plenty of things they were reluctant to show to people of other nations. The Egorovans understood that well, and they weren't trying to force their way through. It was natural for them to wonder why a guide had to take it upon himself to pass on a simple message.

But the Romany Kingdom had its own problems to deal with.

"Well, you see... I just happened to remember that there were some documents I forgot to hand over to you all." The lie came easily to Seiichirou's lips.

The Egorovans looked at the bundle of documents in Seiichirou's arms. *Okay, so he's a bit dim-witted,* they thought, and left it at that.

"I'll come with you. You've got a lot to carry." Orjef, secretly Seiichirou's bodyguard, stood up as well.

Thank goodness he managed to play along. Seiichirou was deeply grateful.

If worst came to worst, they would need to stash *him* away by force.

Owing to its numerous previous offenses—er, distinguishing results, the Sorcery Department was sequestered away at the very corner of the palace. Seiichirou was slightly out of breath by the time he arrived.

"Please excuse me! It's Kondou from the Accounting Department! Is Ist here?!"

The court mages were bewildered when Seiichirou flung open the door moments after knocking, but they calmed when they saw it was a familiar face.

"Is something the matter, Kondo?" asked one sorcerer.

"Huh? Weren't you and Qusta supposed to be guiding the Egorovans around today?" said another.

Seiichirou swept his gaze around the lackadaisical crowd, but did not find Ist among them. He would have cheered if Ist had gone out, but there was still the possibility that the man was buried somewhere in the mess of reference books and magic tools in the room. "Where is Ist, may I ask?"

"He's in the back research room," said a familiar high-pitched voice.

Seiichirou's eyes turned to the boy with dark brown hair. "Oh, Sigma, are you here to observe?"

"Yes. I don't have school at the church today."

Sigma was a proper child—he had just turned twelve the other day. He was born in the lower district and once ran a stall selling toys and other trinkets he'd carved himself. His craftsman father had passed away when he was young, and the boy apprenticed as a woodworker to help make ends meet. Seiichirou had reached out to the youth when he spotted something resembling an abacus among his wares. One thing led to another, and now he was attending a private school sponsored by the prince and the Holy Maiden at the church.

Sometime in the near future, the royal family planned to announce him as the first commoner scholarship student, but he already had special permission to enter the Sorcery Department because he was good at communicating with Ist. Plus, he'd always had an interest in magic tools. Although Seiichirou wanted such a smart and efficient boy like Sigma to join the Accounting Department, Ist had gotten to him first.

"So Ist is in the back?" Seiichirou asked, pointing at the very farthest room.

Sigma nodded.

The Royal Sorcery Department was divided into several smaller rooms that could be reached from the main area. Alongside storage spaces for restricted documents and materials, there were rooms for private research. The back room had all kinds of uses: separating oneself from the other sorcerers, containing spell effects to prevent other objects from being altered, or simply focusing deeply on research.

"Okay, I'm blocking it off," Seiichirou said.

No sooner did the words leave his mouth than he started pushing a large worktable.

"Huh?" Everyone's eyes widened in shock.

"What are you doing? There's no time! Orjef, hurry up and bring over that table! Two's better than one!"

"R-right." The only other person in the room who understood what was going on obeyed Seiichirou without question.

"What's going on, Mister? Ist won't be able to come out if you block the way, right?!" cried Sigma.

"That's exactly why I'm doing it."

Ist could easily blow the door away with magic if he so wished, but the idea probably wouldn't even occur to him if he didn't know why he was blocked in. Hopefully, his thought process would be "The door's locked? Well, whatever."

And so it would be as long as nothing outside piqued his interest. Seiichirou decided that now was the best time to seal it, while Ist was still unaware. The Egorovans would only be in the Sorcery Department for a short time. The barrier just needed to hold until they were gone.

"The Egorovan group will be here in a matter of minutes! Hide anything you don't want them seeing! Oh, and try to move whatever you can and make this place presentable!"

Seiichirou's words finally snapped the sorcerers out of their confusion. They jumped in unison.

"The Egorovan diplomats?! Weren't they supposed to be coming here tomorrow?!"

"Hey, isn't a member of their royal family part of the group?! Oh crap! He's gonna see me in *this*?!"

"What's with the sudden change of plan?!"

Everyone had cries of surprise on their lips, though they swiftly started packing their written notes and materials. There was a lot to do, given that the whole place looked dreadful.

"Who cares how you look?! The classified information comes first! You don't want other countries seeing it! And don't assume they won't understand what they see. They have a magic tool expert in their party!" Seiichirou shouted, hurrying the sorcerers along.

Even as Orjef watched on in exasperation, he didn't fail to add to the barricade pile.

"Oh, so you *can* yell at the top of your lungs..."

∀∀∀

By the time Zoltan escorted the Egorovans to the Sorcery Department, the sorcerers had somehow managed to clear up enough space to walk through, tidied the jam-packed desks, ventilated the area, and—most importantly—barricaded the farthest research room. They even used magic to keep the objects in front of the door in place. The reason they didn't use magic to seal off the entire doorway was because Ist would sense the energy, which could very well pique his interest and prompt him to break the barrier.

As the Egorovans peered around in interest, Qusta stood behind them, appearing visibly relieved. When his eyes met Seiichirou's, the two of them silently nodded to each other.

"So this is Romany's Sorcery Department, eh?"

"It's quite small."

Although there were more people around these days, the Royal Sorcery Department had been short-staffed prior to Seiichirou's intervention. Given that he planned to expand the department even further, it probably *was* a good idea to look into physically expanding the space. Seiichirou added "ask the higher-ups about this" to his mental list of things to do.

"We have a number of smaller rooms, which our sorcerers use for research," Qusta explained, since Zoltan hardly ever used those.

Even Seiichirou, a frequent visitor, knew nothing about magic or how the rooms were arranged. He decided to step back; this wasn't where he was needed.

"What is this?" someone asked.

"Oh, that's the nap room Kondo made for us. Right, Kondo?"

"……Um, yes."

Seiichirou's sentiments were wasted when someone called for him straight away.

"The nap room! I'm a big fan," gushed one of the researchers.

"Yes, because some of us forget to go home when we're absorbed in work!" said another.

"It's good for waiting out magic stagnation."

They were all babbling excitedly.

"Aren't you from the Accounting Department? Why were you involved in the Sorcery Department's facilities?" Lars asked the obvious question.

Seiichirou hesitated for a moment but decided to answer honestly. "Well, you see, I often come here, and I would see the sorcerers sleeping on the floor… I figured that sleeping on a proper bed would rejuvenate the body more quickly and lead to greater efficiency."

This was something Seiichirou had learned through trial and error from his previous world. Sleeping on the floor or at his desk would always leave him aching somewhere. Even worse, the sleep was never good enough to rid him of fatigue. He tried all sorts of strategies, like curling up in the corner of a room, sleeping on the toilet, and laying out two or even three chairs. He had wished for a nap room on many such occasions—but sadly, the company never heeded his requests.

But now the shoe was on the other foot. When he saw the sorcerers on the floor, a wave of nostalgia had come over him. When he installed work desks for the new employees, he took the opportunity to order simple beds as well. The higher-ups gave him permission, of course—although admittedly, the budgeting mostly came down to Seiichirou. When one of the research rooms became a permanent napping area, he felt fulfilled, as if he had finally ticked something off his bucket list.

"And that's not all! Kondo's responsible for a bunch of other conveniences, like a regular food stock and a magic tool that automatically cleans the room. It really makes it easy to focus on our jobs!" the sorcerers enthused.

In contrast to the sparkly-eyed sorcerers, Zoltan and Orjef scowled at Seiichirou. This was the correct response.

"You set up a bunch of things to make them work all day?" Orjef muttered.

Seiichirou pretended not to hear him.

He was helping further the research into movement spells by making the Sorcery Department an easier environment to work in.

At the same time, he was using them to fulfill his own dreams: an easy source of food and nutrition, a nap room where they could get a proper sleep, a machine—erm, magical tool—that would automatically keep the rooms clean. Yes, it was every workaholic's ideal.

Of course, this could only make sense to someone with Seiichirou's particular brand of obsession. Fortunately, the research nuts at the Sorcery Department were kindred spirits in that sense.

One of the research nuts in question heard Orjef's muttering.

"Not at all," he insisted, coming to Seiichirou's defense. "We're nothing but grateful to Kondo for increasing our budget! We never had much money before."

The Egorovan sorcerers, who seemed to be a bunch of research fanatics themselves, cocked their heads at that.

"But isn't he just an accountant? He doesn't possess the special powers of a sorcerer. Why praise him for doing the obvious?" asked Donato, and the others in his group nodded emphatically as well.

From this, it was all too clear that Egorova valued its technicians and sorcerers highly. It made sense to those coming from a frigid land, where magic was essential for withstanding the cold.

"Yes, but you need money to do research, don't you? We've only made leaps and bounds in our movement spells because we have the funds for it. So you can say we owe all this progress to Kondo!"

"Not at all. You're the ones who put in the hard work." Seiichirou tried to quiet the sorcerers. Even he thought that they were laying it on a bit thick, but that didn't stop the flood of gratitude.

Since the Egorovan mages didn't look pleased, Seiichirou failed to notice Lars peering at him with a smile.

Meanwhile, something appeared to catch Luciano's attention.

"Who's that kid?" He spoke up. "I've been wondering for a while."

He was pointing at Sigma. With his white shirt and long beige shorts, he was the odd one out among all the Royal Sorcery Department uniforms. Sigma's shoulders jolted at the sudden attention.

Needless to say, Sigma didn't have a uniform because he wasn't a member of the department, but he had to at least be presentable to go in and out of the palace. Seiichirou had given him a set of shirts and such. He took it from the public funds, of course, because it was a necessity. This was more than fair in his opinion, since that hare-brained prince was using the country's dime to pay for the Holy Maiden's dresses and accessories. In the end, Yua asked to return them, putting most of that money back into the kingdom's coffers.

Sigma sent Seiichirou an imploring look. Although he generally had a good head on his shoulders, he understandably stiffened up around the nobility.

"This boy is a very skilled craftsman," Seiichirou said. "He has been given special permission to enter the Sorcery Department to assist with the research on magic tools and to further his own education."

"Oho! A future magic tool expert! He must be quite skilled indeed to have access to the palace at his age!" Georgi clapped his hands.

Next to him, Donato frowned. "But is he not of common birth? Are peasant children allowed inside royal research facilities?"

What if he leaked information or stole expensive materials and tools? Donato did not put this question into words, but Sigma understood the implication and looked at his feet.

Seiichirou thought *they* were more of a liability for barging into a highly confidential area without an appointment, but they were guests, so he did not say this aloud.

"Yes, well, he does not normally come and go so freely! He just happened to be here today! To observe!" Zoltan insisted.

The Romany sorcerers grimaced at his weaselly tone. Unlike their flaky boss, the promising young boy who showed up nearly every day had long since become one of their own. The fact that he could have proper conversations with *Ist* of all people made him invaluable. Sigma gave a little smile when the sorcerers patted him wordlessly on the shoulder, which made Seiichirou breathe a sigh of relief.

"He must have a great affinity for magic tools and manipulating magic to be granted access as a commoner!" Georgi looked very taken with Sigma, and young Luciano's eyes sparkled, too. Only Donato put much stock in blood, it seemed.

Just when Seiichirou was thinking that this was turning out surprisingly well, Sigma responded, "Oh no, um… I don't have much magic. I can't manipulate it at all."

"What?!" Georgi's naturally loud voice boomed even more vociferously. "How can you be a magic tool maker when you can't use magic?! It's absurd! What is going on in this country?!"

Sigma clammed up again at the reproachful remark. To make matters worse, none of his reliable sorcerer friends spoke up. They were all studious yet weak-willed sorts, and so all they could do was watch on, perturbed. Had Ist been around, he would have argued back, oblivious to the silent strain in the atmosphere.

But he wasn't, because Seiichirou had locked him away.

And so, with no other form of recourse, Seiichirou came to Sigma's aid.

"It is quite possible to work on magical tools without everyone involved being proficient in magic."

"What did you say?! You dare talk like an expert?!"

The man had poured decades of blood and sweat into pursuing his craft. Moreover, he was an important guest. Seiichirou could not afford to anger him.

"My apologies, I am merely an accountant and can only speak about the financial side. However, I can assemble the budget for the Sorcery Department to pursue its research."

"What of it?"

"I delegate the work to the right people for the job."

"What do you mean?" The frown was covering Georgi's entire face.

Seiichirou tried his very best to be patient and complimentary toward the man he was speaking to.

"Compared to your nation, the Romany Kingdom does not

possess as many individuals with both exemplary magic control and a robust knowledge of magic tools. As a nation with a wealth of magic tools, Egorova can have the best of both worlds."

"Hm, I suppose." Georgi didn't look too satisfied with that explanation. Neither did Donato or Luciano. Only Lars's smile remained unchanged.

"So here, the technicians and sorcerers focus on their respective crafts. By having them work together to create magic tools, they make up for what the other lacks."

"Hmm..."

"It is also difficult to find good people."

Indeed. Because magic came down almost entirely to innate talent, sorcerers and magic technicians were in terribly short supply. Egorova was unusual in its abundance.

This thought reminded Seiichirou that Egorova apparently had plenty of mines to extract magic stones from. Through human intervention, they could be used as a magic source. Much like how Seiichirou had only gradually developed resistance to magic after coming to Romany, perhaps people who lived in magicule-heavy regions possessed more magical power?

It occurred to Seiichirou that, if this assumption held true, then it was possible to address the labor shortage by artificially increasing people's magic capacity.

I'd love to ask Ist about this straight away...but that's not happening right now. Seiichirou calmed himself upon remembering the sorcerer he had locked up. *I can always do it after the Egorovans go home... Besides, I can ask Ciro about stuff related to the body.*

Ciro was the director of the Medical Bureau. He'd been looking out for Seiichirou ever since that one time he collapsed and Aresh dragged him in for a checkup.

While Seiichirou was expanding his mental list of tasks, Sigma withstood Georgi's barrage of questions.

"But how much are you able to achieve with your level of magic?"

"Well, um, we made a device that can measure magic power."

"Oh? This thing? So it changes color depending on the magic flow?"

"It has kelsil in it, you see, and…"

"Oho! It expands?! So *that's* how you get it to change color from the pressure! Interesting!" Georgi shouted, instantly grasping the mechanism behind the magic-measuring device Ist and Sigma had created.

This time, his tone was not reproachful, which left Sigma at a loss. "I-indeed," the boy replied falteringly, although he also seemed happy to talk about magic tools.

"Can I have a look, too?!" Luciano raised his hand.

Behind him, Donato looked interested as well. So they *were* just research nuts in the end.

"Wow, it's so simple yet elegant," said Luciano.

"Yes, I tried to make it so that anyone could use it…"

"Oho, a very pauper-like way of thinking," remarked Donato.

"It's important to make things easy to understand," Georgi commented.

"Yes, we have magic-measuring devices in our country, too, but they're made entirely differently," Luciano said as he brought out an object that looked like a finely made pocket watch. Sigma's creation looked more like a thermometer.

"How does your device work?" asked Sigma.

Georgi coughed. "Well, you see, you inscribe a chant on the magic ore here…"

"Wow! What a high-level technique!"

The other sorcerers started to gather around Sigma.

Great, thought Seiichirou, delighted at the demonstration. *Keep it coming.*

"Hey, it's showing on your face," Orjef whispered a warning.

"Huh? What is?" Seiichirou tilted his head without an ounce of self-awareness.

"That 'hell yeah' look you've got right now."

Seiichirou wasn't doing anything that went against the Romany

Kingdom's interests, so he just put on a bright, fake smile. "How imprudent of me."

"So you're not even denying it." Orjef sighed. "Well, whatever. Looks like this will go on for ages, so let's just talk about that other thing tomorrow."

"Yes, I suppose we should." Seiichirou nodded as he watched the lively discussion play out between the research nuts—er, talented technicians and sorcerers.

Despite the late start and the significant change in schedule, the current situation was ideal. If he waited for this to end and *then* talked to Orjef, he would probably get home during the Wood Hour (approximately nine in the evening).

"Then shall we talk tomorrow morning?" Seiichirou suggested. He had the feeling that nothing about this task was going to proceed according to schedule.

The same thought must have occurred to Orjef, because after a moment, he nodded.

ᐯᐯᐯ

"So how was it?" Lars asked.

After the tour and discussion at the Sorcery Department, the four Egorovans had a meal alone and chatted about their day in their provided guest room.

"Interesting," said Georgi. "Their technological prowess wouldn't make a dent in ours, but they make up for it with their imagination."

"Although I question the wisdom of involving the peasantry, I suppose the research did have some merit," said Donato.

They had evidently enjoyed themselves, though their faith in their own country remained unshaken. Lars's lips curved into a smile before he turned to the youngest member of their entourage, who was seated slightly apart from them.

"And how was it for you, Lufi?"

Luciano's cheeks were red, and the young sorcerer's adorable lips were twisted into a slight pout.

"It was enlightening. But…I was surprised that a boy without much magic was allowed into a court sorcerer's research area."

"Oh?" said Lars. "But you're young yourself, and yet here you are—a member of a foreign delegation."

"But I-I…! Are you saying I don't have talent?" Luciano looked down, dejected.

Lars and the others exchanged glances.

"Not at all," said Lars. "You are a talented sorcerer."

"Yes," said Donato, "I am sure that you will carry our nation's future."

"You won't get anywhere comparing yourself to others," said Georgi. "Besides, that kid's going to be a magic tool technician, not a sorcerer."

Among the royal siblings, Luciano had always possessed the most magical energy and a studious nature, which helped with learning new spells. Luciano was so talented, in fact, that there were hardly any obstacles to his participation in the tour to Romany. But this was all still relative to age—seeing a boy without connections make actual contributions to another country's Royal Sorcery Department was a blow to Luciano's confidence.

"If it bothers you, then take this opportunity to absorb as much as you can and let it fuel your growth," Lars said quietly.

Luciano nodded silently.

"Was there anything that piqued your interest, Your Highness?" asked Donato.

After giving a brief show of mulling it over, Lars smiled.

"Yes, I'm interested in *him*. The accountant."

The other men scowled upon hearing this.

"That peasant?" said Donato.

"He didn't leave a very strong impression…," Luciano commented.

"He said that he only had money on his mind," Georgi remarked.

The researchers had very typical reactions.

"The documents he handed out at the start were very well put together and easy to read," Lars continued without breaking his smile. "I believe he's a very capable man."

"But he can't use a lick of magic, right?"

"The Director of the Sorcery Department said he was only here because he put those documents together."

"My goodness... You're kicking up such a fuss when we haven't received even half the documentation. You didn't even read the papers he gave us, did you?"

The three research nuts stiffened.

Lars sighed as he eyed them. These three were bound to fixate on the magic side of the equation and let the other important details slip by. It was why Lars, a man with no magical talent, was the leader of the delegation.

When the subject of this tour came up, Lars thought of it as an unpleasant job, but he had his own objective in coming here. Unlike the other members, the movement spell research was just an afterthought to him.

"Do you know what our spy said the man was doing before today's gathering?"

Nobody had an answer to Lars's question. They just looked at each other.

"He was in the crown prince's personal quarters. They even had lunch together."

"What?! But isn't he supposed to be a commoner?!" The three of them were stunned.

Lars's smile deepened—it was just the reaction he'd expected. "Now, I don't know what exactly they discussed, but there's no question that he is on good terms with the prince."

At that point, Luciano blinked up at Lars. "Elder Brother! I remember! That man was at the dinner party..."

As he responded with a wordless smile, Lars's mind connected the dots.

Successful research into movement spells.

The Holy Maiden's purification.

A bastard prince.

A man of common birth, who was on friendly terms with both the crown prince and the bastard.

Not for the first time, Lars was glad that he chose to come to Romany.

CHAPTER FOUR

Misunderstood

As Seiichirou had expected, Aresh stayed in his room that night and never showed his face. Part of that was because Seiichirou came home late, but Aresh was supposed to have the next day off work. Seiichirou had assumed that he would at least show up the next morning, but Milan the maid told him that he left the house in a rush after breakfast.

Seiichirou's first destination was all too obvious.

"Is Orjef here?!"

The knights of the Third Royal Order gaped at the otherworlder who came barging into their station. Some knights, who saw their captain's darling as the source of their current problems, glared at him with hostility, but Seiichirou simply waltzed up to Orjef and pulled him into Aresh's office without a second thought.

"Have you heard anything about Aresh going to his family home?"

Orjef was surprised. Although they had promised to talk this morning, Seiichirou came in much earlier than he had expected— and he'd gone straight to the Knight's Station instead of their meeting place. But when he heard Seiichirou's question, Orjef calmed. He understood what this was about.

"No, that's news to me...but what a surprise. Never thought I'd see you so flustered."

Seiichirou blinked. It was only after Orjef pointed it out that he realized that he'd let his emotions get ahead of him.

"Sorry. I acted rashly," he apologized with embarrassment.

This display was so unusual for him that Orjef let out a snort of laughter. Seiichirou looked away uncomfortably, which struck Orjef as even *more* out of character, but it was also a bit of a relief because it meant that Aresh's feelings weren't one-sided.

"Let me just check. You and Aresh *are* in a romantic relationship, right?"

Seiichirou seemed to have expected this question because he nodded without much fuss. "Yes."

When Orjef thought about it, their relationship had been fishy from the start.

Even if Seiichirou had been summoned to this land by mistake, Aresh had no reason to be so dedicated to looking after him. It had been someone else's job to keep an eye on Seiichirou in the first place, and yet Aresh insisted on minding Seiichirou himself. Not to mention that he even bought a house for the otherworlder to live in after he had told Orjef for years that he couldn't be bothered to leave his family home. Even beyond that, he zealously backed the otherworlder's policy suggestions and took on a monster-slaying job that nobody asked him to do. He'd changed for the better, and it was all because of Seiichirou.

Seiichirou also matched the traits Aresh had mentioned when he'd once asked Orjef for romantic advice: *"Older," "works at the palace,"* and *"passionate about their job."* Honestly, why hadn't Orjef connected the dots sooner? This man was the only person in Aresh's vicinity who fit the bill.

It came as a shock to Orjef, who had always thought he was savvy about relationships, but, well... Maybe it was because Seiichirou had always given off the impression that he was married to his job. This made Orjef wonder if perhaps Aresh's feelings were one-sided, but between the lapel pin and Seiichirou's current emotional display, that didn't seem to be the case.

Happy for you, Aresh...

Orjef couldn't help but get misty-eyed, but when he recalled the grueling marches Aresh had put them through between the purifying expeditions and the monster exterminations, he decided that his younger cousin deserved a *bit* of resentment. At the same time, he remembered that he hadn't called for Seiichirou just so that he could make fun of Aresh.

Besides, the situation seemed to be changing.

"I didn't hear about Aresh going back home, but I can more or less imagine why he did," he said.

"You can?!" Seiichirou's gaze zipped back to Orjef in surprise.

Orjef poked the other man's chest. "It's 'cause of that lapel pin from the dinner party. Anyone would've guessed what was up between you two. Not many people in this country have purple in their appearance."

Who else got along well with the otherworlder *and* had the money to prepare a silver flower for him? That narrowed it down to just one person.

Not to mention that the party was a gathering of influential nobles. It was inevitable that word would reach Aresh's family, the marquess house of Indolark.

"......Oh, I...see......"

In other words, Aresh's family had summoned him because of his relationship with Seiichirou.

The whole business with the lapel pin had been Aresh's decision. Although Seiichirou had his own problems with that, the idea that he was a burden to Aresh was...well, troubling, to say the least.

Wait, no! I was the one who wanted to take this slow! Aresh got ahead of himself!

This was about *their* relationship, after all. It was a problem that Aresh had not breathed a word to him about it going public beforehand. Why was he only hearing about it from other people after the fact? Although Aresh might have assumed that intra-nobility politics was outside Seiichirou's domain, Seiichirou could have at least done his research and come up with ideas if he'd been given the heads-up.

"If you're asking me about this, then I guess Aresh hasn't told you?" Orjef said.

Seiichirou didn't want to just nod to that, so he averted his gaze.

Orjef sighed. "Well, you guys were arguing, right? Geez, leave it to Aresh to make a mess of things..."

"What did you say?"

"Oh...whatever. Let me vent." That reminded Seiichirou—Orjef had been wanting to talk to him *before* Aresh left the house. "It was the day after the dinner party. Aresh doesn't normally give hands-on instructions to the knights, but this time he did, and...boy, was it rough."

Although Aresh trained regularly, he hardly ever showed his subordinates what to do. When he offered his guidance, the knights who admired him jumped at the opportunity...only to be swiftly disillusioned. The training regimen was on another level entirely— far too strict for the average person.

To top it off, Aresh's scowl afterward was thirty percent worse than usual. It was as if one could see a dark aura emanating from him. Time and again, Orjef felt the need to say something, but stopped himself before the words left his mouth. On an emotional level, he was drained well before lunch.

Aresh's moping made it all too obvious that something had happened, and it wasn't too difficult to figure out what might have been the cause.

"So what happened between you two?" Orjef asked bluntly. No doubt he felt the right to pry given that Seiichirou had caused him trouble, and he'd volunteered information of his own.

So Seiichirou answered frankly. "You see..."

A few minutes later, Orjef collapsed against his captain's office table. Without the table's support, Orjef would have been flat on the floor.

"So basically...he did all that without your consent..."

"Yes... That sums it up."

That guy had lost his mind!

Experiencing love for the first time must have knocked a screw loose!

Aresh's expressionless face from when they were children circled through Orjef's mind.

"I'm so sorry about my cousin..." Orjef bowed his head.

Now it was Seiichirou's turn to feel flustered. He hadn't expected an apology.

"Er, no, he hasn't really been any...trou..." He tried to finish the sentence, but then he realized it was too much of a lie.

"Ha... No need to push yourself..."

"No, I mean... Yes, he has caused trouble, but his feelings...are not a burden to me!"

The problem was that Aresh had made a decision without discussing or explaining any of it. Seiichirou wanted to stress that Aresh's feelings in and of themselves were not the issue.

"I'm kinda relieved to hear that."

Orjef had only been thinking about Aresh's actions. Looking back on it rationally, there was always the possibility that he'd forced his feelings onto Seiichirou, but that thankfully wasn't the case. Orjef was glad that his relative was no criminal.

Meanwhile, Seiichirou was secretly overcome with emotion.

Between what Yurius said the day before and the attitude of Aresh's servants, Seiichirou had gotten the impression that everyone thought it was obvious that Aresh should propose to him, and that Aresh was the victim here. It was as if Seiichirou was the only one with a different idea of what was "normal," and it made him remember how lonely it felt when he first came to this world. He'd been expecting Orjef to reproach him, too, and so the apology took him by surprise.

Although Seiichirou had heard that Orjef and Aresh were only distantly related, they were the vice commander and commander of the same Royal Order. Between their blood and work ties, one could certainly say that Orjef was the closest person to Aresh. Seiichirou was relieved to have him on his side, but...

"Phew... People always said Aresh left his emotions in his mother's womb. Glad he managed to find someone to love him, warts and all."

"I don't know how to respond to that."

Since they had time, Seiichirou waited for Orjef to change into his uniform. They chatted as they walked to their next destination.

"What do you suppose Aresh's family thinks?"

"Who knows? I've never had that much to do with them."

Orjef and Aresh's mothers were sisters. Although that made them cousins, their mothers came from very different stations. Aresh's was born from their grandfather's first wife, while Orjef's was born from the second wife, so although the two men were related by blood, they didn't spend much time together until Aresh joined the Royal Order.

From what Seiichirou understood, House Indolark was stationed in the capital, although their main residence was in a region near the sea. Aresh's mother, two older brothers, and one older sister lived there.

"Aresh's older siblings are all married, and there have never been any sleazy rumors around Aresh. I doubt they'll give him a hard time without hearing him out."

Orjef seemed to think that they would react much like he did: incredulous that Aresh of all people had developed feelings for someone.

But Seiichirou was perturbed. Even if that was the case, *he* was the partner in question. A man from another world.

Regardless of this country's tolerance for same-sex relationships, there was still a mountain of other problems, chief among them the impromptu announcement at a dinner party. Seiichirou would have liked to take the time to introduce himself to Aresh's parents first...

Wait, why am I assuming that we're going to get married?!

Seiichirou had jumped to thinking about the most effective, conflict-free method of getting things done, except that marriage wasn't necessarily his goal in the first place. Aresh was infecting him.

Then again, it wasn't as if he wanted to break up, either. A part of him certainly wanted Aresh's parents to acknowledge their relationship, but...

"By the way," Seiichirou said, after a long pause, "what did you think of the Egorovan envoys?"

"Now, *that's* a sudden change of topic!"

Well, it *was* the very next thing on the agenda. *I'm not running away,* Seiichirou told himself as he switched his brain into work mode.

"Well, whatever," said Orjef with a sigh. "The magic tool expert seemed passionate about the research. The sorcerer was a cookie-cutter noble, but his enthusiasm for the craft was genuine."

Seiichirou shared the same opinion. He nodded, waiting for Orjef to continue.

"Their bodyguards were as skilled as you'd expect. The real wild-cards are...those other two."

"You're counting Luciano?" asked Seiichirou. He had assumed that only Prince Lars would have caught Orjef's interest.

"Yeah. Of course, I've heard a lot of things about Prince Lars, like how he's got a faction backing him for the throne even though he's the son of a concubine."

"The son of a concubine *and* he's the third born?" Seiichirou had done some basic research, but he was only familiar with the surface-level facts.

"Yeah, but it's not like there's a problem with the other princes. Prince Lars is just that talented."

Although he wasn't blatantly angling for the throne, he nonchalantly demonstrated his competence in many different areas, from philanthropy to regional inspections and reforms. Before long, he ended up gathering clout through important tasks like the magic stone extraction work.

"Now that you mention it, he did seem to get along with the technician and the sorcerer," said Seiichirou.

The two were respectful toward Lars as a prince, but also strangely familiar with him as well, which implied a prior acquaintance.

"In Egorova, you need spells and magic tools to extract the magic ore. If a lower-ranked prince can get on good terms with either group, he can jump up the line of succession. That is, if he's got something the others don't."

"Interesting…"

From what Seiichirou was hearing, Lars was doing very well for himself. By carefully laying the foundations and seizing connections with the influential technicians, he was setting himself up as a wise and savvy ruler. That had to be one of the reasons he decided to lead the diplomatic delegation.

Looking back, Lars had read Seiichirou's documents with keen interest. Even when his fellow envoys went off the rails, he only let them do as they pleased after paying careful attention to his surroundings. People like him were natural leaders.

We'll need Prince Lars for future diplomatic dealings… No, wait. Would relying on him cause friction with the other factions?

Seiichirou gave the matter some thought before shrugging. It wasn't his job to worry about diplomacy. Camile and the other higher-ups had more knowledge and political savvy up their sleeves to set the stage for future success. Seiichirou's job was to ensure that the current tour ran smoothly.

Anyway, Seiichirou had a grasp on Lars's involvement, but Luciano's presence raised some questions.

As far as Seiichirou could see, the boy had an interest in movement spells and had insisted on joining the delegation as a relative to the royal family… This made him the privileged young master of the group, so to speak. Although his youth was evident not just in his appearance but in the way he spoke and acted, his zeal for magic was genuine. The questions he asked the Romany court sorcerers were just as astute as any expert's.

"But still, the others were awfully polite to him…too polite, even," Orjef remarked. "I feel like I've seen that kid somewhere before…"

"You have?" Seiichirou cocked his head, wondering if Orjef was talking about Luciano's relation to the royal family.

But Orjef gave him an exasperated look. "You're surprisingly useless…"

"This is outside my area of expertise, so I must defer to others," Seiichirou replied.

Let the most suitable person do the job, he was trying to say.

Only for Orjef to hit him with "I wouldn't say that about a guy who can be with Aresh."

He wasn't going to let Seiichirou live that down.

▽▽▽

Perhaps the Egorovans were satisfied after getting their fill of the Sorcery Department, or maybe Lars's scolding had done the trick, because the group obediently read the documents today. Lars in particular had a lot of questions, which Seiichirou and Qusta took responsibility for answering. Zoltan would always respond to any query about the Sorcery Department with "Qusta will explain in more detail!", which was a waste of time, but other than that it all went smoothly.

The problem arose after lunch.

The guests had been given their own dining space. It was all well and good for them to use this time to chat with the tour guides, until someone mentioned Sigma. Luciano was the one who brought it up, but it was Lars who pressed the subject.

"I heard yesterday that the church is running a private school for common-born children."

Although Seiichirou was the one who spearheaded the project, his job was to praise the nation. He shot Orjef a look to say, "Leave this to me."

"Yes, Prince Yurius believes that the commoners are in need of education," he said.

"His Highness himself?" Donato sounded impressed.

"Indeed. He believes that commoners should have the opportunity to learn simple things such as reading, arithmetic, and etiquette to nurture the next generation of working citizens."

"The commoners, hm? What purpose does that serve?"

"I believe the boy we met yesterday will be a promising technician," said Georgi.

"Yeah. He might not come from nobility or have much magic, but he's already achieving things," Luciano remarked.

The two of them seemed to have quite a favorable impression of Sigma and were happy to chat about him. Only Lars seemed to have a different idea about where to steer the conversation.

As he cut finely into his garegas, a dish wrapped in pie dough and fried, he lifted his gaze.

"I heard that it was the current Holy Maiden who proposed the idea."

Ah, so that's his angle, Seiichirou nodded to himself as he stabbed a fork through his salad.

Romany was not yet aware of how Egorova planned to use movement spells. Given those circumstances, the kingdom was unwilling to give them access to the Holy Maiden. If by some terrible happenstance Seiichirou's identity as an otherworlder was revealed, handing *him* over was the better option. He guessed that this was one of the reasons he was chosen as a guide. He was just as valuable as Yua in the sense that he was living proof that a movement spell could summon a person from another world.

"You're well-informed," said Seiichirou. "Indeed, Her Holiness and His Highness are leading the project."

"The current holy maiden is quite a go-getter, I see."

"Yes. Although she was unfamiliar with our magical methods, she is an extremely hardworking and benevolent soul."

"Ah, but I suppose she is familiar with our magic now." Lars was not giving up easily.

Zoltan was the one who answered. "Why, yes, but she is still not yet fit to appear before other nations! Much less royalty!" he said, deflecting Lars's implication with a laugh.

Camile or Yurius must have cautioned him not to let Lars cross paths with Yua. Seiichirou was grateful for the intervention, but they weren't out of the woods yet.

"Is that so? What a shame. But I am very interested in this private school for uneducated commoners. Would you be able to take us there?"

All eyes on the Romany side turned to Seiichirou.

Seiichirou stood up, trying very hard not to make his confusion evident in his gaze. "We cannot make suitable arrangements for you at short notice, so please allow me to speak with the church first."

He bowed, left the dining hall, and then broke into a speedy power walk.

He knew the private school's schedule, but he didn't know which days Yua and Yurius visited. First, he had to check their schedules, *and* he had to inform the church...!

It was day three of the diplomatic mission.

Not a single day so far had gone according to plan—what a pain in the neck.

Once Seiichirou managed to hear about Yurius and Yua's movements through the Second Royal Order, he told them not to approach the church that day. Then he sent a message to the church, and in practically no time at all, both the Egorovan and Romany delegates headed to the same destination in separate carriages.

"What made you want to see the education facility so suddenly, Your Highness?" Donato asked as he made himself comfortable on the sofa. The Egorovan carriage had quite a large and opulent seating area, which was good enough for something the Romany side had prepared on short notice.

Lars had told them the day before to listen carefully to what the Romany side explained today.

"There was something I was a little curious about," he said.

"Are you talking about the current holy maiden?"

The Holy Maiden appeared once every hundred years in the Romany Kingdom to purify the miasma. Other nations were privy to this legend, and in Egorova there was much talk about how Romany had revived its ancient summoning magic to bring forth its current Holy Maiden from another world.

"I'm interested in their purification and summoning magic, too, but I get the impression they don't want us to meet this holy maiden," said Donato.

"Oh, is that why you got the idea to suddenly visit a place she often goes?" Luciano asked.

Lars laughed and shook his head. "I'd never be so underhanded... Oh, why are you all looking away? Anyway, we only have seven days here, so I won't get hung up about the holy maiden."

It was too soon for her to appear at diplomatic junctions. If they were going to unveil her, it would be with much fanfare. Lars wasn't planning on cutting ahead of schedule.

"I've also considered the idea of opening an educational facility for commoners, so I'm interested in seeing how theirs works," he said.

"'Also,' you say. So there's something else?" Luciano asked.

The corner of Lars's lip turned up. "Apparently, a certain illegitimate son from the Royal Accounting Department is a teacher at the private school."

"What a coincidence!"

According to their spy, Norbert regularly taught arithmetic while juggling his work at the Accounting Department.

"So even the royal family is directly involved... They're quite serious about educating the peasants, it seems." Donato frowned as if he could not grasp their reasoning.

The smile faded from Lars's lips. "That's one way of thinking about it. His motives for getting involved might be different from those of the crown prince."

The Romany guides had mentioned that the Holy Maiden and crown prince sponsored the private school. However, the kingdom was bound to suffer a financial burden were the project to expand.

Then there was the king's bastard son, who took the lowest seat at the dinner party. Did he get involved in the church's private school out of his own volition, or was someone else behind it?

"The Royal Accounting Department...that's where that guide is from," Luciano said.

"Kondo, yes. I find him very interesting."

"You had a lot of praise for his paperwork."

Indeed, upon closer inspection, the documents (which had turned into a bigger stack than the day before) covered a wide breadth while being easy to digest. It would have taken a lot of time and effort for a single person to compile, which lent credence to the idea that the Accounting Department *as a whole* had prepared them beforehand.

"That's part of it, but I also got the impression yesterday that he's the one in charge of the tour group."

The listless-looking man was the quickest to respond whenever the Egorovan side diverted from the itinerary.

"No way. Isn't he just doing all the running around because he's a grunt?"

"Even still, he's got a sharp intuition and he's quick at his job. I'd find a worker like him rather handy to have around." Although he came for the movement spells, Lars smiled at the unexpected discovery.

Knowing very well that the prince always got his hands on what he wanted, Georgi and Donato exchanged glances. They felt sorry for the poor accountant.

But then Luciano said, as if only just struck by the thought, "Oh, you mustn't, Elder... Your Highness. He has a partner in this country."

"Oh, really?"

The man had not given off any such impression today or the day before.

Luciano nodded firmly. "Yes, he had a purple gem in his silver flower accessory at the dinner party."

"A flower... The mias flower signifies 'eternity' in Romany, if I recall. I suppose that means he is married or betrothed, then?"

"Yes, and he had spinels on his arm cuffs."

"Well, well... He must have quite the zealous partner indeed."

"Spinels are quite rare jewels, aren't they? They've got to be wealthy."

As the four Egorovans recalled the visage of the man who had been with them until just a short while ago, they got the impression that some things didn't add up. But they were satisfied with the idea, at least, that Kondo's partner was a hopeless romantic, had plenty of money to spare, and had purple in their appearance.

"I suppose it would be difficult to poach him if he has a partner," Lars mused.

"If you're that insistent upon it, why don't you poach his partner along with him?"

"No, someone with that kind of money has to be an influential noble. I doubt they'd be willing to part ways with their country."

But still, Lars wondered just who the man's partner was.

"Welcome. I hope you have not been waiting long." Siegvold greeted them at the capital's church, which wasn't terribly far from the palace.

Siegvold was the straitlaced and slightly overzealous priest who had assisted Seiichirou back when he was auditing the church. He liked to refer to Seiichirou as a "disciple of Abran." Although he was the eldest son of the influential Marquess Erwell, he was sent to the church when he was young because of his poor magic control, which spurred his blind faith in the Abran religion. Apparently, when he discovered that praying to a magic stone calmed him down (by absorbing his magic), he and his family decided that he would devote his life to serving God.

"It's nice to see you again, Priest Siegvold. Apologies for the sudden imposition."

"No, Disciple—erm, Mr. Seiichirou—I'm always happy to oblige your requests."

When Seiichirou turned to introduce Siegvold to the Egorovans, the four members of the delegation were staring at the two of them with wide eyes. He found that puzzling.

"Your Highness, um…this is Priest Siegvold, a priest who serves the Romany capital's church," said Seiichirou aloud. Mentally, he was asking himself what on earth had them so shocked.

Lars was the first to gather his wits.

"I apologize for the sudden visit," he said as he smiled and offered a hand. "I am Lars Eric, from Egorova."

"I am Siegvold, a priest. Please make yourselves at home."

They shook hands amicably. The sight of the two attractive men of differing heights made for an appealing picture. Yua might have squealed if she'd been around. Although she'd calmed down considerably as of late, she still had a habit of gushing over beautiful people. It was one of the reasons why she wasn't quite ready to be in public.

"You've come to observe the private school in the relief house, yes?" said Siegvold. "The children have been taught the basics of etiquette, but please do inform me if anyone inconveniences you."

"Oh no, we're the inconveniences here. I would never take offense."

Seiichirou was relieved to hear Lars say this. Although the children were studying etiquette, almost all of them came from peasant backgrounds. The relief house children were better, but still too young to know how to conduct themselves in front of foreign royalty. Seiichirou felt like giving Siegvold a thumbs-up for securing Lars's word.

He couldn't actually do that, of course, so he settled for whispering his gratitude when Zoltan ushered Lars's group ahead. "Thank you, Mr. Siegvold."

"No need to thank me. It's my responsibility to look after the children. More importantly, how are you doing, Mr. Seiichirou? It

must be quite a handful for you to guide foreign visitors around when you're already so busy."

"Ha-ha, I'm fine. My plate won't be full for too long."

"Good to hear. Take care of yourself, yes?"

The schedule was quite relaxed to accommodate the royalty in the group. On the flip side, *preparing* for the tour had been very taxing, and there were a lot of out-of-the-blue requests from day one.

But grumbling about it would change nothing, so Seiichirou smiled and pressed on.

"It should be time for Group Three's arithmetic lesson about now. Have there been any changes to the plan?"

"No, the lesson has only just started, so I believe it should be fine for the visitors to sit in."

Come to think of it, Seiichirou had a feeling that Norbert was today's tutor. It was the perfect opportunity to check on how things were going.

He was so consumed by his thoughts that he did not notice that the Egorovans were eyeing his friendly attitude with Siegvold with keen interest.

"Purple..." they muttered.

"By the way, Mr. Seiichirou, how are you holding up here in the relief house?" Siegvold asked out of concern for Seiichirou's weakness to magic and magicules. The church had a higher magic density than other places because it stored the sacred object, an important magic tool, and had barrier spells cast around it.

"Don't worry, I'm fine. I'm not here during prayer time, and the effect should be slight because I have a barrier on me."

Aresh had cast his extra-heavy-duty barrier just three days ago. That was practically no time at all compared to how long Aresh had been absent during the purification expeditions and monster extermination mission. The barrier still had plenty of punch.

This thought sparked a realization: *It's...only been three days.*

Just three days had passed since the fight after the dinner party.

Even though Aresh had spent much more time away on his military dispatches, they hadn't been living together back then. Three days without seeing his face felt like such a long time now.

In the past, Seiichirou would go two or three weeks at a time without seeing his partner whenever he was consumed with work. This would cause them to break up, of course, but his busy schedule always made him forget about the other person straight away. No, maybe it was more accurate to say that the thought never even crossed his mind. For better or worse, work controlled his life, leaving no room for tender feelings.

Why am I thinking about this when I'm guiding important foreign guests? There's a lot weighing on this job...

It was strange to Seiichirou how much Aresh dominated his thoughts, but that didn't change the fact that he had an important job to do. He refocused his mind.

"O-oh, I see... A barrier, hm?"

Meanwhile, Siegvold responded to Seiichirou by turning slightly red in the face and averting his gaze.

Although Siegvold possessed a lot of magic, he wasn't too good at sensing it. He hadn't noticed when Seiichirou had a barrier around him before. So when Seiichirou got magic-sickness, Ist showed him how "barrier spells" and "magic acclimatization" worked. Remembering this, Siegvold pieced together how Seiichirou got his barrier.

Mercifully, Seiichirou had no idea what was going on in Siegvold's head. Since they were now almost at the relief house, Seiichirou excused himself to the Egorovans and went on ahead to the classroom to check in.

As they watched him go, the Egorovans nodded to each other. They'd seen enough of Seiichirou and Siegvold's interaction to draw their own conclusions.

The school was just finishing up its arithmetic lesson.

The children were divided into groups catering to their academic levels. There were about twenty in each group, a mix of orphans and commoners. Since many couldn't afford paper or pens, the woodwork and metalwork studios donated thin tree bark and inkless pens to carve with. The townsfolk offered their full support, given that the local children were studying for free. The church was quite the bustling scene these days, with more commoners coming and going than ever.

"Nice. They're well-behaved," Orjef murmured.

"They're all different ages," Luciano commented.

Seiichirou nodded. "School is an invaluable opportunity for the common-born children. Their parents are very encouraging as well, since it affects their future. Because we are only teaching the fundamentals, the groups are not sorted by age."

"But wouldn't some kids learn faster than others?" asked Orjef. Even if they started at the same point, a five-year-old and a twelve-year-old picked things up at a different pace.

"The lessons have only just started, so they are taking things step by step. The school plans to adjust the groups based on their progress in the near future."

"I see..."

Since the children wouldn't be progressing to higher education, the idea was to create an environment for easy learning. Special classes would be made for promising children who became the next state-sponsored students in Sigma's footsteps.

"I see you value thoroughness and ability over age," Lars said to Seiichirou directly.

Seiichirou glanced at Orjef and Zoltan, and then replied, "Of course. This is not just a philanthropic effort but a matter of raising talent for the country."

The arithmetic lesson ended without incident, at which point Seiichirou called the tutor over.

"Oh, hey! What brings you here, Sei?" Norbert made no effort to hide his displeasure. Although he'd realized immediately that other people were observing, he couldn't stop the class. The only thing he'd heard was that important people from another country had come to observe.

"You know I'm a guide. You can figure it out," said Seiichirou.

"I thought it would just be the foreign guests." Norbert whined. He was basically saying that he was more uncomfortable with Seiichirou watching him than foreign royalty.

Zoltan desperately waved his hand. "Anyway! Won't you introduce yourself to His Highness Prince Lars?"

"Oh, right, sorry. I am Norbert Blanc. I was at the dinner party, though I doubt you'd remember me."

"Ah, yes, I know you. I am Lars Eric. Pleased to make your acquaintance."

When Lars took the reins and offered his own hand in greeting, Norbert, Zoltan, and Orjef all turned wide-eyed. The prince of a great nation had chosen to greet a lowly civil official like an equal. Even if Norbert was from a count's family, it was still shocking.

Norbert hesitated and looked at Seiichirou, but it wasn't as if Seiichirou had the foggiest idea what was going on. In any case, Norbert clearly couldn't ignore Lars's outstretched hand. Seiichirou's eyes flickered in that direction, silently urging his subordinate to return the handshake.

And so Norbert timidly put his hand out.

"Phew, that was nerve-racking! Prince Lars is way more down-to-earth than the rumors make him sound," a relieved Norbert said to Seiichirou and Orjef later, after Zoltan had escorted Lars and his group to the church's inner garden.

"Down-to-earth... I don't know about that," said Orjef.

"Huh? You don't think so?"

"It's hard to say. Well, he is pretty casual with the technician and sorcerer in his party, so I guess he's down-to-earth in that sense?"

Orjef's comment reminded Seiichirou of their conversation from that morning. Lars was indeed casual with certain people. He knew exactly how to treat those who would be "useful" to him in the future—which implied that Norbert fell into that category. But what about him had piqued Lars's interest?

Then Seiichirou suddenly remembered: *Oh, right. He's technically royalty…*

It was easy to forget because of the way Norbert normally acted. Only some of Romany's nobility were privy to Norbert's bloodline—did the leader of the Egorovan delegation stumble upon this knowledge, or did he go out of his way to dig it up?

"Anyway, it sure was a surprise to see you show up out of the blue, Sei!" Norbert said, which reminded Seiichirou…

"Sixty-five points."

"You're grading me?! I was hoping you'd let me off the hook…"

"You speak too quickly. While in front of people, you speak one-point-five times faster than you think, so you have to enunciate. Also, your classes need a tighter focus. Show me your lesson plan later."

"Shucks…"

"You two sure are chummy…" It was Orjef's first time seeing Seiichirou speak without any deference whatsoever. He was a bit worried about what Aresh might think.

Just as Seiichirou was lecturing Norbert, he felt a tug on his cloak. Turning around, he saw a boy with fluffy light green hair, who was about a head shorter than him.

"Oh, Selio."

The young priest-in-training had guided Seiichirou around back when he was investigating the church. Between his fluffy hair and long eyebrows, he was as cute as a girl, though his attitude was not nearly as pleasant.

"Hey, you… You should've said hi to the church people if you were coming."

Selio was not part of today's school group, if Seiichirou's memory served correctly, and so he must have come running after he heard about the visit.

"Ah, sorry. I didn't have any business with the church today."

"Y-yeah, but you still should've said *something!* It's not like I'd force you to come inside or anything."

Seiichirou felt deeply moved that their relationship had come so far that Selio knew about his condition and even showed concern for him.

"Sorry. Next time I'll come when you're having a lesson."

"Okay, but…when would that be?"

"I can't say off the top of my head, but…I'm sure it will be soon."

"Really? Definitely? Do you swear to Abran?"

Seiichirou thought it was a bit much to swear to the god who had kidnapped him and Yua from their world without so much as a by-your-leave, though he decided to nod along.

"Oh man, I look away for one second and you've gone and made more work," Norbert pointed out.

Seiichirou was about to argue when he noticed that Lars and his cadre had returned.

"Hello, Kondo. I see you have a good reputation here at this school as well."

"I suppose so. I taught some lessons in counting when the school was first getting off the ground."

"Oh, did you? By the way, I heard Norbert and the priest call you 'Sei.' Is that your family name?"

Crap.

The visit had been so off the cuff that Seiichirou had forgotten to ask people not to call him that. He got the feeling that he would be exposed immediately if he froze up and told a lie, so he decided to just tell the truth.

"Kondou is my family name, and Seiichirou is my given name."

"Ah, so Kondo is your surname. Your name is Sei… Pardon me, could you say it again?"

"Seiichirou."

"Sei…chiro?"

People in this world in general, not just Romany, found it difficult to pronounce Japanese names, it seemed. To be fair, Seiichirou's name was a mouthful even in Japan.

"That's right."

"Seichiro, then. All right, I've committed it to memory."

A dazzling smile lit up the man's handsome, doll-like face. Even Seiichirou, who was used to seeing Aresh, found Lars too blinding to look at without squinting. Beauty was a curse indeed.

"But I must say that your partner is quite possessive to restrict others from calling you by your first name," Lars said with a meaningful look.

Seiichirou almost combusted on the spot.

The moment Lars and his group were out of the area, Selio tugged on Seiichirou's cloak relentlessly as if to say, "What partner? *Who?*" Seiichirou decided to go home. Behind him, Norbert burst out laughing, which was highly aggravating to say the least. Seiichirou decided to give him some new work when he got back to the Accounting Department.

They visited the church just after lunch, so it wasn't terribly late by the time Seiichirou got home. He wondered if Aresh was back yet.

"Welcome home, Mr. Seiichirou." Valtom the butler had come to the door to greet him.

"Thanks. I'm back," Seiichirou replied.

The ever-sensible vassal figured out what Seiichirou was thinking just by his gaze.

"If you are looking for Aresh, he has not yet returned."

"Oh? Um... I see." Seiichirou's first impulse was to deny his intentions—it was embarrassing, after all, for someone else to see right through him. However, since he wasn't hurting anyone by inquiring about Aresh, he decided to just come clean and ask the most knowledgeable person in the room. "Do you know when he will return?"

"It is hard to say... He sent a message saying that he will be staying with his family for the foreseeable future."

"Excuse me?!" Seiichirou couldn't help but exclaim at this unexpected answer.

So Aresh went back to his family the day after they had a fight, and now he was staying there for "the foreseeable future"? Was he an actual child?!

And here I was thinking about him while I was on the job...

Okay, that part was all Seiichirou's doing and had nothing to do with Aresh. He was pretty much fooling himself there.

Seiichirou collected his thoughts and took a deep breath.

If Aresh went to his parents' house after they had a fight, then the logical thing for Seiichirou to do was pay him a visit and apologize, but that probably wasn't how it worked here. It would be strange for a commoner and otherworlder like himself to visit a marquess out of the blue. And besides, Aresh was an adult. He wouldn't dump all the emotional labor onto Seiichirou so he could sort out his feelings alone.

He is a little...no, very childish in some ways, but...

Seiichirou knew that Aresh was generally considerate of Seiichirou's place in noble society. He could trust that.

Which left one thing for Seiichirou to do.

"Very well, I understand. Please inform me when you know when he will return."

"But of course."

He had a mountain of tasks ahead of him. Tomorrow they would be visiting the Sorcery Department again, and although he didn't foresee another abrupt schedule change, he had to stay on his toes. He had to plot his next course while Zoltan and Qusta handled the touring and explanations.

Seiichirou had somewhere he needed to be before that tour, so he decided to rest early.

Having a lot of work meant that he didn't have to deal with intrusive thoughts.

Seiichirou arrived at the palace early the next morning. The tour with the Egorovans would start after the Light Hour, but Seiichirou showed up at the Wood Hour, two hours before. Although he was curious about how things were going at the Accounting Department, he had another destination in mind.

He was walking down a corridor with a high ceiling. Although one could see a magnificent garden through the humongous wood-framed windows, the sight barely even registered to Seiichirou. He simply made a beeline for the first floor of the west wing, which was near the main tower.

More often than not, he was dragged to this place without volition or consciousness, but he still knew exactly where it was.

"Excuse me, is the director here?" he asked the white-coated members of the Medical Bureau.

They led him into one of the back areas: Ciro's personal operating room and study. As always, every inch of the high walls was crammed with books. Seiichirou wondered if the people who had a checkup here ever had something to say about it.

"Huh? Kondo?! Did you hear about it from Aresh? It's not done yet!" Ciro Quellbus, a man with gold-green glasses and dirty blond hair, took one look at Seiichirou before gaping in shock.

"What do you mean, 'It's not done yet'?" Seiichirou responded, puzzled by the man's choice of words.

"Huh? Aresh didn't tell you about the medicine? What did you come here for, then?"

Seiichirou wanted to ask about his theory: Did living in a region rich with magic and magicules increase a person's magical power?

But that all felt very much beside the point after that weird conversation opening.

"I came to ask your thoughts about something, but what's this about medicine? Does it have something to do with Aresh?"

"Oh, now I've done it. Aresh is going to bite my head off."

Seiichirou was just guessing here, but it sounded like Ciro had let something slip that Aresh had asked him to do in secret. Now he couldn't just let the man off the hook. When Seiichirou repeated his question, Ciro talked easily. Perhaps he wasn't so afraid of Aresh after all.

"He asked me to make a cure for magic-sickness and poisoning."

"Magic poisoning, you say?" Seiichirou wondered if it was for him.

Most inhabitants of this world had innate magicule tolerance, likely because of exposure since birth. This invalidated the need for a medicinal cure for magicule poisoning. The same thing went for magic-sickness.

But Seiichirou's level of magic resistance was only just barely good enough for everyday activities, even if it had improved by leaps and bounds since his arrival. He couldn't consume magicule-heavy indulgences, nor could he approach magic-dense areas with ease. Although Aresh's barrier allowed him to enter the church and Sorcery Department without issue, he would probably break out into a fever without it.

"He said that although he can normally take care of you, he can't when he's on military duty and whatnot."

The Third Royal Order dealt chiefly with monster exterminations. Since monsters often appeared in remote areas, Aresh could be gone for long stretches of time. Although he hadn't been on any major campaigns thus far because of the Holy Maiden's purification expeditions, that would likely change in the future. Seiichirou had been told that monsters became more active during the warmer seasons.

"......" Seiichirou said nothing.

Aresh had always counted on casting a barrier once a week before Seiichirou went to a risky area. This meant that he would insist on spending time in bed together, which was nice and all, but...this was about Seiichirou's body and no one else's. It should have just been a matter of Seiichirou looking out for himself. All he really needed to do was stay away from places dense with magicules.

And yet he went to the church and Sorcery Department anyway—because it was his job.

Although Aresh was always telling Seiichirou to cut down on work and take care of his body, he never told Seiichirou to quit. He understood and respected that work was how Seiichirou asserted his identity.

Sure, he might have a childish side, and he nags and does things without asking, but...

Seiichirou feigned a cough to hide his burning cheeks and looked away. As his mind worked to subdue the flush on his face, he asked Ciro the question that had driven him to the Medical Bureau in the first place.

"You think the magicules in the environment can increase a person's magical power?" Ciro repeated.

"The possibility crossed my mind after I interacted with the Egorovans."

"I've never considered it before." Ciro crossed his arms and plopped himself on the sofa. At his urging, Seiichirou took the seat across from him. "People have always said that magic power is hereditary, hence why the nobility have more of it."

Since being able to use magic was a sign of status and one had to be taught how to control it, only the nobility were placed into environments where they could learn that. Occasionally, some people like Siegvold demonstrated exceptional magical power. For this reason, the common-born children who possessed a lot of magic but lacked the ability to control it were often adopted into the church.

"If people share the same blood, it means they're more likely to be raised in the same environment," Seiichirou commented.

"Yes, I suppose you could say that."

"It's still just a hypothesis at this stage, but can I ask you to look into it for me? We might be able to address the labor shortage by increasing people's magical power."

"So in other words..." Ciro's spectacles glinted. "We won't have to fight the church to get healers!"

Healing spells required exquisite magic control, which meant they could only be used by those who had been specifically taught how to do so. Yua, the Holy Maiden, was a perfect example: she had received the finest education possible from a master of the craft. Because of this, the country's two biggest authorities—the church and the palace—frequently squabbled over the small talent pool.

Currently, they resorted to using local town healers, who only had enough power to cast basic spells.

"Yes, if we can gather people with a lot of magical energy, we can start a school to teach them how to control it," said Seiichirou.

The nobility mainly attended academies where they were taught a wide variety of pursuits. Most of this was irrelevant for people who were aiming to become healers. It was basically the difference between university and vocational school.

"Given that this is a matter of recruiting talent, I will consult with the prime minister about it. May I tell him that I have your support?" asked Seiichirou.

"Oh yes! Be my guest!"

At this point, Seiichirou went quiet and turned back to face Ciro.

"I'd like you to exert due diligence in your experiments. Nobody knows what a sudden magic influx could do to a person's body. It could be a human rights issue."

"I understand what you're saying about a magic influx, but what do you mean about human rights?"

"Given that a person's employment prospects will increase with the more magical power they possess, some may force themselves to accumulate more of it."

For example, a household with financial troubles might force its children into dangerous, high-density areas. People could start selling themselves in the name of inflating their magic.

"Hmm, I see your point, but that's their prerogative. Would you really stall the project because of what *some* people might do?"

Having come from a nation that prioritized human rights, Seiichirou had a very different worldview from Ciro. Most people in this kingdom probably thought like Ciro, while Seiichirou was the overly sensitive one, but he wasn't going to concede on this point.

"No, we can't let people burn themselves out. Human resources are finite. Besides, it would be a bad look if the citizens associated shady deals with a state-sanctioned project. The nation is built on the people's trust." Seiichirou's own country had once driven millions to die because of its flawed leadership. This knowledge compelled him to steer away from perfectly avoidable tragedies.

"I must say, Kondo, you have an interesting way of thinking. That's all well and good, but aren't you taking on too much of the burden yourself? Aresh has been telling me to tell *you* to mind your health."

"I'm fine."

"Where do you get the confidence to say that...? You're still escorting the Egorovans around today, aren't you?"

As much as he understood Ciro's concern, Seiichirou had his pride.

"I hardly have anything to do today."

They were going to the Sorcery Department, where the research nuts were bound to keep everyone occupied. And Ist would be absent, since Seiichirou had put in a request to the First Royal Order. Everything would be just like last time, he thought.

Yes, even Seiichirou was prone to wishful thinking.

[CHAPTER FIVE]

Informed

Much like the previous visit, Seiichirou stood some distance away from the experts as they geeked out. He was chatting with Orjef and Lars when he heard a sudden shout. The soprano pitch of a boy whose voice had not yet broken told him exactly who it was.

"What happened?" Lars demanded as he rushed over and peeled Luciano away from Sigma.

Seiichirou hurried over to Sigma's side as well.

"What's wrong, Luciano? This isn't like you." Lars gently grabbed Luciano by the wrist, halting his lunge at Sigma.

"I mean, he...he...!" Luciano was too emotional to be coherent.

"What happened?" Seiichirou asked Sigma quietly. The peasant boy's face was devoid of color. Although he was diffident around people of higher status, it wasn't a surprise that he would attract the ire of a pompous young foreigner like Luciano. Seiichirou didn't suspect that Sigma had made some kind of intractable faux pas. "It's okay," Seiichirou assured him.

Sigma opened his mouth timidly. "He asked me about the magic tool from the day before yesterday, so I explained it again."

By "the magic tool from the day before yesterday," he had to be talking about the magic-measuring device. Seiichirou nodded, nudging Sigma to continue. The boy cast a glance at Luciano before turning back to Seiichirou.

"Then...he asked me how I came up with the idea," he continued falteringly. "When I said Ist and I made it together, he got mad all of a sudden…"

"Huh…"

The only new thing Sigma had mentioned was Ist.

Which meant that… *No, it can't be…*

"How can a nobody like you work with a master like him?!" yelled Luciano.

"Seriously?" Seiichirou's reaction was too soft for anyone but Sigma to hear.

After they somehow managed to mollify Luciano and leave the disorderly Sorcery Department behind them, Seiichirou—well, more like everyone on the Romany side—clutched their heads in their hands.

"So…may I ask…is our Ist well-known in your country?" asked Zoltan nervously.

"Well, of course," Donato replied crisply. "He's discovered new magic, revived older magic, and simplified existing spells. With so many accomplishments under his belt, who *wouldn't* know him?"

Seriously?

It finally sank in for Seiichirou. He knew that Ist was a talented sorcerer, which was how he'd climbed the ranks to assistant director despite his merchant family background. But from Romany's perspective, Ist's conduct was so uncontrollable that he was basically left to his own devices to stop him from making a public mess of things. This was partly because Romany was unconcerned about magic research outside the fields of offensive spells (for killing monsters) and barrier spells (for protecting the capital), which led to the Third Royal Order getting the lion's share of the praise while the Sorcery Department got the short end of the stick. Magical knowledge hadn't even spread far among the populace in general.

Yet because of the long leash he was given, Ist had managed to achieve a great deal on a shoestring budget. This had all come as a surprise to Seiichirou since magic was outside his area of expertise (sorry, Ist). He would have upped the funds straight away if he'd known.

"But, well, you see... We haven't exactly been publicizing his results," was Zoltan's excuse for being blindsided.

"You don't need to publicize it. Sorcerers know these things," Donato pointed out bluntly.

He did have a point. Zoltan barely ever showed up at the Sorcery Department, and whenever Ist achieved something after holing himself up in his lab, he was generally quite pleased with himself and made no effort to hide it.

Wow, Ist can write a thesis? Seiichirou thought, rather rudely.

"Ist has marvelous insight and creativity," Donato went on. "I assumed that these new movement spells are largely based on his research, so I was hoping that he would give a lecture..."

"Luciano is a particularly big fan. He asked to participate in this tour so that he could meet and talk with—" Lars began.

"Y-you don't have to spell it all out!" a red-faced Luciano insisted, acting very much his age. "But I'm sure that a fellow of Ist's standing has no time to meet with us..."

Actually, he's under lock and key because he's a liability in public.

"And so it appears that Luciano lost his composure after hearing that the boy collaborated with Ist," said Lars. "I cannot apologize enough."

Zoltan and Orjef were both flustered by the frank apology. They couldn't brush away words that came from a prince's mouth.

As the two nobles smoothed things over, Seiichirou and Qusta were on the sidelines exchanging glances.

What do we do?

What do we do, indeed?

"I apologize for making a request right after our rudeness, but would there be any way to get Luciano in touch with Ist?" asked Lars.

They couldn't turn down a direct request from royalty.

"Um... Ist has business outside the capital at the moment..."

This was true. He, with other researchers, was away in a backwater region on an environmental survey. (He had been in a back room the day before yesterday, though.)

"Will he return within the duration of our stay?" Lars asked the obvious question.

The Romany tour guides gulped.

Sadly...Ist would be back the next day.

If they lied and got found out, it would cause a diplomatic issue. But letting them meet Ist would also cause a diplomatic issue.

Which was the lesser of the two evils? Seiichirou decided to give up and let Zoltan do all the thinking. It was up to the boss to take responsibility for their subordinates.

And so Ist ended up being included in the symposium at the Sorcery Department, scheduled for the day after tomorrow.

"I'm wiped..."

Seiichirou was surprised by his own words—it was the first time he'd said them in a while.

The Egorovan delegation was full of eccentrics, and they'd insisted that they would forgive any impoliteness. This was good enough for most people, but Ist wasn't *most people*.

It'd be nice to have something over the Egorovan side for a worst-case scenario, Seiichirou thought as he opened the door to the mansion.

"I'm home...," he muttered as he went inside.

Neither Valtom nor Milan were waiting for him like they usually did. Figuring that their hands were probably tied with something else, Seiichirou weighed the idea of heading straight to his room rather than hunting for them.

Then, he spotted someone on the stairs in the entrance hall—it wasn't Valtom or Milan.

An unfamiliar woman descended toward him in elegant heels. With her blue-streaked black hair, her luscious pale skin, and her deep indigo-blue eyes, she had the look of a woman with confidence. Long eyelashes bordered her sharp eyes. She was, in other words, a beautiful woman. One could easily tell from the design of her dress that she belonged to the upper echelons of society.

As she stood on the landing and peered down at Seiichirou, the beautiful woman parted her red lips to say...

"You're late."

Given that this was Aresh's mansion, it stood to reason that this woman was his guest, but Aresh himself was nowhere to be seen. Valtom or Milan would have told Seiichirou if Aresh was home. So the woman was probably in a position where she could invite herself in.

Just then, Valtom appeared behind her and soundlessly made his way to Seiichirou.

"This is Erene, Aresh's older sister," he whispered into Seiichirou's ear.

Why...? Why won't anyone let me do my job...?

∀∀∀

"Lufi, how long do you plan to be giddy?" Even Lars couldn't help but make a glib remark when he slipped into his room and spotted Luciano humming.

Luciano looked back at him curiously, apparently oblivious to the humming.

"You're grinning a little too much," said Lars. "It's obvious how eager you are to meet your idol."

Luciano instantly turned red. "N-no way! Absolutely not!" The protests sounded feeble.

As the older brother, Lars thought it was rather endearing. Luciano normally had the calm and composed expression of someone years older.

"What about you, Elder Brother? You were talking to that accounting guy that whole time," Luciano pointed out.

Lars smiled at this attempt to turn the tables. Luciano was quite right in saying that Lars had spoken solely to the man from the Accounting Department. "I enjoy his quick and astute responses to my questions."

Lars thought that any conversation with a capable person was worthwhile. *But...* Lars eyed Luciano.

"This isn't Egorova, so you have to compose yourself when you're outside the room," he warned.

Luciano deflated. "I can't ease up in Egorova, either."

Lars nodded. Luciano was right. No member of royalty could afford to let their guard down inside the royal palace. That was especially the case for people like Lars and Luciano, who stood out despite their low position in the line of succession. There were any number of people who would attempt to drag them down. Part of the reason Luciano had insisted on following Lars to Romany was for the opportunity to relax.

"But we have important things to do tomorrow, so pull yourself together," said Lars.

"Fine," said Luciano, after pouting for some time.

Tomorrow would be the one day on their seven-day excursion when they wouldn't be accompanied by their guides.

Donato and Georgi said that they were planning on taking a stroll around town even though Lars and Luciano had other plans. In fact, it was no exaggeration to say that *this* was their real mission— the cultural exchange tour was just a pretext.

Lars personally was interested in other things, too, like the king's bastard child. But...

"I think it's very important to meet my sister's future spouse," he said.

"I...think so, too, Elder Brother."

The smile on Luciano's lips was like that of a meek young girl.

∀∀∀

The tinkling sound of knives and forks broke the silence in the room. Seiichirou was sitting at the wide dinner table, directly opposite Aresh's sister—a perfect stranger until mere moments ago.

After Seiichirou sputtered out a greeting to the sudden

newcomer, Valtom and the other servants tactfully suggested a meal, and so there they were.

Seiichirou was honestly grateful to them. One could be forgiven for not saying much while they were eating. He used this time to kick his brain into full gear, figure out what was going on, and plot his next course.

"Your cooking is as delightful as ever," Erene said amiably to Pavel.

"Thank you very much."

"You're still welcome to join my house."

"I appreciate the offer."

Oh, of course, thought Seiichirou as he watched this conversation. *If she's Aresh's sister, then she must have eaten the cooking of Pavel and his mentor.*

He found himself a little curious about this woman who had grown up with Aresh.

"You're quite a light eater," Erene spoke to him suddenly.

Seiichirou almost dropped his knife, but he caught himself just in time.

"Ah, yes," he said reticently.

His palate had expanded thanks to Pavel's hard work, but that didn't stop him from having a small stomach. He was still eating more now than when he lived in Japan, though his portions were about the same as Erene's, a noblewoman. She was probably surprised at the gulf between Seiichirou and Aresh, a young knight with a voracious appetite.

Seiichirou's eyes flitted over her again. Now that he knew that she was Aresh's sister, he could sort of see the resemblance in the way they carried themselves. Her black-blue hair and indigo eyes weren't the same color as her brother's, but then again, Seiichirou had heard that purple eyes were rare.

Her makeup made her look older, but she was probably younger than Seiichirou. Aresh had told him before that he had two older brothers, followed by one older sister. This meant that Erene was the closest of his siblings to his age, which probably put her in her mid-twenties. She was already married, if Seiichirou recalled correctly.

Regardless, Seiichirou had never interacted with a noblewoman—Aresh's sister or no—and this crippling lack of experience left him at a loss about what to do. Although he could get away with not speaking during a meal, no dinner lasted forever.

Tea was served after dinner, marking the beginning of social pleasantries. Erene wasted no time opening her mouth.

"You are not guiding the delegation tomorrow, I hear."

Seiichirou wondered why she was choosing to ask about that. But it wasn't a secret or anything, and it was quite likely that the nobles all knew about things like this, so Seiichirou nodded.

"That's right. However, I do have plans to meet up with the other guides to discuss the results thus far and our upcoming schedule."

It probably sounded as if Seiichirou was preemptively brushing off an invitation, though he wasn't particularly lying. He and Qusta planned to discuss how things went off the rails over the past three days. They also had to talk about D-Day—er, how to get Ist to behave.

After that, Seiichirou had an appointment with Camile, where they would discuss the issue of increasing an individual's magic capacity. He needed to get his documentation together before the end of the day...

Erene's eyebrows furrowed at Seiichirou's words. She was very similar to Aresh in how she expressed her displeasure.

"Well, whatever," she said after an uncomfortable pause. "I'm sure you're aware that my parents summoned Aresh the other day?"

"I am, yes." His absence was very much noticed.

"Do you know why he was summoned?"

"...I have an inkling." Orjef had mentioned it earlier. It was pretty much guaranteed that it had something to do with Seiichirou's accessory at the dinner party.

"I just happened to be at the family estate at the time." Apparently, Erene had been staying with her family because her husband was on a long work trip. "Our parents and I already knew that Aresh was acting as a guardian to the man who was summoned alongside the Holy Maiden."

Of course they would know, given that he had moved out of their house and bought one of his own.

"I also heard some peculiar rumors...but who would have thought...?" Erene turned her piercing gaze on Seiichirou, which naturally made him sit up straight.

Seiichirou hadn't been contemplating marriage when the lapel pin incident happened, but he was already thirty. Setting aside the whole "other world" and "getting back home" thing, he was at the perfect age for settling down—and so was Aresh, by this world's standards. Seiichirou would have had to meet Aresh's relatives eventually, regardless of the whole marriage thing.

He would have preferred for it to happen after he was done with this high-stakes, diplomacy-impacting job, but beggars couldn't be choosers.

"I apologize for failing to give my regards until now. Allow me to reintroduce myself. I am Seiichirou Kondou, assistant director of the Royal Accounting Department. As you know, I was summoned by accident from another world alongside the Holy Maiden. Aresh has been an enormous help to me, and I owe him a tremendous debt." Seiichirou performed a deep bow from his seat, to which Erene made no reply. But he had to say it. "He and I are also seeing each other romantically."

When he lifted his gaze, Erene's indigo eyes were boring straight into him. Her expression...was unreadable. Aresh was always easy to figure out despite his blank expressions, but Erene was a cipher to Seiichirou.

"I know that under regular circumstances, Aresh and I should have paid our respects at your family home, but my hands are currently tied with the Egorovan delegation. I thought that when this task was done..."

Although Seiichirou knew it was unwise to show up alone at a marquess's house, he at least wanted to indicate his desire to do so. Just then, however, he thought he saw Erene's eyes narrow as she sipped her tea.

"You know nothing."

"Excuse me?"

Erene clanged her cup against the saucer.

"Are you unaware of why the Egorovan delegation came here?"

"Well... I assumed they wanted to inspect our movement spells as a pretext to initiate talks about exchanging magic..."

"Diplomacy does not begin and end at sharing magical techniques. Do you not know the simplest way of establishing international relations?"

Well, of course he didn't. He dealt with numbers, not diplomacy. From Seiichirou's cursory knowledge of history, the "simplest way" was probably marriage between royalty and nobility and whatnot...

"...Wait."

As her eyes drilled holes into Seiichirou's face, Erene continued: "Do you know what the Egorovan prince plans to do tomorrow?"

"He means to speak with Romany nobility...," answered Seiichirou. *No way.*

"Yes, he will be at House Indolark to discuss marriage with the fourth princess."

And that's why Aresh won't be coming home, her high-pitched voice declared without emotion.

"...ndo. Kondo!"

Seiichirou blinked and snapped his head up.

Qusta was peering at him from across the table, his small eyes betraying their concern. Seiichirou remembered that the two of them were currently using a compact room in the palace to talk about the Egorovan delegation.

"S-sorry!" He hurriedly flipped through his papers to see how far they had gotten. They'd finished discussing the tour thus far and were about to look over the schedule for the remaining two days.

"Shall we take a short break?" Qusta suggested.

Figuring that he would need some time to regain his concentration, Seiichirou agreed. Dining was permitted there, so Qusta asked a palace maid to bring over some tea without missing a beat. Although he gave off the air of an amiable middle manager, Qusta had all the refinement and grace of a born noble.

"Is there something worrying you? Besides Ist, I mean," he added playfully, to which Seiichirou chuckled.

He could feel the knot in his chest loosening somewhat. He couldn't dump his personal problems on someone from work, but there *was* something he was curious to ask Qusta about as a noble.

"Are you married, Qusta?" Seiichirou asked, giving in to the temptation.

"Oh? Well, yes. I haven't been for terribly long, though, despite my advanced age," Qusta said with lighthearted self-deprecation. He was in his mid-thirties, which was late for a nobleman in this country to marry. He looked like someone who already had two or three children, and he knew it.

"I see. Is your wife a member of the nobility, too?"

"Yes, she is. She is of a higher-ranked family, and I am merely the third son of a count, so our courtship took quite a roundabout route. Well, fortunately, we are married now, so we can look back on those times and laugh."

"I suppose matches among the nobility can be quite complicated..."

Having come from another world, Seiichirou obviously didn't possess an ounce of noble lineage. His prospects were already sunk.

Er, not that he necessarily *wanted* to get married. But still.

"Do nobles get betrothed from a young age?"

"They do if it means securing an heir for a prominent family. I am just a third son, however, and I spent my student days absorbed in research, so I was a rather late bloomer in that regard..." Qusta laughed. He had probably assumed he had missed the window for marriage and would stay a bachelor forever.

Similarly, Aresh had never breathed a word about being engaged despite coming from a marquess family. Surely it would have come up when he and Seiichirou started living together.

At the same time, it was no secret that Aresh had many admirers vying for his hand in marriage. Even as the third son, his striking looks and good pedigree were more than enough. The fact that he was the brilliant commander of the Third Royal Order was icing on the cake. He was a catch—from both a political angle and an aesthetic one.

Given the wealth and standing of a marquess family, Aresh was privileged enough that he could turn down almost any marriage offer that came his way. But Seiichirou could imagine that it would be a very different story if it was foreign royalty who came knocking.

"Thank you for taking time out of your busy schedule for me."

"Oh no. I was wanting a status report."

Seiichirou sat across from Camile. He was by now very well accustomed to the indigo-blue curtains and the antique table in the prime minister's office.

Although Seiichirou had submitted a schedule beforehand, it had gone by the wayside to accommodate the Egorovans' demands. It had been a good idea to arrange an intermediary meeting.

"Hm... Prince Lars has quite a keen interest in the affairs of our state, from what I can see," said Camile.

"I got that impression as well. Although the others are here for the spells and magic tool research, Prince Lars has been observing Romany's statecraft as a whole. I also feel that everyone besides Donato looks favorably on recruiting people based on merit rather than social standing."

"Hmm..." Camile scrunched his face in thought as he flicked through Seiichirou's papers.

The biggest issue from Camile's perspective was who had the reins over Egorova's politics. Seiichirou knew little about the circumstances in Egorova and merely stated his personal impression of the individuals. He was a finance man, no more, no less.

"So? Is there anything else you wish to tell me?" Camile asked suddenly.

For a moment, Seiichirou was flustered by the abrupt question, but he collected himself and presented the documents he had written the night before.

"Yes. There's this... I have a theory based on my observations of the Egorovans and the relief house children. Ciro of the Medical Bureau has agreed to help me investigate."

Camile's blue-gray eyes widened as he peered at the sheaf of papers. "'A Proposal to Expand Magical Capacity Through Environmental Magic and Magicules'? I see you're at it again..."

There was a note of exasperation in Camile's voice as he sighed and rubbed his temples. Seiichirou felt sheepish. He was a stranger to this world's conventional logic; maybe his idea was *too* out there.

But then again, a specialist like Ciro had said there was merit to the idea. Plus, there was still a shortage of qualified magic users, even if they were able to educate the commoners to a degree.

Given that the Romany Kingdom planned to suppress the miasma in the forest without the Holy Maiden henceforth, they needed to work with other countries. In that sense, there were plenty of people with high magical capacity around, but they couldn't increase the talent pool if magic was seen as a purely genetic talent. It was worth testing to see if a person's training and living environment made an impact.

"Although my idea may seem a little unconventional, the nobility of certain regions are overrepresented among the children at the relief house and the members of the Sorcery Department. One could interpret a correlation between high magical capacity and said regions..."

"What are you trying to say? That their talents come not from blood but the land itself?" Camile asked in a low voice.

For a moment, Seiichirou's breath caught in his throat.

Magic was an important measure of status in this world. One's job prospects would change depending on how much magic they were capable of wielding, and even the academies catering to nobles divided their classes based on this distinction. Because of this, there was apparently an association between high magical capacity and family pedigree. A project which fundamentally rejected that premise was perhaps a bit too ahead of its time.

But there was no other way of speeding up magic research. And so Seiichirou bowed his head, knowing that he was getting ahead of himself in his haste to realize his goals.

"I apologize... I stepped out of line as an outsider..."

"There's never a dull moment with you."

"Excuse me?" When Seiichirou lifted his head, he saw a familiar sight: Camile desperately attempting to stifle his laughter.

"You're a funny one! Imagine the uproar among the nobles if things happened your way!"

"R-right..."

Seiichirou had forgotten that Camile was a maverick—and one who wielded a frightening level of power and authority, at that.

"But I suspect that magicule-dense areas will have poor effects on the body," Camile went on. "I suggest starting the experiments on prison inmates."

"That would be unwise, Your Excellency."

"How so?"

Having anticipated Camile's suggestion to a degree, Seiichirou took a deep breath and straightened his posture. He argued that it was terribly inefficient for the people in power to experiment on prisoners and the weak as if they were expendable pawns.

"The nobles should be the ones to participate—provided that their safety can be assured to the utmost degree, of course."

"What makes you think that?"

"Magic is very important to the nobles, yes? In that case, they should be the ones taking the lead. Having them participate only after the fact may risk widening the gap between the haves and the have-nots. By involving themselves in the earliest stage and exposing themselves to the dangers, there will be no unfairness in the process."

"You have a point..."

If the privileged only jumped in after they could get a practical benefit out of it, they would use their existing authority to monopolize it. This would further entrench the biases in noble society.

"Also, given that magicule-dense regions generally suffer from magical beast attacks, I suggest state funding for the regional lords cooperating in the project."

They couldn't just help themselves to the land without asking, and plenty of the local nobles already had a lot of magic. If they could teach magic control to those nobles at the same time, it would mitigate the risk of anyone's magic going berserk.

"You're suggesting this as a form of rural support," said Camile.

"Exactly. I'd also like to try it with different age groups, if possible. It would be useful to know whether adolescents can grow their magic more quickly, and so forth."

"Hm. I understand what you're getting at, although I imagine that it would not be so simple for the nobles to relinquish their children..."

"That is where your power comes in, Your Excellency. If you could advocate for the advantages of this project..."

"The nerve of you, Seiichirou...," said Camile, failing to suppress his smile this time.

Seiichirou answered with an evil grin of his own, forcing a bark of laughter from Camile's lips.

"Good grief...and here I thought you'd use this opportunity to ask me about the *other* thing," he said exasperatedly, after he had finished laughing.

"What thing?" Seiichirou cocked his head as Camile directed a maid to pour them another cup of tea.

"The marriage proposal to House Indolark."

"So you knew about it," said Seiichirou.

Camile nodded as if it was the most obvious thing in the world. "Who do you think I am? Of course I'd know which members of our nobility would receive a visit from foreign royalty."

He was right.

Which begged the question of why he never said a word of this to Seiichirou.

The answer was, of course, "Because I didn't need to tell you."

"I see," Seiichirou said.

"Is that all you have to say? Isn't there anything you want to ask me?"

"Nothing in particular."

It was pointless listening to other people's commentary.

A brief silence ensued. "I see," Camile said. "Very well, then. I'll arrange a meeting with Director Quellbus and Director Zoltan in the coming days to discuss your proposal."

"Thank you. Please excuse me, then."

Seiichirou quietly bowed and left the room.

As he made his way home, he wondered if Aresh's sister was there.

Valtom greeted him at the door. At the same time, Seiichirou spied Erene on the stairs and held back a sigh.

"What's with that look?" she asked.

"Er..." Seiichirou turned his face away, not feeling like explaining himself. "Is Aresh...?" he began to ask Valtom, only for the butler to shake his head wordlessly.

Today was another disappointment.

"I see."

At this point, Seiichirou switched gears and headed up the stairs to his room. Erene shot him a look, but he didn't want to bother with her today. Tomorrow, he would have to present Ist in front of foreign royalty. He didn't have the spirit or energy to entertain someone else.

"Ah…" Erene made a noise as if she wanted to say something.

Seiichirou stopped. He wasn't so apathetic as to ignore her entirely. "What is it?"

She took her sweet time to respond. When Seiichirou lost patience and urged her to continue, she made a sour face. "How was work today?"

"I'm afraid I cannot disclose matters concerning foreign royalty," he replied, as if he was affronted by the very notion of what she was asking, even though she had demonstrated yesterday that she more or less knew the whole deal.

Erene's brows furrowed. Evidently, she was put out, although she could not outright say so.

"Oh, really! Fine, then. Go make yourself at home."

Seiichirou did not need her to tell him that. He bowed, and then retreated into his room. As he sank into a chair and sighed, Milan brought him a change of clothes.

"Are you weary, Mr. Seiichirou?"

"No…" At first, he tried to deny it, but then he thought better of it. "Well, yes."

When he first came to this world, he threw himself into his work, believing that nobody was on his side. Only Aresh showed him careful consideration, he'd thought, but it turned out that Aresh's servants were deeply kindhearted as well.

Pavel the chef always poured his heart into Seiichirou's meals, and Milan the maid kept Seiichirou's autonomy in mind as she unassumingly assisted him in all sorts of mundanities. Valtom the butler could be described as stern, but Seiichirou was second only to his master Aresh in his list of priorities.

Part of it was because this was the place he returned to, but Seiichirou could not help but see all these other people in the house with a familial sort of warmth. So this time, instead of deflecting Milan's concern, he answered her frankly.

"What did Lady Erene come here for?"

Implicit in Seiichirou's question was "When will she leave?" Milan put one of her plump hands to her cheek and tilted her head. "She said that she would stay here to entertain herself while her husband is busy at work."

"So she decided to sojourn at her brother's house while he's not around?"

"Her husband works at the royal palace. I suppose she wants to feel a little closer to him…"

Seiichirou sighed.

So her husband worked at the palace? And she forced her way into Aresh's house because it happened to be nearby? But that didn't make sense when House Indolark had its own estate within the capital. Aresh was at *that* house—why did she come to a place where she knew he wouldn't be?

Seiichirou wondered if it was so that she could deter him by telling him about Aresh's engagement, but that didn't seem quite right, either. For one thing, she had no right to tell Seiichirou to leave the house—Valtom and the others would never allow it in Aresh's absence. Besides, Erene had never actually uttered anything of the sort.

Although Aresh spoke little about his family, Seiichirou knew that Erene was the third-born child and the only daughter. He wondered where the sole girl stood in a noble house full of boys. The next heir was already secured, and there was a spare in reserve. Not to mention that her younger brother was exceedingly talented in his own right.

"Erene is very beautiful and a hard worker, but next to Aresh…" Milan knew Aresh and Erene from their childhoods because she had once served as a maid at the Indolark house. Milan had stepped back from work to have a child of her own, and Aresh reached out to her once the early child-rearing had passed. The rest, as they say, was history.

People had referred to Aresh as a prodigy for as long as he could remember. He excelled at everything he touched: fighting, magic, and academics. Meanwhile, people told Erene that martial prowess was unnecessary for her as a girl. She poured everything into her books so that she would not be outdone by her younger brother. Apparently, she was twenty-six, which made her four years Aresh's senior.

Unfortunately for her, she lacked the magic to pursue a career in research. Her brother, on the other hand, became the youngest commander ever of the prestigious Third Royal Order.

"Do they...not get along?" Seiichirou asked.

"Oh no, I wouldn't say that. Erene has always doted on Aresh as her only little brother, ever since they were children. But although she means well, she finds it somewhat difficult to express herself... Aresh is like that, too, of course..."

In his mind's eye, Seiichirou saw a tiny Aresh sulking as his older sister fussed over him.

Early the next day, Seiichirou departed for work before Erene could catch him. He met up with Orjef, and the two of them made their way over to the Sorcery Department.

"Is that sorcerer you're so worried about really the same guy the Egorovans say is a genius?" asked Orjef.

"Our side knows Ist's talents, too. It's why he's the assistant director."

Sadly, his achievements were completely counterbalanced by his actions.

"I've heard the rumors, but what specifically should I be looking out for?" Orjef did not know Ist directly. He probably had a hard time imagining what kind of person he was because of all the conflicting impressions.

"Let's see... Well, first off, he's not interested in other people. If you try to tell him something, it won't get through right away. You have to repeat yourself a few times." This was generally because he had other things on the brain. Either he didn't hear what you said, or it didn't register in his mind. "Oh, and he's very chatty about the things he's interested in. He'll forget the right way to address people when he's excited. That, and...ah, yes, he feels like a five-year-old in a grown man's body."

"A five-year-old..."

He basically had no capacity for looking after himself. He was always getting his things dirty and then using them anyway. In that sense, he was very much like one of Seiichirou's cousins back in Japan.

"And yet he's a genius sorcerer and the assistant director?" said Orjef.

"Yes. He is a genius sorcerer *and* the assistant director."

For all his antics, he was still the assistant director.

"He's not very brawny, but he also doesn't have much mental control. He can tap into a surprisingly deep well of strength when he spots something that catches his interest. I ask that you restrain him by force during those times."

"O...kay...," said Orjef, sounding thoroughly weirded out, but just when Seiichirou was breathing a sigh of relief about securing the vice commander's assistance, Orjef squinted at Seiichirou's face. "Hey, by the way, you've got this awful pallor. You all right?"

"This is how I always look," Seiichirou gave his usual response. He was *very* used to people telling him that he looked unwell.

But Orjef cocked his head. "Nah, you seem more listless than usual... I mean, you always look unusually bad, but..."

Was he trying to pick a fight?

"Well, anyway, try and lighten up for me, would you? You're a real help, and I'm scared of how Aresh would react if something were to happen to you."

"...I will endeavor to try."

As they were talking, they spotted a well-dressed group approaching from the other end of the hallway—it was Lars and the Egorovan cohort. Zoltan and Qusta were serving as their guides.

"Good morning." Seiichirou put a hand to his lower chest, the formal greeting in Romany.

"A good morning to you, too, Seichiro." Lars unexpectedly referred to him by his first name, his usual dazzling smile on his lips.

Luciano, meanwhile, was glowering. It was a far cry from the other day's jubilation about meeting Ist.

Orjef noticed it, too. "Is something the matter, Lord Luciano? Are you feeling unwell?" he asked.

Luciano lifted his head and shot a slightly uncertain look in Lars's direction.

"There was something of a small disappointment... Ah, yes. Seichirou, may I ask you for some advice?" Lars said as they walked to the Sorcery Department.

"Me?" Seiichirou looked back over his shoulder.

"Yes. You are engaged to a member of the nobility in this country, yes? I heard about it. Yesterday, we visited a noble to issue a marriage proposal, but we were turned down."

"Scandalous! Which house would have the nerve to turn down a proposal from Egorovan royalty?!" Zoltan fumed. He had no idea, evidently.

"It was the son of Marquess Indolark," said Lars.

"What?" Orjef glanced furtively at Seiichirou.

"Excuse me?" Qusta turned his head as well.

Marquess Indolark had just one unmarried son: Aresh.

Seiichirou kept his face blank, even as he inwardly winced at the piercing stares.

"He said something about getting engaged recently, but we are very keen on having a man with his talents... And so, given that I've heard that you have won the affection of a member of this country's nobility, may I ask how you achieved it?"

As everyone turned to look at Seiichirou, each with their own worldly concerns, the man in question chose emptiness.

Today's job was to prevent the unruly Ist from acting up in front of foreign royalty, which was hard enough to begin with, but Seiichirou was exhausted before it had even started. He warded off Lars's question with a half-baked "It depends on the person, so I'm afraid I cannot be of much help."

Then Zoltan fumed: "Prince Lars asked you a question! Answer it seriously!"

Qusta rushed in to mollify the director while Orjef spoke up to minimize the awkwardness. As much as Seiichirou could see they were looking out for him, he frankly found their stares more piercing than Lars's or Zoltan's.

"Did you propose the marriage on behalf of another member of the royal family?" Orjef asked Lars in an attempt to change the topic.

"Ah, yes!" Zoltan chimed in, evidently eager to hear the details.

"Yes, for my younger sister, the fourth-born princess. Given that we foresee a long-term relationship with Romany, I believe marriage ties are inevitable."

"The fourth princess! Now that is indeed an honor! Would you care for me to introduce you to eligible high-ranking members of our nobility?" Zoltan suggested eagerly.

"The fourth princess...?" Seiichirou wondered aloud.

Zoltan's reaction made sense—by playing matchmaker to a marriage involving foreign royalty, he would be serving a valuable diplomatic role, even if it meant shouldering long-term responsibility as a go-between.

"That is a fine idea, but can you find anyone more suitable than Commander Indolark?" Luciano pointed out, quite rightly. With his sterling reputation, abundance of money, and status as an unmarried man, the commander of the Third Royal Order seemed like almost *too* perfect a match.

Lars and Luciano were evidently unwilling to give up on Aresh. Seiichirou could feel Orjef and Qusta's eyes burning holes through his head.

Ugh, can I just go to bed already?

Just as Seiichirou was beginning to get fed up, the group finally arrived at the Sorcery Department.

Unlike the previous impromptu visit, the department was fairly tidy this time, thanks to the heads-up they received beforehand. The sorcerers who came out to greet them had also cleaned themselves up a bit, which made Seiichirou and Zoltan sigh in relief.

"So, um…what about Ist?" Luciano looked around restlessly. His face had been pale before, but now his cheeks were flushed pink.

"Isn't there something to do first, Luciano?" said Lars.

"Oh…right. Sorry. Would you allow me to apologize to the boy from the other day?"

By "the boy from the other day," he had to be talking about Sigma. Luciano had done a bit of growing up in his own way after that incident, it seemed.

"Oh, you needn't go out of your way to apologize…" Zoltan began.

"No, I want to. Please let me," Luciano answered firmly.

Unfortunately, neither Sigma nor Ist were anywhere to be seen. In Sigma's case, it was because he was simply an ordinary civilian who was allowed to drop by according to his own schedule. He wasn't always at the Sorcery Department. In fact, he might have been told to stay away today after the ire he drew last time. Judging by Zoltan's flustered conversation with a subordinate, Seiichirou suspected that this might indeed have been the case.

But the real issue was that Ist wasn't there.

"Wh-what is the meaning of this?! You told him to be on time, didn't you?!"

"Y-yes, of course!"

But there was no one to blame other than the absent sorcerer himself.

Zoltan normally had a deft hand at handling Ist, but he seemed to have been too preoccupied with his guide duties to take on the mantle. If Seiichirou had been in his shoes, he would have tied up Ist ahead of time and thrown him somewhere within easy reach.

Bam!

The door abruptly opened with a *crash*. The Egorovan guards tensed and readied themselves.

All eyes were on the door as it swung open without any delicacy whatsoever. Then a familiar pair of peridot eyes fell on Seiichirou.

"There you are!" the person shouted cheerfully. "Hey, Kondo! Give me money!!"

With a conversation opener highly reminiscent of his first meeting with Seiichirou, Ist made his debut before the Egorovan delegation.

CHAPTER SIX

Appeared

"No."

Right there in front of the dumbfounded crowd, Ist's drowsy eyes blinked multiple times in succession.

"Huh? Really? Why not?"

His expression said that it hadn't occurred to him that he could get shot down, but this wasn't the first time they'd had this conversation. There was no way Seiichirou would say "yes" without a second thought. He was surprised that Ist was surprised.

The bigger issue was that this was not one of Seiichirou's routine visits to the Sorcery Department.

"Waaah! Stop it, Ist! Have you forgotten that we have important guests from a foreign country today?!" cried a familiar brown-haired boy behind Ist.

Zoltan was the first to recover his wits. "I-IIIIIIst! You...you cur! First, you come late, and now you... Aaaaargh! Forget it! Greet the guests from Egorova!"

He barged right up to Ist, fully prepared to give him a piece of his mind, only to change his tune and shove the sorcerer from behind. This was the smart choice. Ist never listened to lectures.

"Huh? What...? Oh, right. Okay. So, uh, I'm Ist, assistant director of the Royal Sorcery Department."

As Ist made a bow that would pass absolutely nobody's muster,

Zoltan shook behind him. He was clearly one second away from exploding.

"I am Lars Eric Egorova, from Egorova." Lars took the lead.

"A-and I'm Luciano Delidov!" Luciano hurried to chime in. Donato and Georgi then introduced themselves in turn.

Although the Egorovans were surprised, they didn't seem affronted, fortunately. Luciano's eyes in particular were sparkling. Lars gave the boy a subtle nudge, bringing him back to earth so he spotted the person behind Ist.

It was Sigma, and he seemed more uncomfortable than anyone else in the room.

"Er, um…"

Sigma flinched in response to Luciano's voice. This seemed to galvanize Luciano further, because he stepped right up to the other boy.

"I-I apologize for my rudeness to you the other day."

"Huh? Um?" The sudden apology from a noble had Sigma in disbelief.

"I was jealous that you got to work with Ist, and I was cruel to you when you did nothing to deserve it. I am really sorry."

"Wha—?! Er, um, it's not a big de—"

"Can you forgive me?"

Meeting the upturned eyes of a pretty young boy oozing with class, Sigma's face turned bright red. He nodded several times over.

"Well, now that that's all settled… Kondo, give me money."

"I said no."

Meanwhile, the adult who had entered the room made another demand, only to get shot down again.

"Huh? What?" said Ist.

"Don't go 'Huh? What?'! You think you can ignore the Egorovans just because you've said hello?! They have gone through a lot of trouble to meet you!" Zoltan was normally unafraid to resort to his fists, though he kept his hands at his sides in front of the Egorovan delegation. He was, however, still visibly shaking.

"Oh, but it's rare for Kondo to show up here. And I need money quick," Ist argued vehemently.

"Yes, and I've told you on many occasions that you need to explain what you plan to use the money on." Sensing that Ist had a concrete goal in mind this time instead of his usual "I need a bigger budget" sentiment, Seiichirou did a quick bow to the Egorovans and approached the sorcerer.

Whenever Ist got like this, talking to him about anything was pointless. Seiichirou had to address the root of whatever was on his mind, or else the situation would get further out of hand. Seiichirou would have liked him to submit a written proposal, but that was asking a bit much of Ist, so he generally heard the man out verbally.

"I saw this useful-looking magic tool in town, so I bought it," said Ist.

"When you were on that inspection yesterday? What would it be useful for?"

Ist would have been away in a rural town, ostensibly for an inspection but mainly to keep him away from the Egorovan delegation.

"Movement spells," said Ist.

It was as if a sudden chill filled the room. Seiichirou did not have to look over his shoulder to know that the Egorovans were staring right at them.

"We can talk about this later, Ist..."

"Aww, but you're always so busy, Kondo. If I don't ask you about it now, you'll never hear me out. So, yeah, you use the tool as a substitute for the medium in dimension-crossing magic. I figure it could send you back to your original world."

Seiichirou sputtered.

This was his mistake. He should have at least taken Ist to a different room. Then again, would their eager guests have allowed Seiichirou to peel Ist away?

Now what? The wheels turned frantically in Seiichirou's mind, but before he could figure something out, someone else interjected.

"Seiichirou, are you from a different world?"

Lars's words resounded throughout the Sorcery Department.

Crap. How am I supposed to answer that? Given that an honest answer would reveal the Romany Kingdom's mistake, it wasn't for Seiichirou to decide. A part of him thought, *They summoned me without asking. Why should I have to cover for their screw-up?* but he suppressed that thought, knowing that he'd have to deal with the fallout.

As this internal war raged in Seiichirou's head, a certain somebody answered the question without a care in the world.

"Yep. Kondo got summoned here alongside the Holy Maiden. He knows a lot of interesting things. Has plenty of neat ideas, too!"

Even if it was futile, they really, *really* should have prepped Ist before throwing him into the fray. Seiichirou's entire group felt this deeply in their souls.

Alas, the scheme was foiled, and they would have to make do.

As much as that sounded like a villain's line, it perfectly encapsulated Seiichirou's mindset. As difficult as it was to accept on a personal level, Seiichirou's summoning was treated simply as "an unforeseen accident." The kingdom offered its "cordial protection," and Seiichirou was working entirely of his own volition.

So he remained unmoving in the face of the Egorovans' barrage of questions.

"I am simply a palace official, and I cannot answer your questions without the state's permission. Please direct your queries to the higher authorities."

A public servant couldn't answer questions on a topic he wasn't authorized to speak about. Seiichirou could trot out that excuse to salvage the situation.

Indeed. The tour would end the next day. Even if the Egorovans did rush to make a request, they would not get permission immediately. Besides, if they left the Sorcery Department now, they would be cutting short their time with the celebrity sorcerer they were so eager to meet.

"In any case, I believe there was something you wished to ask Ist?" said Seiichirou.

"Oh, r-right!" Luciano was the first to approach Ist, with Donato on his heels.

For his part, Ist was probably satisfied after saying his piece, because he accepted the two sorcerers' presence. Well, he probably assumed Seiichirou had approved the funds without them actually talking about it. But Seiichirou did not want to correct him on that here, lest Ist's mind swing back in that direction. *Let sleeping dogs lie,* he decided.

"Who would have thought you were from another world?" Only Lars approached Seiichirou.

"His situation is not yet public knowledge outside the kingdom," Orjef interjected, "so I ask that you keep it a secret."

"Very well. Now I see why you, the esteemed vice commander of the Third Royal Order, was tasked with his protection." Orjef smiled without affirming or denying the prince's comment. "...Duly noted. I shall refrain from further inquiry at the moment."

Lars made a theatrical show of defeat.

Not for the first time, it occurred to Seiichirou how perfect Orjef was for this job in terms of his administrative position and social standing.

"But I must say..." Lars's jade green eyes, framed by his long silver eyelashes, peered directly at Seiichirou. "I find it remarkable that a man from another world, without any connections or means in this country, has managed to become a civil official and even a guide to foreign guests..."

"I would not say that I lack connections... If anything, I suppose that being from another world has made me stand out."

A lower-class citizen could pick themselves up by their bootstraps and still find it practically impossible to get their foot in the palace door, while Seiichirou got into the Royal Accounting

Department the moment he asked. This was probably because it was easier to keep an eye on him within the confines of the palace than if they had released him into the wild.

On the other hand, Seiichirou had enacted reforms which caught the prime minister's eye and earned him a swift promotion, but Seiichirou thought of this as just doing his job. Without Camile or Aresh's backing, his proposals would have gone nowhere, just like in Japan. If not for the magicule and magic poisoning, Seiichirou found it much easier to do his job here compared to back there.

"That alone does not explain the quality of your work. Case in point: I've never seen anyone put documents together like you do." Lars seemed to be quite taken with Seiichirou's administrative skills. It was a nice thing to hear, quite honestly. The prince's reputation preceded him, but Seiichirou was genuinely impressed at his knack with people. "Given your talents and charm, I can see how you were wedded within such a short time frame," Lars went on.

Snap.

Seiichirou was so frozen that one could almost *hear* the sound of his limbs clicking to the spot.

Orjef hurried to his aid. "He…is not wedded…"

"Oh, really? But you were wearing a lapel pin at the dinner party… Ah, I see. You're still engaged."

Did he manage to see the pin all that distance away? Or did someone else inform him of it?

"I was fortunate enough to meet your partner," Lars continued. "He is an upstanding individual indeed…"

No, "fortune" has nothing to do with it. You just went out and met him. The accusation almost slipped out of Seiichirou's throat, but he swallowed it just in time. He felt that something was off.

Did Lars make that marriage offer to Aresh while knowing he was Seiichirou's partner? Or did he only find out after he met Aresh?

Anyway, Seiichirou couldn't get over how Lars was praising his partner right after indicating he had no intention of giving up on the marriage proposal. Something about this didn't add up.

"Who exactly are you…?"

"Kondo! I need your help!" Someone cut into the conversation before Seiichirou could finish his sentence. It was Qusta.

"What's the sudden commotion?" Seiichirou asked, although there was really only one thing Qusta would need help for in this situation.

Turning his gaze to the source of the trouble, Seiichirou saw Ist surrounded by a throng of pale-faced Romany sorcerers. Only Zoltan's face had color—it was beetroot red, in fact. He was frantically trying to cover Ist's mouth.

Meanwhile, the Egorovans all watched on with sparkling eyes.

Well, to be precise, they were just as pale-faced as the royal sorcerers. But their eyes were still sparkling.

This could only mean one thing…

"Orjef! Restrain him!" Seiichirou cried.

"Huh? Oh, okay!" Orjef was momentarily flummoxed, but then he remembered the conversation they'd had before they arrived. He promptly got to work holding Ist down and covering his mouth.

"Oh no! What are you doing to Ist?!" Luciano's voice rang out in reproach—although it was Seiichirou who had more right to complain. Ist was undoubtedly a menace.

"Director Zoltan…what exactly happened?" Seiichirou asked.

Zoltan groaned. "Ist was about to tell the guests about the new techniques and how the movement spells work…"

Called it.

There was slight reluctance in Zoltan's tone, but he seemed aware that Seiichirou was the one most capable of getting this situation under control.

That said, Ist wasn't the type to blithely leak confidential information. Putting aside the question of whether he recognized the information as "confidential," it wasn't in his character to tell just anyone about the spells he was researching.

"Did you offer your opinions on the spells?" Seiichirou directed that question to the Egorovans.

But it was Ist, still being restrained by Orjef, who started wriggling in response. Naturally, he couldn't overpower the vice commander of Romany's strongest knights. Seiichirou gave the signal to Orjef to at least uncover his mouth.

"Yeah! You hit the nail on the head, Kondo! These people are amazing! I was really racking my brain over how to protect living creatures against non-physical impediments. The basic movement spells just don't account for it, you see. The ancient summoning spell used a special medium to fulfill that role, but there's only one of those in existence. That's why I was looking for a substitute. Anyway, talking with these fellows made me realize that you can use a barrier spell to fortify your spirit."

"Orjef."

"Mfff!"

Ist's mouth was sealed once more, cutting off the sorcerer's breathless rant.

"Listen, Ist. The ancient magic and the spells for moving humans are Romany state secrets. You can't tell people from other countries about them just yet. Is that clear?" Seiichirou's eyes swept over Ist. "I suspect not, so I will say it again. Listen carefully. Do not tell anyone about the ancient magic and the movement spells. Do you understand?"

Ist's head bobbed up and down.

Seiichirou sighed and looked back over his shoulder. The research-obsessed Egorovans looked very unhappy.

"Progress should not be confined by country!"

"Yeah, we could have helped Ist with his dilemma!"

"This research will make its mark in magic textbooks for years to come!"

Seiichirou did not reply to that.

"Prince Lars." He turned his gaze to the back of the group.

Lars's handsome face was scrunched in consternation even as his lips formed a smile.

"From the Egorovan perspective, this visit is merely an

opportunity to get a taste of Romany's magic culture. Any serious inquiry will come later."

Yeah, listen to him. Seiichirou and the others nodded.

But then…

"I promise to use my authority to secure further cultural exchanges with Romany. Would you be willing to allow us to participate in your movement spell research?"

"Your Highness!" The three Egorovans' eyes lit up in glee.

"Nice!" Ist positively glowed as well, and so did the Romany sorcerers.

"Eld… Prince Lars!" Luciano cried out excitedly.

The research nuts had complete tunnel vision. Who was supposed to deal with *this*?

At the very least…it's not my problem.

"We will consult with the authorities," was all Seiichirou could say.

Zoltan went to report to Camile, marking the end of the day's activities. The higher-ups were having an emergency meeting, apparently.

Still, they couldn't leave Ist and the Egorovans to their own devices in the Sorcery Department, nor could they lock Ist up again, so the guests went out into town for the second day in a row. Orjef and a group of Second Royal Order knights went off to serve as their bodyguards, leaving Seiichirou to go home and wait for the official decision.

It isn't even the Fire Hour yet, thought Seiichirou, though unusually for him, he didn't feel like doing other work. Obediently, he climbed into a carriage and made his way back to the mansion, where he crossed paths with the gardener who came by once a week.

"Oh, hey there. Rare to see you home so early," said the heartylooking man. Apparently, he was quite popular in his field and tended to multiple nobles' gardens. That said, he generally only came by during the day, so Seiichirou had only met him about three times.

"It's been quite a day… Ah, you've done very nice work."

The gardener nodded placidly, not prying any further. "Thanks. You've come at a good time, by the way. Mr. Aresh just got back."

Seiichirou's heart jolted at the unexpected news. Even though Aresh had only been away for three days, making it four since Seiichirou had last seen his face, he could feel his heart racing.

When he entered the mansion, Valtom came to the door to tell him that Aresh was home. Although Seiichirou already knew this, he reacted as if it was news to him. Valtom said that Aresh was in his room, so Seiichirou went up to the second floor. He didn't see Erene around, although he forgot to ask Valtom whether she had left.

He was about to knock on Aresh's door when he remembered that he was still in his uniform. Just as he turned around to go change, the door swung open.

"You're back?" Aresh sounded surprised.

Seiichirou was about to say, "That's what I should be saying to you," when he remembered that he almost never came home from work early. That was the source of Aresh's shock.

"Yes," he said, turning back around to face his partner.

Aresh was wearing a simple shirt. Although it wasn't his uniform, he certainly would not have come home in this outfit, which meant that he had already changed into his indoor clothes.

Aresh opened the door wide, making room for Seiichirou to enter. Seiichirou, however, did not budge an inch.

"What? Not coming in?" asked Aresh, sensing something amiss.

"…Am I allowed to?" Seiichirou asked quietly.

Aresh blinked, and then his cheeks twitched in an almost imperceptible sign of discomfort. "Sorry," he said after a pause. "Come in."

Seiichirou walked in, and Aresh closed the door behind him. The next moment, Seiichirou felt a pair of arms wrap around him from behind. Strong arms, accompanied by warmth and the subtle scent of Aresh.

Aresh breathed heavily against his neck.

He must have sensed Seiichirou squirming, because his voice sounded slightly huffy.

"Hey…can't you stay still?"

"Erm, not from this direction…"

"What direction?"

"Could you just let go of me for a moment?"

Seiichirou was being petulant, but Aresh released him without complaint.

Then Seiichirou turned around.

"I'd prefer we face each other."

He spread his arms—and was greeted with an even stronger embrace than before.

Because of the height gap between them, Seiichirou's head would fall against Aresh's shoulder whenever they hugged while facing each other. This time, Seiichirou leaned in, taking in Aresh's scent. After a few minutes of the two of them getting their fill of the other, Aresh finally relaxed his grip, and Seiichirou lifted his head.

Beautiful amethysts.

After spending the past few days looking at Lars, Seiichirou knew that he was beautiful, but Aresh possessed a more primal quality. There was a wildness to him, tempered by his status as a knight. Seiichirou was drawn to that roughness—perhaps he was something of a slave to love.

When Aresh slowly drew his lips close, Seiichirou responded in turn.

It was their first kiss in five days.

Over and over, their lips met, and then Aresh opened his mouth.

"Your barrier is still intact, but I'll reapply it to be safe."

Those words snapped Seiichirou back into reality.

He had reunited with Aresh, and their fight had not left things on a sour note. Plus, Aresh was as considerate about Seiichirou's physical condition as ever. These were all good things.

But wasn't there something they needed to talk about first?

"Before that, isn't there something you need to tell me, Aresh?"

"…Huh?"

Seiichirou was surprised to see Aresh so surprised. "Like I said, don't you have something to tell me?"

"Like what?"

Aresh's expression suggested that he really did not understand.

Seiichirou decided to cut this circular conversation short.

"You never told me why your family summoned you."

He had heard from Erene that the Egorovan royals had approached Aresh's family about an engagement, but Seiichirou should have been involved in this conversation from the start.

He knew that Aresh had turned down the offer. This was something he should have heard directly from Aresh's lips—hence why Seiichirou was asking about it now.

But the answer he received was outside the realm of his expectations.

"It's not something for you to concern yourself with."

"Huh?"

"More importantly, I need to get going again soon. I should reapply the barrier before then," Aresh said as he reached an arm out to pull Seiichirou in.

His lips descended once more...

Crunch.

Aresh's eyes widened in shock—his perfect lips were now lightly coated in blood. Because Seiichirou had bitten him.

Seiichirou used this moment to free himself of Aresh's arms and take several steps back.

"Seiichirou?" Aresh looked surprisingly young in his bewilderment.

But this was no time to gawk at him.

"Oh, I see... I see how it is... *Mr.* Aresh."

Aresh jolted.

He was always insisting that Seiichirou speak to him without formalities. Although Seiichirou didn't drop the politeness entirely, he still referred to Aresh without a title whenever they were in the mansion together. And so the moment he used the word "mister," Aresh could tell that something was amiss.

"I will not be coming home for a while, either," Seiichirou declared.

"Huh? What are you...?"

"I'd like to collect my thoughts. Please excuse me."

And then Seiichirou was out the door, fleeing with all the strength he could muster before Aresh could return to his wits and chase after him.

I'm glad this happened before I changed clothes, he thought.

∨∨∨

Sigma's day started early.

Every morning while his mother made breakfast, he did the laundry and woke up his younger sister. Once, he would have gone to his mentor's woodwork studio after breakfast without fail, but nowadays he only did that twice a week. The rest of the time he spent studying at the church or doing odd jobs at the royal palace. Thanks to a chance meeting with a civil official, he had permission to enter the Royal Sorcery Department. The kingdom's eminent sorcerers spent their days absorbed in research, and Sigma counted himself lucky that he could watch them at work.

It was there that he recently encountered a group of Egorovan visitors, including a member of foreign royalty.

They were surprisingly down-to-earth, but as they were chatting, a noble boy around his age got angry with him. The adults told him it wasn't his fault, and the boy apologized, too, so Sigma decided that it was okay for him to go to the palace today. In fact, the sorcerers had actually asked him to come so that he could keep the assistant director in line while the Egorovans were around.

Ist was a bit of an odd duck, and communicating with others wasn't exactly his forte, but Sigma didn't mind him. As prone as he was to speaking out of the blue and acting on impulse, he was a fun person and talented sorcerer who never seemed to run out of ideas. As far as Sigma was concerned, the civil official who initially reached out to him was way more of a weirdo.

It was still early in the morning when he showed up at the Sorcery Department, and he didn't see anyone around. Although some people would usually be napping around now after pulling an all-nighter, everyone was told to go home this week in order to keep things presentable while the Egorovans were around.

When Sigma checked the nap room just to see if anyone was there, he didn't notice that a man in a familiar brown cloak was leaning against the wall.

"Good morning," said a voice from behind him.

"Whoa!" Sigma jumped, startled. He hadn't expected anyone to be there. "M-Mr. Kondo…"

The man peering down at the shocked Sigma with a drowsy face was the Royal Accounting Department's assistant director—the number one weirdo in Sigma's estimation.

Contrary to Seiichirou's usual listless yet prim-and-proper appearance, his uniform was wrinkled, exposing part of his chest, and his hair was unkempt.

"M-Mr.…I mean, Sir, did you stay here last night?"

"Mm, I did. It was my first time. Pity there's no shower room here."

Realizing that Seiichirou had come to wash his face, Sigma nodded in understanding.

"Everyone here can use cleansing magic."

This was how the Sorcery Department maintained a level of cleanliness, the clutter aside. Alas, this meant that this place was beyond Seiichirou's reach as the ideal working environment.

"But what's the matter? Did, um, something happen to make you stay here?" Sigma cocked his head in confusion.

As he peered down at the boy, a sudden thought occurred to Seiichirou.

"Just some things… Anyway, Sigma, you worked at a wood-working studio, yes? Do you still go there?"

"Huh? Um, yeah. I mean, yes. Not every day, though."

"Then would you be able to put in a word there and..." Seiichirou crouched and whispered something into Sigma's ear.

The boy nodded. "Yes, that would be simple. I could even do it right away... Sir." Although he still struggled with speaking to authority figures, he was doing his best.

Seiichirou pulled a small coin out of his wallet and handed it to Sigma. It was worth about one hundred thousand yen in Japanese terms.

"Then can I leave it to you?"

"Whoa! I bet this is too much!"

"You can keep the change. Tell me if you need more. Thanks."

As Sigma reluctantly pocketed the coin, the door to the Sorcery Department flew open violently.

"Ah! Found you, Sei!" The newcomer was much noisier than Sigma, the literal child. It was Norbert, whose crop of blond hair looked less than impeccable today. "I was looking for you!"

"What's the matter, Norbert? Your hair is looking shabby."

"I didn't have time to style it! Darn it, Sei, why'd you run away from home?"

"...So I take it that Mr. Aresh has sent you sniffing for me like a dog."

"Way to twist the knife! Ugh, and even Sigma is looking at me in disdain! Whyyyy?! Curse you, Sei and Commander Indolark! You guys didn't have to involve me in your spat!"

"A...spat?" Sigma looked up at Seiichirou.

Faced with a child's innocent gaze, Seiichirou was momentarily lost for words. "Not exactly," he mustered finally.

"It's a total lovers' spat! I heard the details!"

"Ugh...he told you?"

"You think he'd squeeze me like a rag and not even tell me a thing? That's beyond the pale! Although I did kind of have to put two and two together."

It seemed that Norbert had asked about what led to Seiichirou fleeing the house in anger. Aresh said that he would have liked to come pick up Seiichirou himself, but he suspected that doing so would have added fuel to the fire. Which was correct.

"That makes me sound like the bad guy," Seiichirou said.

"I don't think you're totally in the wrong, Sei, but wasn't it mean of you to run out of Commander Indolark's house? He's worried about your condition."

"...I didn't *run out*. I'm just putting some space between us so that we can cool our heads."

"Couldn't you have just walked into a different room?"

"No. Our bedrooms are connected, and Aresh has the key... Oh." Seiichirou stopped when he realized he had said a bit too much of the truth.

Sigma's face had turned red and he was fidgeting restlessly. This wasn't something for a child to hear.

Norbert winced. "Anyway, didn't Commander Indolark say no to that offer?"

"That's not the issue here."

"Huh?"

Norbert had totally assumed that Seiichirou was anxious about the royal marriage offer. Then it occurred to him: *Wait, Sei never gets emotional about anything. His nerves are made of orichalcum.*

When Norbert recalled how Seiichirou was the kind of man who carefully weighed up each and every problem and devised countermeasures for all of them, his head tilted further in confusion. "So what got you so mad?"

"I was displeased with his sloppy communicating."

"Huh?" Norbert said dumbly, upon being hit with the same words Seiichirou gave him whenever he screwed up at his job.

Was this whole thing about work?

"Communication is vital in everything," Seiichirou said.

"Um...sure, but maybe he was trying not to worry you?"

"Me, worry? Rubbish. He turned down the offer. And if he were in a position where it was difficult to refuse, that would be all the more reason to inform me. We could have devised a plan."

Seiichirou was right, in Norbert's opinion. But...well. Something about what he was saying didn't sit right with Norbert.

"Hmm, I...guess so? But maybe he wanted to sort it out by himself since it was *his* problem, and uh..." Norbert struggled to make his case, to which Seiichirou reacted with a sour expression.

He did not argue, however. It was not because he accepted Norbert's logic. He simply thought it was pointless to debate the matter, and so he did not bother trying.

"I see how it is... *He* thinks little of me, and so does everyone else."

"That's not true..."

Having made his displeasure known, Seiichirou picked up his cloak, signaling the end of the conversation.

Norbert was not quite ready to back down here, not after being shaken from sleep by a communication spell well before his normal waking hours and getting dispatched on this mission.

"Yeah, Commander Indolark could have said more, but you're not being reasonable, either."

When Norbert imagined what it would be like to have a romantic partner with such a cold and dispassionate attitude...he would probably conclude that the other person did not love him. In that sense, Aresh had nerves of steel.

"...Shut up."

Seiichirou flicked Norbert on the forehead. What an inscrutable fellow.

∀∀∀

That day, the Egorovan delegation gathered in the conference room with their guides. Prime Minister Camile and Yurius, who handled relations with Egorova, were also in attendance. Ist was in the research room, having been deemed unsuitable for the conference.

"After deliberating on the Egorovans' request yesterday, we have found that our kingdom would also benefit greatly from collaborative research into movement spells," announced Yurius, to the obvious delight of the Egorovan sorcerers and the slight ambivalence of the Romanians.

Seiichirou twirled his magic pen as the situation unfolded exactly as predicted. The fundamental purpose of this tour was for the Romany Kingdom to determine whether Egorova, as a nation of magical technology, was worth having diplomatic relations with. Although the outcome happened faster than expected, Egorova had basically passed the test.

But a problem still remained.

"In the future, we would like to conduct experiments with Egorova's bountiful magic stones..."

"No, I believe that should only happen after your side has proven its hypothesis..."

It was still up in the air who would take the lead in the negotiations.

Romany could have bought itself some time had the Egorovans gone home and submitted their request after the fact, but because they were skipping right ahead to discussing a collaboration, Romany had almost nothing to bring to the table. Egorova had far more magic stones and research facilities at its disposal. If the research was situated there, then Romany would be handing over all its knowledge of the ancient magic to the other country, which would definitely mean Egorova held the reins. In the worst-case scenario, Romany would just be helping Egorova with *its* research. This was why Camile, Yurius, and Zoltan argued firmly for the Egorovans to return to their country first.

In the end, after a very long discussion, the Egorovans agreed to report the matter to their home country and resume talks after their side had permission for the collaboration. To that end, they decided to depart for Egorova at once instead of the following morning as originally planned. The sorcerers were *that* eager to get permission to start their research. Their guards and carriage drivers eyed their eager expressions with growing dread.

"Seiichirou," Camile called out before he left the conference room. "Depending on how things shake out, we might need your plan. Can I ask you to put your focus on that?"

Seiichirou nodded in response to the man's hushed whisper. Given that any research into the relationship between magicules and magic capacity needed magicule-dense areas to experiment in, Egorova's cooperation would be a boon.

Once Camile was gone, Lars finished up his conversation with Yurius and came over to Seiichirou for some reason.

"Seichiro."

Seiichirou's heart could not help but harden in suspicion upon hearing his name spoken with such familiarity, but he gave the prince a smooth bow anyway.

"I wanted to chat with you before I left. Do you have some time?" Although his departure had been pushed forward, Lars himself would not be involved in the preparations. He had time while things were done around him.

"I do." Seiichirou nodded.

Lars invited him to the terrace. "It really took me by surprise to find out that you were from another world," he said, his silver hair swaying in the breeze.

The only thing Seiichirou could say to that was, "Is that so?"

"I was thinking of scouting you because of your talents as a civil official, but that's not feasible anymore." Lars was basically saying that no country would be willing to hand over a person who was summoned alongside the Holy Maiden.

"That is flattering of you to say. Thank you."

Lars smiled at Seiichirou's reaction. Seiichirou was similar to

Prince Yurius and Camile in that it was difficult to figure out what he was thinking.

"From what I hear, you are involved in researching a method that combines movement spells and ancient magic to send people to another world. I take it, then, that you are trying to return to your original world?"

Seiichirou's breath caught in his throat.

For a moment, he struggled to form words.

"That's right," he said finally.

It was the reason he had pushed Romany into further advancements as a magical nation.

"You have a partner in this country, yes? And yet you still plan to return?" Lars continued.

Seiichirou felt a chill in his heart.

"I cannot answer personal questions."

His expression was probably full of tension. Lars quickly raised a hand in apology.

"Sorry, I did not mean to upset you."

"Oh, no…"

Seiichirou's normally dispassionate eyes were now brimming with heated emotion. A strained smile broke out on Lars's face.

"I really am sorry. I meant it as a simple question."

Seiichirou thought it intolerable that someone would ask a "simple question" to dig into his private life.

"Your initial plan was to return home. You must not have expected to find a partner here, yes? Personally, I find it difficult to wrap my head around a love that cannot be controlled by reason."

Looking again at Lars's face, there was a slightly forlorn look on his immaculate, doll-like features.

"In my position, I can only see people in terms of how useful they would be to my goals. It is the only way I can think of them. Eventually, I will marry within due course, and I am sure it will be another means to an end." Lars's jade green irises met Seiichirou's black eyes. "I thought the two of us were alike. That's why I wanted to get to know you. How you came to choose love even if it means throwing your plans aside."

The Egorovan delegation left the Romany Kingdom that afternoon. Several knights from Romany accompanied them, ostensibly as protection on their travels.

Aresh was one of them.

CHAPTER SEVEN

Startled

Three days passed after Aresh left with the Egorovan delegation. Given that it took about six days to reach Egorova via carriage, they were probably only about halfway there. In the meantime, Seiichirou worked like he always did. No, if anything, he worked harder than usual—he had been away from the Accounting Department for a while.

"Are you...okay, Sei?" Norbert asked worriedly.

"What are you talking about?" Seiichirou responded flatly, not even bothering to stop his hand.

"Well, you know..." Norbert and the other Accounting Department members watched Seiichirou uneasily as he threw himself into his work.

Pretty much everyone close to Seiichirou knew about his relationship with Aresh, especially after that lapel pin incident. And then, out of nowhere, Aresh went off to guard the Egorovans.

In most scenarios, the idea would have been for him to part ways at the border, but Aresh was hand-picked for this job to establish diplomatic ties. There was no better candidate, after all, than the capable commander of the Romany Kingdom's Third Royal Order, who could slay monsters and make long treks abroad with ease. Some were also aware that, as an individual with political influence, Aresh had received a marriage offer from the Egorovan royalty...

The servants at the mansion, Valtom first and foremost among them, spoke up on Aresh's behalf and tried to comfort Seiichirou. Even Erene, who had gone back to her own mansion after her husband's job concluded, came all the way to the house to tell Seiichirou: "That boy has never been good with words."

But Seiichirou pretended not to notice how they were looking at him. He simply nodded and got back to work.

"It's time for a break, Sei! Lunch! Let's go to the dining hall!" When Seiichirou continued his toils even after the lunch bell sounded, Norbert forcefully dragged him away into the dining hall.

Norbert must have thought it his duty to look after Seiichirou in Aresh's absence. Surely the man would neglect his meals if left to his own devices. Yet before he could shovel any food onto Seiichirou's plate, the workaholic in question wordlessly ate. He had not picked just anything without thought—they were all dishes that were low on magicules, just as the doctor (Aresh) ordered.

"Sei..." Norbert gasped.

Seiichirou did not normally bother with anything *not* work-related and simply took things in stride, and yet here he was, properly internalizing Aresh's devotion.

"Hey, are you guys going to eat?" said a familiar voice.

Seiichirou turned around and saw a man with a black cloak over his left shoulder. "Oh, Orjef."

"Vice Commander Rhoda!" Norbert squeaked.

Orjef chuckled at these two *very* different reactions before taking a tray himself. Seiichirou wondered in dismay if the vice commander was planning to eat with them, though he soon resigned himself to it. Although Orjef had finished playing his part as Seiichirou's bodyguard, Seiichirou knew that Orjef was looking out for him in Aresh's absence.

Besides, Orjef was a good-natured guy. Easy to talk to. Best of all, his sensibilities matched Seiichirou's, as demonstrated when he apologized for Aresh's handling of the lapel pin incident.

Norbert was tense, but the three of them ended up eating together.

"Ugh, Aresh is such a pain in the neck! You won't believe how busy we got after he pulled that vanishing act." Orjef complained lightheartedly about Aresh, which was probably his way of easing the weight on Seiichirou's shoulders. He and Aresh genuinely had no time to talk before the latter departed on his guard duties, though Orjef would probably get by. He'd done the bulk of the administrative work before Aresh met Seiichirou.

"I suppose that was inevitable, given that the Egorovans left in haste." Seiichirou, for his part, kept his face blank. He even sounded like he was sticking up for Aresh.

Orjef exchanged glances with Norbert, who was, to him, only a casual acquaintance at best. They'd both assumed that Seiichirou would be depressed or angry, yet he seemed to be neither. Orjef had thought he was a weird guy when he showed no emotion after that incident with the Third Royal Order members, but when they talked during that recent tour, he got the impression that Seiichirou actually was as expressive as a normal person. Now he swung right back to his initial persona.

The conversation went on. Seiichirou gave proper, full-sentence responses. Although it didn't reach the level of "friendly chatter," it was still a pleasant enough conversation over a meal. They were interrupted, however, by a wave of murmuring around the entrance of the dining hall. When Seiichirou looked over his shoulder to see what was going on, a girl who looked very out of place in the hall in her white and golden skirt was sprinting toward him.

"Good! I found you, Kondou!" cried Yua Shiraishi, the kingdom's Holy Maiden and the only person who could pronounce Seiichirou's name correctly. Her finger was pointed right in his direction.

Seiichirou finished chewing on his vegetables, and then said, "Shiraishi, were you not taught how rude it is to point at people?"

"Oh, sorry!" Yua apologized as she hurriedly lowered her arm.

But then she seemed to remember something.

"I heard the news, Kondou!" she declared as she slammed her

hands against the table. "Aresh is going to marry an Egorovan princess!"

All eyes were on the Holy Maiden after her sudden appearance, and they went wide at this outburst.

Aresh Indolark, commander of the Third Royal Order? True, he was neither married nor betrothed. A prince *had* been part of the recent Egorovan delegation. And now Aresh was accompanying them, supposedly as a guard.

Seiichirou heard the whispers, but he kept a stone-cold face.

"You are incorrect," he refuted Yua bluntly.

"B-but he went with the Egorovan prince after he received a marriage offer, right?"

"Who told you that?"

"Oh, Prince Yurius did."

That infernal prince...! He was reasonably competent in general—except when it came to Yua.

Seiichirou gripped his fork so tightly that a stronger man would have bent it. Mercifully, it remained intact in his grasp, but the fact that he was shaking in anger got across nonetheless.

Orjef rushed to interject. "Your Holiness, please calm yourself! You do not have all the facts."

"Y-yeah!" Norbert chimed in. "Commander Indolark would never entertain marriage talks..."

Yet despite their arguments, Yua's brow remained furrowed.

"But it *is* true that he was scouted for marriage, and that he's gone to accompany them, right?" she retorted.

""Urk."" The two of them flinched.

Behind them, Seiichirou nodded as he put away his tray. "That seems to be the case, yes."

"Is that all you have to say, Kondou?!" Yua was getting ever more worked up in her affront. Pushing the other two men aside, she brought her lovely face within inches of Seiichirou's. Leave it to a high school girl to have perfect skin—you could practically see the sheen from close up. "You're not just gonna roll over and take it, are you? Aren't you two supposed to be an item?!"

Another wave of murmurs filled the dining hall, albeit not quite on the level as the previous round. The regulars were used to seeing Aresh's nanny-ish behavior around Seiichirou at mealtimes, so the prevailing mood in the room was "Oh? So it wasn't my imagination?"

Seiichirou gazed back at Yua, not affirming or denying her words.

"Let's get him back," Romany's Holy Maiden declared with an uncharacteristically composed expression.

""Huh?"" Orjef and Norbert were dumbfounded.

But Yua went on, not paying them any heed. "Let's go to Egorova and take Aresh back!"

"Wh-what are you saying, Your Holiness?" Norbert spluttered. "How do you plan to—?"

"There's no way a foreign country would turn down a visit from the Holy Maiden, right? Kondou can just come with me!" Having kept her Holy Maiden work confined within Romany's borders, Yua had yet to even show her face to other countries. A country that was planning on establishing diplomatic ties with Romany would indeed accept a visit from the Holy Maiden. "What are you waiting for?! Let's go today!"

"What? That's so out of the blue," said Orjef. "You can't just..."

Norbert chimed in. "Not to mention that Sei would never..."

Seiichirou was always coolheaded, logical, and obsessed with efficiency. He would never drop his work to crash his partner's marriage interview in a foreign country, like the protagonist of some teen novel. Norbert was convinced of this.

He looked over his shoulder to find that Seiichirou was standing up, having already put away his cutlery.

"It is a little sooner than I expected, but yes. Let's go."

"What?" said Orjef and Norbert.

"Yippee!" squealed Yua.

"I managed to get ahead on my work over these past three days," said Seiichirou. "I should be able to leave right away if I delegate what remains. Let's go to Egorova."

As a smile bloomed on Yua's face, Orjef's and Norbert's shouts resounded throughout the dining hall.

""What the hellllll?!""

Seiichirou was quick to move.

He had always been the kind of man who covered all his bases. Right from the start, he had made meticulous preparations so that he *could* pass on his work.

Likewise, the Holy Maiden Yua showed an extraordinary capacity to get things done. After securing an immediate appointment with the prince, she and Seiichirou were ushered into a meeting room. Prime Minister Camile was there as well—and so were Orjef and Norbert, befuddled by their confusion. They'd somehow gotten swept up in the momentum from the dining hall.

"The Holy Maiden making a courtesy visit to Egorova...you say..." Yurius looked as if he was gritting his teeth, while Camile seemed somehow amused.

"Yep!" Yua chirped. "If that's how we spin it, the other side won't turn it down."

"But... Nggggh..."

As Yurius groaned and rubbed his temples, Seiichirou went in for the kill.

"Given that both sides have agreed to diplomatic relations, Egorova will inevitably be the first country to make contact with the Holy Maiden."

"Well, yes, but at this stage..."

"What's the problem? It's just a pretext!"

"Yua... You don't need to say the quiet part aloud..." Even Yurius, who normally indulged in Yua's eccentricities, found himself pushing back against her this time.

But Yua was firm and unmoving. "What are you going to do if Aresh marries that Egorovan princess and never comes back?!"

"Urk." For Yurius, it would be a shame indeed to lose a man of Aresh's magical and military talents to another country. But... "Why are you going so far out of your way for Seiichirou?"

He would have understood if Yua was opposed to Aresh moving to another country because she fancied him. He wouldn't have liked it, but it would have made sense. But he could see from Yua's demeanor that she knew about Aresh and Seiichirou's relationship and was trying to get the two of them together.

"In my country, people who get in the way of romance get kicked by a horse and die!" was Yua's response.

"Yua..." Yurius was lost for words.

Judging by that reaction, Seiichirou wondered if something had happened between them. Camile whispered into his ear: "Other nobles have been saying things to His Highness."

"Oh, I see."

So Yurius had proposed to Yua. And because of that, the nobles around him blasted him with criticism.

Judging by what Yua said, she seemed to have feelings for Yurius after all.

"Prince Yurius... I have a lot to think about," she said. "Would you mind waiting until I return for my answer?"

"Yua... Of course."

Predictably, Yurius's resistance shattered quickly.

All that was left was getting permission from Camile, the man who held the political reins.

"Your Excellency, I believe that if you were to send us to Egorova, I can secure Romany's position as the leader of the movement spell research." Seiichirou tried appealing to Camile's political instincts.

But Camile did not react how Seiichirou expected. Instead of stepping out of whispering distance, he simply turned his head in Seiichirou's direction. Seiichirou took a step back in surprise.

Camile raised his hand as he watched Seiichirou in amusement.

"I thought my chance had come, but it seems not," he said in a low, velvety tone as the back of his pointer finger trailed down Seiichirou's cheek.

"That—" Seiichirou began.

"Oh! Oh! There's something I want to ask His Excellency!" Orjef cut in before Seiichirou could get the words out.

"I gotta ask you about work, Sei!" Norbert jumped in as well.

They were obviously trying to peel Camile away from Seiichirou, before Seiichirou's eyes could even widen. Camile let out a chuckle.

"What's this? When did you get so many knights in shining armor?"

"That's not quite it. They're simply on Aresh's side," Seiichirou answered with narrowed eyes. Norbert pouted, but Seiichirou ignored it. He hadn't forgotten how Aresh had ordered Norbert to take Seiichirou to the dining hall or how he had sent him sniffing around for Seiichirou in the nap room.

"Is that so? Then would that make me *your* ally?" Camile said with a flirtatious glance. At some point, Yua, who should have been indulging in her own love scene with the prince, had begun gazing at them with hearts in her eyes. "Is there something I can do for you, Seiichirou?" asked Camile with a sultry tone.

Seiichirou responded:

"If you could sign this document, that would be great, thanks."

∨∨∨

In the end, they didn't get going on the same day as Yua had hoped. There were still preparations to make. But the next morning, a hastily assembled "Holy Maiden's Procession" gathered in front of the palace gates.

There were two carriages and five knights to protect them. Four knights were from the Second Royal Order, who specialized in protecting the kingdom's key figures.

The other person was…

"I knew this would happen. I knew it. But how the hell is this going to work?!"

...Orjef, Vice Commander of the Third Royal Order, bemoaning the circumstances.

Although this meant that both the commander and vice commander would be absent, this apparently wasn't a problem, given that the Third Royal Order took frequent expeditions away from the capital. Admittedly, the severe lack of prep time did cause its own issues, though they were not insurmountable.

"They've got a lot of magic stones over there. They might even have some texts I've never seen before!"

Next to Orjef was Ist, assistant director of the Sorcery Department, as jubilant as a child on an excursion. He must have heard about the trip from somewhere because he strode right up to Seiichirou and demanded to come along.

"But why me...?" A pale-faced Sigma clutched his bag, trembling. He'd been there when Ist had made his demand, and here he was again today, getting dragged into the fray.

"It's a good opportunity to broaden your horizons, don't you think?" Seiichirou said nonchalantly. Inwardly, he was grateful to Sigma for being Ist's guardian. Although there was something silly about a thirty-year-old needing a twelve-year-old's guidance, this was Ist they were talking about.

"Nah, I'm the one who should be wondering what I'm doing here..."

Norbert, who had been glued to Seiichirou's side the whole time, had joined the group under Yurius's orders. The fact that he was technically royalty probably had something to do with it. This didn't have much to do with Seiichirou, so he just shrugged and let it happen.

"Aren't you a bit *too* callous with me, Sei?" Norbert whined.

"It's my way of showing affection."

"Uh...well, in that case..." Seiichirou's frivolous young subordinate blushed.

Today, his hair was done up properly. The Accounting Department would be going without two of its members, but this was fine since Seiichirou had written down instructions for their colleagues.

"Anyway, Sei, what's that?" Norbert pointed at Seiichirou's face, which was covered below his eyes.

Indeed, Seiichirou was wearing a thin, dark cloth as a mask.

"I'm told this cloth is made from a plant called rafket. It's not one hundred percent effective, but it can stop magicules from getting into my lungs."

The plant was apparently cultivated in Plasas, a kingdom to the south where magicules were sparse. It could be used to purify magicules to some small degree.

"Cool," said Norbert. "But wait, that reminds me...are you gonna be okay?! I heard magicules are way denser in Egorova compared to Romany!"

"I've accounted for that."

Namely, the purifying mask...plus the medicine for diluting magic and reducing the symptoms of magic poisoning. He got it from the Medical Bureau director Ciro, who made it on Aresh's request. Ciro had been reluctant to hand it over, saying that it was still in the trial phase and didn't have a strong impact, but Seiichirou convinced him that it was better than nothing. Ciro also gave him the mask as another means of protecting himself.

"Most of Egorova's magicule-dense areas are in the mines, so I doubt I'll keel over straight away in the capital," Seiichirou said.

"Well, sure, but don't push yourself, okay? Tell me as soon as you feel unwell."

Norbert kept bugging him about this, so Seiichirou told him, "Yeah, yeah. I get it."

As all of this was going on, the star of the show arrived with a knight and lady-in-waiting in tow. It was Yua—clad in a refined, light blue one-piece dress—and one other person: a beautiful lady oozing with elegance in her purple dress and her tied-up black-blue hair.

The sharp-eyed lady—Erene—must have heard about this trip on the grapevine, because on the night Yua made her proposal, she came to Aresh's mansion and said, "You ought to bring a noble along with you."

And thus she pushed her way—er, cordially invited herself—into the group.

"So you're Aresh's older sister!" said Yua. "I can see the resemblance. You're gorgeous!"

"Why, thank you, Your Holiness."

"Oh, you can just call me Yua, not Your Holiness."

"Well, then, Lady Yua, let's pray for our safe travels."

The refined ladies in the group hit it off marvelously. Without further ado, Yua, Erene, Orjef, and the lady-in-waiting went into one carriage while Seiichirou, Norbert, Ist, and Sigma took the other.

It took six days to reach Egorova's capital by carriage. This only applied, however, to carriages outfitted with special magic tools for royalty. With all of Romany's wisdom and know-how, the journey would still take ten days. To make matters worse, Egorova's mountainous landscape meant that any carriage unfit for steep climbs would have to take detours.

Having come from a world of cars, bullet trains, and airplanes, Seiichirou was still not terribly used to carriages. He hadn't traveled any long distance since the Demon Forest. Even if horses were faster than humans, the weight of luggage and the frequent rest stops slowed progress considerably. They had changed horses at towns along the way to the Demon Forest, but they lacked the preparations to pull that off this time.

Seiichirou had expected that the trip would take over ten days—once upon a time.

"Let's take the shortest route! We can make it in three days!" declared Romany's Holy Maiden.

Everyone else gaped at her as if she was off her rocker, save for one person with sparkling eyes. Needless to say, it was Ist.

"I'd love to get there quick, too. How do you plan on doing it? What's the method?"

"I'll cast healing magic on the horses! Then they can keep going without breaks!"

What is she, a drill sergeant? Seiichirou winced at Yua's suggestion, but the others looked surprisingly receptive. Apparently, since healers were a precious resource, nobody had thought to use them for these purposes.

"Oh, I can use healing magic, too," Ist enthused.

It bore mentioning that their group included the Holy Maiden and the kingdom's foremost sorcerer.

"Help out, too, Orjef. You can use a bit of magic," Erene demanded huffily. This reminded Seiichirou that if Orjef was Aresh's cousin, then he was Erene's cousin as well.

"Don't ask for the impossible!" Orjef retorted. "I'm no healing magic expert!"

"Useless. What are you even doing here?"

"You know I'm a guard, right?!"

As he watched the bickering cousins and the buoyant Yua and Ist, Seiichirou decided to revise his opinion. He wanted to reach their destination as fast as possible, too.

"If there are multiple types of magic you can use, are you able to cast something that slows fatigue instead of just healing?" Seiichirou asked.

"What do you mean, 'slows fatigue'?" Yua asked curiously.

"Ohhh, what's this?!" said Ist. "Are you up to something, Kondo?! Let me in on it!"

"Calm down, Ist. We haven't even left yet, and you're too worked up." The twelve-year-old restrained the thirty-year-old baby.

Feeling grateful for Sigma's service, Seiichirou pulled a large scroll out of his luggage.

"This piqued my interest when I was researching Egorova. The shortest route is between these mountains."

Seeing where Seiichirou was pointing, Orjef's eyes boggled. His regular monster-slaying excursions and trips to remote areas and frontier lands gave him a robust grasp of geography.

"Hey! How do you know about that?! It's not common knowledge in the kingdom!"

"Huh? What is it?" Yua cocked her head.

"There is a tunnel here connecting Romany and Egorova," Seiichirou explained flatly.

"Whoa! That's convenient! Why aren't we using it already?"

"Because it caved in over a hundred years ago, making it impossible to get through."

"Oh."

"Yeah," said Norbert. "I heard about that. It was built a long time ago as a trade route between Egorova and Romany for importing food and whatnot, but when Egorova decided it could make do on its own with its magic tools, the tunnel was left in disrepair and now it's unusable."

Leave it to a member of the royal family to know history. Orjef, who had actually seen the tunnel for himself, nodded along to Norbert's explanation.

"But that doesn't mean there's no way through at all, does it?" Seiichirou said.

After all, they had the kingdom's best and brightest with them.

Seeing the smile on Seiichirou's lips, the entire group realized that he was completely and utterly serious. They were stunned into silence.

And so, through the combined efforts of Yua's healing and purification magic, Ist's weight-lightening and strengthening magic, and Orjef's earth magic, they were able to keep the horses strong and healthy while clearing the path ahead of them. Orjef and Ist also teamed up on gravity spells to clear enough space for the carriages to get through. With that, they actually did manage to reach Egorova in three days.

∨∨∨

"You think things are gonna be okay with us making such a sudden entrance?" Norbert asked.

"We're fine," said Seiichirou. "We sent a notice via magic ahead of time."

However, given that they only sent a message before they left and another one the day before they arrived, it was certainly possible that the Egorovan side would refuse to trust it.

When they announced to the palace gatekeeper that the Holy Maiden had arrived, he looked like he'd been bowled over for a second before he hurriedly scampered off. The group entrusted their carriages to palace staff and were escorted to a small room that looked like a lobby.

Normally, VIPs would have been given their own rooms in the palace immediately upon arrival, but the wires had gotten crossed, it seemed. Seeing an obviously noble lady sitting in a room meant for merchants to make deals with the palace made for quite an amusing picture.

"Oh, right, Mist—er, I mean, Sir," said Sigma, breaking the awkward silence in the room. "I forgot to give you that thing you asked for. Here it is."

The boy who looked most comfortable in their current surroundings seemed to have relaxed a little because he pulled a small box out of his bag and handed it to Seiichirou.

"Ah, so it's done. Great timing."

"Yeah, I told you it was simple. I was gonna give it to you straight away, but I forgot after all the stuff that happened. Sorry."

True, he did get pulled along into the Holy Maiden's impromptu courtesy call to a foreign nation in a magic-enhanced carriage that practically zipped them to their destination. Little wonder he was confused.

"What's that?" Seemingly unruffled about being in a foreign palace, Norbert peered over Seiichirou's shoulder at the box on his palm.

It was purple, square, and sturdy-looking.

"A secret," Seiichirou said.

"What?! C'mon, tell meeeee!"

As this kerfuffle was going on, there was a loud metal clanking sound, accompanied by the hasty entrance of several armored knights. Behind them was a familiar slender man who seemed out of breath.

"Phew... Th-that's them, all right! The Romany court magician, the knight, and the civil official..." The wheezing man was Donato, the sorcerer from the Egorovan delegation. Apparently, the palace had gotten someone who had actually been to Romany to identify them.

"So that's the actual Holy Maiden...?"

"B-but how'd she get here so fast?!"

Even after receiving confirmation, the Egorovans were still flabbergasted. They could not hide their confusion over how Seiichirou's group had shown up a mere day after them.

Just when Seiichirou was thinking that they were wasting their time sitting around, Erene elegantly stood up from the stone chair that had looked so out of place against her class.

"I am Erene Rein, member of Count Rein's house and daughter of Marquess Indolark of the Romany Kingdom. I understand your need to confirm our identities, though I was wondering how long you were planning on keeping us cooped up here. The Holy Maiden is weary from her journey. I pray you welcome her in haste."

Her voice rang out with authority.

Silence came over the room, so heavy that one could hear a pin drop, and then the Egorovans practically fell over themselves to show their guests through the palace.

Oh, so that's *what she meant by 'we need a noble'*, thought Seiichirou as he gazed at Norbert, supposedly also a member of a count's family.

They were ushered into a lavish reception room that could not have been more different from their previous accommodations. The ceiling was decorated in golden patterns, and the furniture was awash in yellow and red. The chandeliers were also beautiful in their intricacy. Judging by how the light beamed at unnatural angles, they might have been magic tools.

Although the Egorovan palace was made of stone, giving it a more rustic look than Romany's, the interior was sparkling. Seiichirou had gotten the impression from the fine detail in the Egorovans' clothing that their magic tools and technology allowed for impressive advancements in their handicrafts and manual work. Perhaps that only made sense for a cold, mountain-locked country.

Several sofas and chairs surrounded a table. Yua and Erene took the front sofa while Seiichirou, Orjef, and Norbert sat on the chairs. Sigma insisted on standing with the attendants at first, but when Seiichirou asked him to catch Ist who was scurrying about the room, they both sat down on the back sofa.

After a round of tea, a manservant opened the door and Lars strode in, clad in an even more resplendent outfit than what he wore in Romany. He had a feeling that this clothing probably featured a traditional design native to Egorova.

A girl in a black shirt and dress came in after him. The shirt had red and gold embroidery, while the skirt was laced with red and green. Her luscious, neatly trimmed black hair fell past her shoulders. And she had the same jade green eyes as Lars.

"Wait? What? Whaaat?!"

Unsurprisingly, Sigma's eyes went wide as saucers.

Because that face belonged to Luciano, the boy who came to Romany as an Egorovan envoy. There were no two ways about it.

Lars smiled awkwardly at the gaping visitors.

"I apologize for keeping you waiting. It is a pleasure to meet you, Your Holiness. And you as well, Lady Rein. I am Lars Eric Egorova, third prince of Egorova. And this is…"

Gently, he nudged Luciano's back. The boy…er, girl, took a step forward, clutched the ends of her skirt, and curtsied elegantly.

"I am Lufina Cujeltika Egorova, *third* princess of Egorova."

"Wha—?!"

Seiichirou could tell that Sigma had turned to stone behind him, though he wasn't particularly shaken himself. The other adults were surprised, though a look of understanding came over their faces. Yua, who was seeing the girl for the first time, simply nodded.

They'd been told initially that Luciano was a boy with blood ties to the royal family. It wasn't a huge leap for her to be bona fide royalty. Given that she was at an androgynous-looking age, concealing her gender was the easiest way to go incognito.

"I knew I'd seen her somewhere before...," Orjef muttered.

"Did you not realize when you met her?" Erene needled him. Apparently, it was typical for members of a marquess family to study the portraits and family trees of foreign royalty.

Norbert, who was technically royalty himself, quickly looked away when Seiichirou glanced at him. He hadn't clocked it, either, it seemed.

"But I must say, I never imagined that Romany's Holy Maiden would visit our kingdom on such short notice."

Lars was questioning why the Holy Maiden would suddenly choose to make her first foreign visit, as well as her uncanny travel speed.

"Well, our nations will be collaborating on magic technology," Yua said. "I would love to lend my assistance."

"Consider it a testament to the great trust Egorova has earned within Romany," said Erene.

"High praise, indeed." Lars's gaze swept over the guests from Romany once more, briefly stopping at Norbert, but when he spotted the masked Seiichirou further along, his eyes widened ever so slightly. "In any case, I am sure you are weary from your travels. Please, do take your time to rest. Romany's Holy Maiden will always be welcome in Egorova. His Majesty and many others would love to extend their greetings, so I hope that you stay the night."

He was all but saying that things were in a rush at the moment and they needed time to prepare. Seiichirou felt bad for him, but he was in a hurry, too.

"My apologies, but before we get settled, I would like to meet with the guards who accompanied you from Romany. Would you happen to know where they are right now?" Erene called out to Lars just as he was about to leave the room.

For a moment, Lars made eye contact with Luciano...er, Lufina. Lufina briefly lowered her gaze before turning to Erene.

"If you are referring to Commander Indolark, he is presently meeting with my younger sister, the fourth princess."

Alas, the marriage interview was already underway.

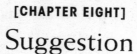

CHAPTER EIGHT

Suggestion

Aresh was in conversation with Egorova's fourth princess, whom the kingdom was offering up as a marriage partner.

Nobody in the room failed to understand the significance of this, but Erene still held her ground.

"Oh, then please allow us to sit in. I would love to meet the princess who might become my brother's spouse."

At the "brother's spouse" part, Norbert and Orjef cast anxious looks in Seiichirou's direction. But what point was there in getting worked up about it now?

"Yes, but…" Lars sounded reluctant.

"I'd like to meet her, too, please." Yua added her weight to the ring.

Judging that it would be unwise to keep refusing Romany's guest of honor and Aresh's older sister, Lars capitulated easily.

"Oh, but my sister is sickly, so you might be subjected to an unpleasant sight…," Lufina said worriedly.

"Don't worry, that would be our fault for barging in on her anyway," answered Yua, who could have stood to be a bit more concerned.

The women took the lead, while Lars and the men hung back behind them. Ist trailed last, gawking at everything in his path. Sigma valiantly dragged him along to keep up with the group.

Seiichirou made a mental note to himself to give Sigma a bonus allowance when they got back.

"I'm honored that you would make such a long trip to visit us. Thank you, Mr. Rhoda," said Lars.

"Oh no, we ought to apologize for the sudden visit. I heard after the fact that our commander was chosen to be a guard..."

Orjef apologized; he was no good at mind games and probing people. Lars and his group had probably already figured out why the Holy Maiden's courtesy visit was happening so abruptly without any of the usual red tape.

Lars's immaculate eyebrows creased into a frown. "No, we're the ones who imposed first. Although I should mention that it was Commander Indolark himself who suggested coming to Egorova."

"What, really?!" Norbert yelled in surprise.

To be fair, it was hard for anyone to drag Aresh of all people anywhere, let alone out of his country. Seiichirou had more or less imagined that he had chosen to do so of his own volition.

"But we are also guilty of not discarding our hopes regarding the proposal." Lars paused there and looked at Seiichirou. "I'm surprised you came as well. I can see that your talents extend to negotiation."

Seiichirou could see that the ladies had stopped in front of a door, which told him that Aresh and the fourth princess were probably inside. Lars, Orjef, and the others came to a halt, too.

An Egorovan maid knocked on the door. Lufina announced their presence, and the path opened for them. The ladies entered the room first, and Seiichirou took a step after them.

At the same time, he opened his mouth to speak.

"No, I'm just here to take back my man."

"What?"

The room was simpler than the reception lounge. That said, it was still a palace room, which meant that it was furnished with luxury items.

Seiichirou's target was sitting at the far end of the room, his black-clad back facing the door. The princess was sitting across from him at a table, and she stood up when she spotted the newcomers. The man directly in front of her turned around a beat later.

"Lufina," the princess called out her sister's name with a bell-like voice.

The man in front of her swung his large frame around at that moment.

And then...

"What are you doing here?!"

He rushed straight over to Seiichirou, completely ignoring Lufina, Erene, and even Lars.

"Don't you know what kind of place this is?! Why the hell would you come here when your barrier is fading? Do you have a death wish?!" Aresh barked at him, his large hands planted on Seiichirou's shoulders.

Any normal person—no, even a Romany knight—would have shrunk in the face of such a formidable man, but Seiichirou was unmoving.

"I came to talk to a certain someone who doesn't bother communicating," he retorted. "I did take precautions, you know."

"Precautions?"

"The prototype from Ciro."

For one, Seiichirou wasn't supposed to talk without wearing the special mask. Aresh's frown deepened when Seiichirou produced the medicine. Yet, before Aresh could resume his lecture, someone else touched him on the shoulder from behind.

"You've got some nerve ignoring me, Aresh."

Upon being subjected to a sharp gaze not dissimilar to his own, Aresh's frown transformed from "worried" to "annoyed."

"What are *you* doing here, Erene?"

"What a way to speak to your older sister. Who do you think is responsible for getting you two in the same room without a hitch?"

Instead of focusing on the familiar squabble between the two intimidatingly beautiful siblings, Orjef seemed more preoccupied with the fourth princess.

Not that his reaction was surprising.

If the third princess, Lufina, was around twelve, then the fourth princess had to be even younger. It wasn't so unusual for royal and noble marriages to be decided from an early age to preserve bloodlines and family names. Age gaps were common enough. Seiichirou knew this.

But still...

"Um... May I ask how old the fourth princess is?" Seiichirou heard Norbert ask Lars hesitantly. This was what everyone was dying to know.

Lars parted his perfectly shaped lips. "She will be four this year."

"Bwah! Ngh! Urk! Ahem!" Orjef's mouth produced a series of strangled noises. He hurriedly shut his mouth and pretended it was all a cough.

But no, Seiichirou understood.

He knew about age gaps and arranged marriages.

But it was still *extremely funny* to see the tall and imposing Aresh next to a three-year-old girl.

"Orjef...I have some words for you later." Aresh, who should have been preoccupied in his verbal sparring with Erene, turned to glare at his cousin. The smile instantly vanished from Orjef's lips.

"Er, don't you have something to say to me first?" Seiichirou spoke up.

Aresh fell silent.

Lufina gazed in surprise at the suddenly cowed Aresh, but then she seemed to remember something and ran over to the fourth princess's sofa. "Sofia!"

Lars was also quick to rush over to his sisters.

The fourth princess, named Sofia, had the same silver hair as Lars. It hung in a braid past her shoulders. Coupled with her spotless skin, she was quite a pretty young girl, but her wide, bluish-purple eyes were downcast, her face had a terrible pallor, and her breathing was ragged.

"What...?"

"Apologies, but my sister is sickly. She might have gotten anxious from seeing new faces. Call a healer over right away," Lars told an attendant as he clutched Sofia's tiny body.

"I can use healing magic." Yua raised her hand.

"Wait." Seiichirou took a step forward, stopping Yua in her tracks.

"What are you—?"

Seiichirou approached the young princess and peered at her tentatively so as not to appear rude.

The pallor, the sweat, the labored breathing. It all looked familiar...no, it *was* familiar. He'd experienced it with his own body. Seiichirou looked back at Aresh. A look of understanding came over him when their eyes met.

"This...is magic poisoning!" they declared.

"Magic poisoning...?" the others in the room muttered, not looking quite convinced of this out-of-the-blue diagnosis.

Seiichirou ignored them and pulled out the medicine Ciro had given him, but then he thought better of it and handed Lars one of his extra masks instead. "This mask will absorb magicules. This is a spare, so I haven't used it yet. Please give it to Her Highness."

"What?" Lars blinked, and then said hesitantly, "All right."

Seiichirou turned to Yua next. "Shiraishi, please cast purification before you use your healing magic. You can limit it to this room."

"Huh? Oh, sure. Okay."

If Sofia was as weak to magicules as Seiichirou was, then the first order of business was ridding the room of magicules.

Yua clapped her hands together as if she was in prayer and chanted a song-like spell. In that instant, a wind blew in the room. People who weren't normally conscious of magicules wouldn't be able to tell, but Seiichirou could see at once that the air was now clear.

Sofia's breathing stabilized at that same moment.

"What is...going on...?" Lars gaped at the girl in his arms. Lufina looked similarly shocked.

In lieu of a response, Seiichirou's knees buckled, for the

aftereffects of the purification magic left him slightly reeling. Aresh caught Seiichirou in his arms.

"Ah, my apologies," Seiichirou said. "Your Highness Prince Lars, allow me to inform you that Her Highness the Fourth Princess most likely has a weakness to magicules."

Sofia's condition had settled, but given her tender age, the servants still took care in handling her. She was soon carried off to her bedroom to rest.

Seiichirou and the others returned to the reception room, where they chatted once more with Lars and Lufina. Erene, Yua, Aresh, and Seiichirou took the front seats. Seiichirou tried to stand back, but Aresh forced him to sit next to him.

"Sofia has never possessed much magic, and her frailty often confines her to bed," Lars explained.

One could see the Egorovan's strong bias toward magic and technical prowess in his words. It made sense for a nation founded on its magic research and tools. Here in this frigid, mountainous land, one could genuinely say that technological progress meant everything.

Given that one needed magical power to research magic tools, Egorova's nobility regarded a person's magical capacity as a mark of status.

"Sofia...was born from a foreign mistress," Lufina said hesitantly, prompting Norbert to lift his head.

A bastard child born from an immigrant woman with no connection to nobility or royalty. Even if she was regarded as a member of the royal family, the girl's low birth and meager magic coupled with her sickly body meant that she occupied an extremely precarious position.

"Given her frail constitution...there were some who suggested marrying her off into a prominent rural clan or a wealthy merchant family before she got much older."

She was considered *that* useless to the royal family. Lars would resent the nobles who said as much for the rest of his life.

Then came the talks about a cultural exchange with the Romany Kingdom. Although Lars wasn't terribly proficient at magic himself, his political acumen was the strongest among his brothers, and so it was suggested that he lead the diplomatic delegation. Part of it, of course, was so that he could score some personal achievements and for Lufina to learn from the Romanian sorcerer she so deeply admired, but the two of them were worried for Sofia at the same time.

Neither the third prince nor the third princess had much family pedigree to lean on. Lars's mother did not come from a particularly highborn house, and Lufina was the daughter of a noblewoman whose family owned an abundance of magic stone mines. The two siblings had always gotten along well because of that, and they extended the same sympathies toward Sofia.

When they heard that Romany had a milder climate than Egorova and that it possessed a magically talented knight force with a young, unmarried, and talented commander from a prominent noble family, they sounded him out as a match for Sofia.

"If she got shuffled off into the hinterlands as a political pawn, who knows if she would even be allowed to live?" said Lars. "We thought that surely a high-ranking knight in Romany would not treat her so poorly in the interest of future diplomatic relations."

"I apologize for pushing our decision onto you," Lufina said.

Apparently, the two of them had been dogmatic about the engagement.

"I really am sorry. Our intelligence informed us that you were not betrothed…," Lars said as he glanced at Aresh and Seiichirou sitting intimately close to each other. "I assumed that Seiichirou's partner was that priest…"

Aresh's purple eyes flashed angrily. "The priest? You mean Siegvold? I don't understand. What were you doing for them to come to that conclusion?"

"Nothing," said Seiichirou. "The Egorovans asked to see the private school, and I just spoke a little with Priest Siegvold as I was guiding them around."

"How would *that* make them draw assumptions?"

"I don't know. Why don't you ask them? They're right there."

"Your lovers' quarrel isn't getting us anywhere. Save it for when you're alone," Erene said flatly, prompting Aresh to frown and fall silent. Seiichirou shut his mouth, too, not wanting others to see his petulant side.

"Oh no, I'm sorry," said Lufina. "Kondo was wearing an amethyst lapel pin at the dinner party, so we just assumed that his partner had purple in their appearance. Then we met the priest and got the wrong idea."

"Now whose fault is that, Mr. Aresh?" said Seiichirou.

"Well, it *did* make them understand that you were taken," Aresh said sullenly.

"Oh, don't give me that..."

"I told you to save it for later." Erene snapped her fan shut.

The two bickering lovers fell quiet once again.

"Anyway, we caused you a great deal of trouble with our plan," Lars said. "I won't be offended if you just forget about the whole marriage offer."

"We are ever so sorry," said Lufina.

"No, I'm just glad we sorted out the misunderstanding. Please lift your heads," Erene insisted.

"There's also, well...the matter of how you healed Sofia," the two Egorovan royals said after they had slowly lifted their heads.

They were curious about how Sofia's pallor had instantly cleared when every previous attempt at healing magic only served to contain her immediate symptoms.

"You asked for a purification spell, yes?" Lars went on. "Does this mean that the Holy Maiden's power can cure Sofia's illness?"

"What? Purification removes the magicules. It's not a cure to illness, I think?" Yua, who had only done what Seiichirou told her to do, cocked her head.

With the conversation evidently going nowhere, Aresh chimed in. "Princess Sofia most likely suffers from magic poisoning. It can happen to people with low magic resistance when their stamina is low or if they go somewhere with a high density of magicules."

"Magic...poisoning?" Lars and Lufina looked confused.

Seiichirou didn't blame them. This was a world where magicules were as natural as air, and Egorova was particularly dense with the stuff. It was like telling an earthling that someone had an allergy to oxygen or nitrogen.

To muddle matters further, healing spells did work on sickly bodies to an extent. A peasant might not have the luxury, but the royals could solve most problems instantly with healing.

"Magicules are part of the air. They are not poison," Aresh explained. "Most people, even those with weak bodies, will not suffer unless they venture to the depths of the magic stone mines or some such place. But there are rare cases where people have low resistance."

And such cases would probably be regarded as inexplicable.

"How do you know all of this?" Lars asked.

Aresh turned his gaze to Seiichirou, who nodded and took up the explanation. "As you know, I was summoned from another world. Because of that, I have hardly any magicule resistance to speak of."

Even then, he'd managed to get by in the Romany Kingdom, which wasn't too dense with magicules, by sticking to small portions of magicule-light foods. But when he got his hands on magicule-heavy indulgences, he rapidly fell ill, and Aresh came to the rescue.

Seiichirou did not go so far as to mention all of that, but he did say, "Princess Sofia's body is still developing. I believe that is why she cannot withstand the magicules in Egorova."

"Oh dear... So you're saying that as long as Sofia is in Egorova..."

"Which is why I have a proposal."

"Hm?" Those who didn't know Seiichirou very well were confused at his sudden assertiveness.

"Oh."

"Ohhhh."

Meanwhile, those who *did* know him well reacted as if they'd seen this all before. Either that or exasperation.

At times like these, Seiichirou got as carried away as Ist.

"Romany is currently launching research into the relationship between magicules and magical energy in the hopes of increasing magical capacity and magicule resistance."

"Increasing magicule resistance?" said Lars. "Really?"

"Indeed. Having almost no resistance myself, I've made do with tools such as these. I would almost certainly have suffered a bout of illness had I come to Egorova without them."

It would have been nigh impossible for a freshly summoned Seiichirou. It was only through Aresh and Pavel's blood, sweat, and tears that his tolerance had managed to increase in a tangible way.

"And I believe that I was able to raise my resistances with minimal periods of illness because I was in Romany, where the magicules are not so dense."

"Wait a second. Are you saying you managed to increase your magical power?" The question came from an unexpected angle.

Seiichirou was a little surprised, though he nodded without his expression so much as flickering.

"Yes. Although magical power is said to be hereditary because it presently has a strong correlation with bloodlines, I believe that it can be raised after the fact."

Which was why he was suggesting that Romany take custody of Princess Sofia as part of their countries' joint efforts at magical research.

"That...would be the best possible outcome," said Lars.

Indeed. By having her participate in research efforts, she would convalesce in a magicule-light land and build her tolerance. This would also spare her from being married off into the hinterlands, and if her magical power did manage to increase, her standing as a royal would improve.

This would also mean Lars's side would owe them a debt and provide a good pretext for Romany taking the lead with the research. To put it cynically, the Egorovan princess would essentially be a hostage. Although she wasn't terribly important from the Egorovan perspective, she was still a princess nonetheless. Lars's side certainly wouldn't abandon her.

Of course, only so many people were worthy of taking custody of a princess, which was why a certain somebody took this opportunity to stand.

"My house can take responsibility for Princess Sofia."

All eyes turned to Erene.

"Seiichirou," she said. "Let me join the experiments, too."

"Huh? Well, I don't see why not..." Seiichirou did not see what a married noblewoman like Erene stood to gain from participating, but there were probably a lot of people who wanted to throw their hat into the ring given that it was a state-sponsored plan.

"Oh, but I'm not sure about sending Sofia alone to Romany..." Lufina sounded ill at ease.

"Not to worry," Norbert answered with his usual lackadaisical tone. "Long as she's got a family who loves her, she'll be just fine!"

He was a king's bastard child, adopted by a retainer. Having sworn to support the royal family, the young man smiled without a care in the world.

Lars thanked them once more and stood up. "I've prepared private rooms for all of you. Please make yourselves at home until dinner."

He was trying to set the scene for a banquet to give himself time to report to the higher authorities.

Aresh chose this moment to speak up. "I hope you'll forgive us for not attending."

Us, not *me*, he said. All eyes turned to Seiichirou.

"As I explained earlier," Aresh said, "this man's body is weak to magicules. He must rest before he returns to Romany."

Aresh's barrier had weakened by then. Although Seiichirou had been fine on the journey to Egorova, the aftereffects of Yua's purification magic left him slightly feverish. As Aresh said, he needed treatment before he went home.

Aresh's attitude was so matter-of-fact that nobody could bring themselves to ask who would be doing this "treatment."

Perceiving this, Lars smiled and said, "Very well. I ask that you take care," before leaving the room.

After that, Ist insisted on seeing the Sorcery Department, so Lufina showed him the way. Sigma went with them, of course. It wasn't terribly dignified, but nobody on the Romany side spoke up strongly against it after what they'd experienced.

"Let us get ready for the dinner party, Lady Yua," said Erene.

"Oh, but I don't have a dress."

"I packed enough for you as well. So shall we be off? Orjef, be our bodyguard."

"What? Why me?"

"You really don't have a shred of wit, do you? *They* don't need a guard, do they? Isn't a knight supposed to protect the dainty ladies?"

Seemingly used to Erene's barbs, Orjef merely glanced at Seiichirou and the others before reluctantly leaving his seat.

"Nor—"

"Oh, I'll just be chilling in my room. Don't mind me!" Norbert avoided looking at Aresh, who was hovering behind Seiichirou.

Evidently, he didn't want to get kicked by a horse and die.

∀∀∀

The room assigned to Aresh had distinctive Egorovan patterns on its walls and carpets, although the actual colors were simple.

Seiichirou gasped—the moment he was inside, the door shut tight and a strong pair of arms enveloped him.

"I'm so glad you're okay...," Aresh murmured in a low voice.

His scent, so distinct from the Egorovan fragrance in the room, threatened to make Seiichirou weak in the knees, but he pushed back against Aresh's burly chest. There was still some unfinished business between them.

Although Seiichirou did not put much force into his arms, Aresh sensed his resistance and relaxed his grip.

"We...still haven't talked it over," Seiichirou said.

Aresh was silent for a very long moment before he said, "Let me heal you first. I'm sure you're fatigued, and not to mention you got hit by the Holy Maiden's magic."

"No. Let's talk."

Although he thought it ridiculous to use his own health as a bludgeon to threaten Aresh with, Seiichirou just knew that he wouldn't be in a state for conversation if Aresh used his magic on him. Besides, he only had a slight fever, which had never deterred him from working in the past. He could put up with this level of discomfort.

Acknowledging the strength of Seiichirou's will, Aresh made him sit down before taking the neighboring seat. It was hard for them to talk while facing one another directly.

"If this is about the marriage offer, I turned it down immediately."

According to Aresh, his family had summoned him to ask about Seiichirou, at which point he announced in no uncertain terms that they were indeed romantic partners. Then his parents told him that a member of the Egorovan royalty would be coming to visit. He couldn't exactly scamper home after that, so he ended up going through with the meeting.

He had not expected Lars to pop the question of marriage. In his mind, his family calling him over and the marriage offer were two entirely separate things.

"My family is my problem, and...I certainly wasn't planning on getting engaged. That's why I didn't feel the need to tell you about it." Aresh looked at Seiichirou's face, his expression screwed up in discomfort. "Sorry," he muttered quietly. Some part of him evidently understood that he had incurred Seiichirou's wrath.

Next, he addressed why he independently decided to go to Egorova.

"I was...looking for a way to send you back to your country...," he admitted.

"Huh?"

Seiichirou's eyes widened at those unexpected words.

Hadn't Aresh been rushing to tie Seiichirou down to this world so that he *wouldn't* return to Earth? What changed his mind?

"Did you...decide that you were better off without me?" Seiichirou asked, not realizing how much his voice was trembling.

"Absolutely not!" Aresh snapped back. "I don't want you to go. But that...that is my selfishness speaking. You were brought to this world suddenly against your will. You cannot see your family, and even the air makes you ill."

By now, Seiichirou had developed some level of magicule resistance, all thanks to Aresh. And because they were now romantic partners, receiving treatment through intimate relations was a non-issue.

But if Aresh had not been there, if they had never formed this connection, then Seiichirou might very well have lost his life.

"I'm sure that those who figured out a way to revive the ancient summoning spell would eventually find a way to send you back to your original world," said Aresh.

"I suppose..."

If the magically gifted commander of the Third Royal Order was saying so, then it had to be true.

Aresh had resigned himself to their eventual parting.

Seiichirou wanted to return to his original world. He wanted to see his parents. He wanted to experience the comfort and safety of the land of his birth.

But...

"That's why I came to Egorova, so that I could find a way for you to travel *between* worlds," Aresh said.

"What?"

For a moment, Seiichirou could not understand what Aresh was saying. He stared at the man before him, his eyes wider than ever before.

Black hair, purple eyes, and a form that exuded masculine beauty. That was Seiichirou's man.

"I believe that our sorcerers will eventually find a way to reverse-engineer the ancient magic and complete a spell that will return you to your original world. You're not the Holy Maiden, and so it would be difficult to pinpoint you and summon you back. Romany's literature deals primarily with the Holy Maiden and her purification, and our magic focuses on offensive spells for dealing with monsters. There is only so much we can achieve. A good thing, then, that our country is opening diplomatic relations with a nation that specializes in magic and technology, but I know that it is easier said than done. It's why I thought of seeing for myself if there were any leads, and then telling you," Aresh said quickly, without pausing for breath.

Seiichirou did not interrupt him. His brain was entirely focused on piecing together what he had just learned.

Wait? So that means...?

The reason Aresh went off to a different country without telling Seiichirou anything was because he knew that Seiichirou would eventually return to his original world and he wanted to find a way to travel between the worlds? So that they *wouldn't* have to part ways forever?

"Did...the Egorovans know about this?"

"No? Given my position, I don't generally have any opportunities to travel to Egorova. I simply used their desire for me to meet the fourth princess as an excuse to go."

Aresh was saying that if they just wanted a meeting, he would do the meeting. Then he would be given free rein, and if it took too long to find what he wanted, he would make up some excuse to go back to Romany. Since their nations would be establishing diplomatic ties, he could do what he pleased. The man was utterly single-minded.

"Why didn't you say a word about this to me?"

"Because it depended on whether I found a method." Aresh averted his gaze uncomfortably. In his mind, he couldn't speak about it if it wasn't definite. He might give Seiichirou false hope or make him homesick.

Seiichirou's lips clenched into a tight line as he pulled out a small box from his breast pocket.

When he presented the box to Aresh, it was the other man's turn to blink in utter non-comprehension.

"Open this, please," Seiichirou said curtly.

Aresh took the box.

He opened the inexpensive-looking lid to find two unadorned silver rings.

"What's this?" He looked up at Seiichirou's still glowering face.

"In Romany, you wear accessories on your chest to indicate that you have a partner, yes?" Seiichirou answered sullenly. "In my country, you give your engagement partner rings engraved with each other's names on the inside and wear them on the finger next to your little finger."

Aresh's long fingers held up the simple rings. He and Seiichirou's first names were engraved inside.

"Everyone underestimates me."

When Aresh looked at Seiichirou again in disbelief, the man was much closer to him than he expected. Seiichirou leaned against him, his expression still a picture of fury.

Aresh collapsed on the chaise under Seiichirou's weight. As Seiichirou glared down at his partner, he continued, "You think I just got *pulled* into this relationship, don't you? Don't you underestimate me."

When Seiichirou's lips descended on his, Aresh accepted them in a dumbfounded haze.

The Egorovan royal palace must have been outfitted with proper soundproofing, because no sound emanated from outside the room. Here, in this dead silent space, one could hear a pin drop.

"Mm...hah..."

As Seiichirou leaned against Aresh, he pushed his tongue inside

the other man's mouth and ran his hands over his body through his shirt.

"Wait...the barrier comes fi—" Aresh broke their lips apart to say, only for Seiichirou to glare at him balefully.

He brought his mouth to Aresh's ear, and...

"Ow—?!"

More shocked than actually pained by having his ear bitten, Aresh could only gaze up at Seiichirou.

"I'm saying I can't wait."

Lust brimmed in those narrowed, insolent eyes. In the face of such naked desire, Aresh summoned all his strength as a knight to lift both himself and Seiichirou off the chair.

"Whoa?!" Seiichirou yelped as Aresh hurled him onto the bed. He didn't even have time to voice a complaint.

Aresh climbed onto the bed too and ripped off his shirt. Then he stripped Seiichirou of his outer garments, pressing their bodies together the moment his shirt was off.

"You've lost weight again...," Aresh grumbled between panting breaths.

"Not that much, surely," Seiichirou answered sullenly as his hands trailed over Aresh. As always, his partner's body was slender and muscular.

Aresh's large hand tracing Seiichirou's skin was already sticky with sweat. As their lips met incessantly, Aresh's hand stroked Seiichirou's chest, making a jolt run through his entire body.

"Ah...!"

As if to confirm something to himself, Aresh pressed his thumb against Seiichirou's nipples. Then, before Seiichirou knew it, Aresh's hands were around his wrists, and it was *his* turn to have his ear licked.

"Ngh... Guh..."

Unlike Seiichirou, Aresh seemed to be in clear control of himself even as he continued his gentle ministrations. Seiichirou lifted his hips, still not ready to go out without a fight.

"Hey..."

Feeling the proof of Seiichirou's arousal brushing against his body, Aresh's expression changed. A satisfied smile flitted across Seiichirou's face, only for Aresh to immediately crush their lips together, stopping his breath short.

Seiichirou tumbled to his side, and Aresh used his legs to pin him in place as he stroked Seiichirou's chest and crotch at the same time. The kisses kept raining down on him. A moan threatened to leave Seiichirou's throat, though he suppressed it. For all his physical inferiority, today was the one day he did not want Aresh taking the lead.

Unfortunately for him, Aresh chanted a spell between his kisses, and the magic made Seiichirou's head spin.

"I told you...to do that later..." Seiichirou tried to object, but Aresh was having none of it.

"You'll just faint if I keep going without it," he insisted as he took off Seiichirou's shoes and pressed their bodies together.

Aresh did have a point, but Seiichirou felt like gnashing his teeth—he wanted to be fully conscious from start to finish this time. *Ah, but...*

Aresh's song-like chant.

His beautiful, husky voice.

His magical power, flowing through Seiichirou.

"...This is so unfair..."

All of it made Seiichirou's mind melt. Perhaps part of it was because of the synergy he had with the man who had saved his life.

The suspension bridge effect.

Imprinting.

Regardless of what it was, it all came down to Aresh himself. *He* was the one who saved Seiichirou's life. Who continued to care about his health. Who got annoyingly insistent about Seiichirou's bad habits. Who respected the man's thoughts and feelings. Whose endless concern gave him a tendency to get stuck in his own head and act on his own. Who was so fatally clumsy with words. Who was quick to get huffy and pout.

Aresh. It was all Aresh.

Seiichirou did not love Aresh because Aresh loved him. That wasn't the extent of it. This capable yet clumsy man was so deeply adorable that it was impossible *not* to love him.

Such feelings belonged to Seiichirou alone.

"Ah! Ah! Aahhh!"

Sweet moans escaped Seiichirou's lips every time he experienced a thrust from behind.

The barrier and healing spells were already in place. In other words, their bodies were joining again and again in earnest. Yet Aresh's energy never flagged. Likewise, Seiichirou should have been experiencing magic-sickness from the healing, but he never once lost consciousness.

The sheets were drenched with sweat and a different kind of bodily fluid. Seiichirou wondered if an Egorovan maid would have to deal with this tomorrow.

"Ngh?!"

His drifting thoughts were interrupted by Aresh slamming powerfully into his deepest part.

"So...you can still think..."

Seiichirou felt Aresh's arms wrap themselves around him.

"No...I...ngh..." As he trembled from the penetration, the breath caught in his throat and his answer died on his lips.

"...I'm close," Aresh whispered into his ear.

His strong arms held Seiichirou in place, and then his heat filled Seiichirou completely.

"Ohhh... Ah...hah..."

As Seiichirou's body trembled within Aresh's embrace, he felt as if the man's breath was also flowing into his ear.

"Haaah...hah..."

It took a long time for Aresh to finish his release. As he accepted it all, Seiichirou began to feel the onset of magic-sickness along with the fatigue of his overtaxed mind and body. He looked up hazily, and the man above him gazed back with gleaming eyes.

In a way, I...feel like I've come home to Romany, a part of Seiichirou thought as he languidly curled up against Aresh's shoulder.

CHAPTER NINE

Decision

The sun looked ever so yellow.

This was not because Seiichirou was not on planet Earth. In other words, it meant the *other* thing—the sun looking brighter after a long bout of nightly activities.

They'd been up all night. No, even until the morning. As Seiichirou lay numb, the view outside the window looked dull and colorless. Well, given that most of Egorova was gray, maybe this was just normal?

While Seiichirou was occupied with his hazy thoughts, Aresh returned to bed with a glass of water in hand.

"What are you zoning out for?" The knight commander looked confused, a testament to the vast physical difference between him and a sickly white-collar worker. For all the healing spells and efforts to get Seiichirou's body accustomed to magic, he was still no macho man at his core.

The magically gifted knight commander had used a spell to make the soiled sheets spotless. While he was at it, he'd cleaned up Seiichirou's body. Understandably, it would have been awkward for them to take an intimate bath together while in a foreign country, which was what they would have done had they been at Aresh's mansion.

"Want some?" As Aresh extended the glass of water to

Seiichirou, Seiichirou noticed the gleaming silver ring on Aresh's left ring finger.

He accepted the glass bashfully, wondering why he was getting embarrassed *now* after everything that had happened.

"The size...doesn't quite fit you. We'll have to get it adjusted when we get back."

He hadn't measured Aresh's finger, and so the ring looked a little loose on him. Although this was better than it not fitting at all, it was still something of a letdown.

"You can do that?"

"There's a craftsman Sigma knows. Let's go see him together next time. Oh, but I suppose that wearing a ring will hinder your work as a knight," said Seiichirou, musing that a ring would get in the way of swinging a sword.

Aresh frowned sullenly. "Are you telling me to take it off?"

"If it's a hindrance, yes? How about wearing it around your neck when you're in training or battle?" Seiichirou said. He'd gotten a simple silver ring thinking that it wouldn't get in the way, but then again, *any* accessory could be a hindrance.

Aresh wasn't having it, though. "No. I won't take it off."

"Well, do what you like." Then Seiichirou muttered what he really thought: "Just please don't lose it."

"I would never!" Aresh was quick to respond.

This was all getting very cheesy, but when Aresh brought his face close, Seiichirou didn't complain. He turned his head in Aresh's direction and closed his eyes...

Bang bang bang bang!

"Is Kondo here?!"

A furious knocking sound rang out—it sounded almost as if someone was trying to batter the door in. Seiichirou almost dropped his glass of water.

"What?" Aresh was *very* disgruntled.

"That sounds like Ist!" Seiichirou knew that he had to stop the noise.

"Oh! Kondo! Hey, hey, I found this cool thing! Let me show you!"

"Hold it! Just wait for a moment!"

Ist was yanking at the locked door. Seiichirou mollified the pouting Aresh as he hurriedly dragged his overtaxed body out of the bed and got dressed.

"Uh… Sorry for making you wait."

A few minutes later, Seiichirou opened the door to find Ist with a bundle of papers in his arms. He was wearing the same clothes as the day before, which were now slightly disheveled. Behind him stood Lufina and Sigma, as well as Lufina's knight and maid.

"Yep, you sure did!" This was quite a thing to say to someone after ambushing their room early in the morning. Seiichirou could see the knight and maid grimace, but this was just par for the course with Ist.

The sorcerer strode right into the room and spread out his papers without even pausing to ask for permission. Seiichirou looked highly displeased, but his expression changed somewhat when he saw the magic circles drawn on the pages.

"I was looking around the Egorovan Sorcery Department yesterday," said Ist, "and it turns out that they've got a slightly different way of writing compared to Romany. In Romany, you list out the external effects of a spell, but here they take the spell's entire composition into account. Look!"

Which was all well and good of him to say, but since Seiichirou couldn't read the words, he couldn't make head or tail of what he was looking at.

"Incredible, right?!" Ist grinned.

"Is it?" was all Seiichirou could say.

"Yeah! I mean, check out this magic circle! This line represents 'fire resistance,' and this one indicates 'wind' and 'flow'! And the positioning says that there's a half-second time lag after activation."

"Sorry, I don't understand the jargon. Could you explain the significance of this, please?"

Seiichirou was always telling Ist to get to the point. He needed a proper breakdown of the results and expected costs before he could organize a budget. Unfortunately, getting Ist to submit lists and reports was too much to ask, so Seiichirou heard him out verbally. Because of this, Ist had developed a habit of telling Seiichirou every little thing.

"Okay, so if we combine the ancient magic formula with that magic tool I mentioned to you earlier, we can send you back to your original world!"

First thing in the morning, Ist dropped a live grenade with a carefree smile.

"I can...go back to my old world?" It was what Seiichirou had been searching for ever since he was kidnapped...er, summoned to this world.

He'd gotten distracted by other things along the way, but it was still the reason why he had worked to make the Holy Maiden obsolete, pushed for magic research, and set up an education system for recruiting potential workers. The collaboration agreement with Egorova would expedite the process even further by securing a reliable supply of magic stones as a power source.

It was everything that he'd worked for, yet Seiichirou still froze when he heard Ist's incredible announcement.

But this was Ist he was speaking to. As far as the sorcerer was concerned, Seiichirou's reaction was irrelevant.

"We'd managed to decipher the magic circles of ancient magic in Romany literature," Ist went on as he unfurled more papers, "but when I realized that Egorova has a different way of drawing magic circles, it made me look back at that ancient spell. You see, I always thought it had a line for tracking someone with the Holy Maiden's power, but if you combine it with this composition here and take the spatial coordinates into account, then instead of tracking—"

"Wait." Aresh physically stopped Ist's rapid-fire lecture. By covering his mouth.

This was the same thing Orjef had done, which made Seiichirou reflect vaguely that knights sure were handy to have around. Between the bombshell reveal, the jargon, and all the activity from the night before, his head still wasn't quite working the way it should.

"You didn't show Egorova the ancient magic circles, did you?" Aresh demanded.

The spell to summon a Holy Maiden from another world was still a state secret. Although Romany had agreed to work with Egorova, they weren't meant to disclose the spell yet.

"Oh, don't worry, it's fine! Ist has the entire circle memorized, so he didn't show anyone the texts! He's not even carrying them with him!" Sigma rushed to Ist's aid.

Relieved, Aresh relaxed. Not missing his chance, Ist slipped out of Aresh's grasp and grabbed the papers.

"Commander Indolark, you must have memorized it, too, yes? See, look, if you put this part with this part and this part, it's exactly the same as the top-right bit in the middle of that magic circle. Right?"

"He's not going to know the whole composition just from one look..." Sigma tried to stop Ist, since Seiichirou was a bit slow to react.

Only for Aresh to give a matter-of-fact nod. "It does look similar, yes."

Oh, right. This man was a genius.

"Is it normal for people in Romany to accurately recall a magic circle they've only seen once?" Lufina asked shakily, to which Sigma frantically shook his head.

Seiichirou elaborated, "Of course not. Those two are special cases. I only have a memory for numbers."

He can memorize numbers at a glance... The boy and girl felt terribly humbled by the existence of yet another outlier, but the girl was still a sorcery prodigy who would one day become the pride of her nation, and the boy was a rising star technician whose talents had earned him state sponsorship despite his humble birth.

Having finally regained his wits, Seiichirou asked the young prodigies, "Have you been with Ist this whole time?"

"Oh no, we haven't."

Apparently, Ist had initially behaved himself when he visited Egorova's Sorcery Department, but he got so engrossed in the documents he was allowed to read that he stopped responding to the Egorovan researchers. He muttered and occasionally made strange noises to himself as he sat in the lab for the entire night. As a princess, Lufina had to make an appearance at the dinner party, so she asked Donato and Georgi from the diplomatic delegation to keep an eye on Ist. This also allowed Sigma to focus entirely surveilling Ist in case he acted out of line.

When Lufina returned to the lab in the morning, Ist shouted, "I did it!" and ran off in search of Seiichirou. Lufina chased after him, bringing the story back to the present.

"I see…," said Seiichirou. "I'm terribly sorry about all the trouble. I must offer you a formal apology later."

"Oh no, our sorcerers were honored to get a close-up view of Ist at work. So, um…is the movement spell complete, then?" Lufina asked.

"In theory, yes," a voice that did not belong to Ist answered. It was Aresh.

"What do you mean?"

"Originally, we could only use the spell to transport inanimate objects. The spell has a different formula depending on the starting point and the destination. The problem was that the target's physical makeup would change because of the coordinates and the influence of the magic."

A living creature needed three layers of protection to preserve their body, soul, and mind, but this would make the corresponding magic circle so dense that it was impossible to render visually.

"But I think we can make it work by combining Egorova's formulas with ours!" Ist chimed in. "We can!"

"The fastest way of doing it was to reverse-engineer the ancient magic circle." Aresh had apparently been convinced that the movement spell would work if they worked backward from the original spell's construction.

"That's the route I wanted to take as well, but I had to rule it out. If there's anything even slightly off about your understanding, you could end up turning a body to mush or destroying someone's soul. But I was able to grasp the picture from the Egorovan circles, so hurrah!"

Seiichirou was deeply relieved to see that Ist was no mad scientist with zero regard for sacrifices. Perhaps he got that from Zoltan. Seiichirou made a mental note to thank the director when he got back to Romany.

"But a movement spell and a returning spell are different, aren't they?" Lufina asked.

Ist had said *"Send you back to your original world."* Ordinary movement did not account for interdimensional travel.

"Yes, but the fundamentals are the same. With the ancient magic, we used the previous Holy Maiden's blood and a purifying magic stone to pinpoint the coordinates. We have a general understanding of the formula for crossing dimensions, so as long as we get the movement spell to work, it wouldn't take too much extra legwork in my opinion," Ist said.

"Hang on," said Aresh. "The magic stone you used as a medium back then crumbled into dust."

This reminded Seiichirou that the two of them had been present at the scene of the Holy Maiden's summoning. Judging by what Aresh was saying, they'd safeguarded the previous Holy Maiden's blood and purifying magic and used them as mediums to summon the current Holy Maiden, but the magic stone had apparently shattered to pieces after the ceremony.

The prevailing theory was that they could open a path to Yua's original world by drawing on her blood and purifying power, but the magic stone was a problem. Given the unique qualities of the Holy Maiden's purification, no ordinary magic stone could contain it. The previous stone was said to be a gift from the gods, and no one knew exactly where it came from.

"That's why I was telling you about the thing I bought as a replacement," Ist said to Seiichirou.

"Oh, right."

"I saw this useful-looking magic tool in town, so I bought it."

"So, yeah, you use the tool as a substitute for the medium in dimension-crossing magic. I figure it could send you back to your original world."

He'd said that. He'd most definitely said that.

Seiichirou had forgotten all about it in the ensuing chaos, but back when the Egorovans were visiting, Ist had ignored them in favor of hounding Seiichirou for money.

"What kind of magic tool was it?"

"It's a communication device, but it's made out of a strange ore. I doubt the makers had it in mind, but it occurred to me that its power can extend across dimensions if combined with the magic formula I came up with and the Holy Maiden's magic."

According to Ist, the town he visited had a unique culture, and the ore was difficult to find in other lands.

"Which town did you go to, again?" Seiichirou asked.

"Agiral, I think it was called."

"What?!" A voice suddenly rang out from a different direction.

One of the doors flung open to reveal Norbert standing there with his mouth agape. Orjef was visible behind him.

"Do you know the place, Norbert?" Seiichirou asked.

"Well, yeah. It's the place my father went to inspect."

Now that he mentioned it, Seiichirou recalled that Norbert's foster father, Count Blanc, had been away until very recently to inspect and engage talks in a land where the royal family's influence was weak. This was one of the reasons Norbert had attended the Egorova welcoming party.

"House Blanc ended up assuming control of the Agiral region, if I recall?"

"Less 'control' and more like 'a system of mutual cooperation.'

Agiral's not planning on opposing the kingdom, so they kind of just got along. We promised to help them out if they're ever in trouble."

Leave it to Count Blanc, a man willing to raise the king's son as his own, to make a good impression on people. He seemed to be particularly good at forging diplomatic relations.

"So can I use the ore and magic tool? Can I? Can I?" asked Ist.

"Let's draw up an official contract for their purchase. I don't expect they'll hold it against the royal family if we can work out a regular system for procuring their local goods."

In the best-case scenario, the kingdom would have a steady supply of research materials and a deepening friendship with Agiral.

"You'll use anything and everything, won't you?" Orjef said exasperatedly.

To this, Seiichirou smirked as if Orjef had said the obvious.

"I am a greedy man, you know."

∨∨∨

Although the Egorovans invited them to stay a little longer, Seiichirou's party returned to Romany that day. They now had a laundry list of urgent matters to report. Seiichirou deemed it necessary to tell Camile and Yurius the news before Yua.

"I regret that I was unable to spend much time with you, but I am sure that there will be opportunities in the future as our countries deepen their friendship," Lars said when he saw them off.

Inwardly, Seiichirou was puzzled. Erene, the Sorcery Department, and other diplomatic officials would be handling the matter of the fourth princess. As for the joint research, the bulk of it would take place at the Sorcery Department. Seiichirou didn't see much opportunity for an accountant like him to meet up with an emissary like the prince.

Lars apparently thought differently. When Seiichirou tried to give a forced smile and a diplomatic response, he took Seiichirou's hand.

"I was never able to understand romantic feelings. But I was struck by how you, a logical-thinking man like me, dove without hesitation into a place where your very life was at risk."

His handsome, doll-like face was ever so slightly flushed, and his jade-green eyes brimmed with emotion.

"I'd love to meet someone who inspires the same passion in me," he said, drawing close. "Someone like you...if possible..."

"Huh?"

As Seiichirou stood there, dumbfounded by the sudden words and actions of this *very* important negotiator, a black wall appeared before him.

Aresh slapped down Lars's hand without any thought toward etiquette whatsoever.

"Hey! Aresh!" Seiichirou panicked.

Likewise, Lufina rushed to pull Lars away. "Elder Brother, you mustn't! That man already has a partner to whom he has dedicated his body and soul!"

Glancing at Lufina, Seiichirou saw that the twelve-year-old princess's face was bright red.

Could it be that...just like the Sorcery Department people, she...?

Indeed, he did cross paths with her immediately after Aresh had cast his barrier and acclimatized Seiichirou to the magic through some very thorough loving...

At this point, Seiichirou went numb. He swore a vow to watch himself before he ever met up with any perceptive sorcerers henceforth.

ᐯᐯᐯ

Three days later, Seiichirou's party was back in Romany—even quicker than the outbound journey. This was because Aresh pooled his formidable magic talents with those of the kingdom's foremost sorcerer. Diana, his reliable mount, also chipped in by pulling their carriage along.

Incidentally, Seiichirou spent the whole trip glued to Aresh's side. After all the exertion of the previous night, he snoozed the entire first day. Norbert, who was in the same carriage as them, apparently spent the whole time trying to look at anything but them.

As soon as they were back, Aresh and Orjef requested a meeting with Camile and Yurius, where they made their report.

The next day, Seiichirou was called into a meeting with Yurius, Camile, Aresh, and Zoltan in attendance. Yua was invited, too, and she stood there looking puzzled. The last time she went to an official meeting was after the purification expedition, where Seiichirou had proposed the barrier plan. That meeting had taken place in the audience chamber, right there in front of the king and a crowd of nobles.

But this time was different. There were only four people to face: Yurius, the crown prince and her sweetheart, Prime Minister Camile, Zoltan from the Royal Sorcery Department, and Aresh, Seiichirou's partner and the commander of the Third Royal Order. This was not a public space, and both Yua and Seiichirou would have their individual opinions respected here.

"I can return to my world…?"

Unlike Seiichirou, who appreciated the Romany Kingdom's discretion, Yua reacted to the news with pure astonishment.

"Not immediately," said Aresh.

Zoltan elaborated: "We have merely established the means. There is still much research to do and many experiments to repeat before it comes to fruition. In the meantime, I ask you to consider your plans."

Zoltan was the Sorcery Department's representative instead of Ist because everyone figured that Yua probably wouldn't ask about the technical details.

"How long…are we talking?" she asked.

"I would say it will take about a year," said Camile.

Yua gasped upon hearing a concrete number.

A year—that was not an absurd amount of time. A year could go by in a flash. Considering that it had already been almost a year since they had come to this world, time truly did fly.

"To return or not to return...the decision is up to you."

Yua's head jerked up at Yurius's words. There was something bittersweet about his gaze.

"Speaking purely for myself, I don't want you to go back...but we dragged the two of you to this land without your permission. After all the help you have given us, we have no right to tie you down any further."

In fact, Yurius was saying he should be applying his entire efforts into getting them back home. Knowing this, Yua's eyes brimmed with tears of happiness...and sadness at the same time. She did not say a word.

"Hey, Kondou," Yua called out to him the moment they were out of the conference room. Having anticipated this, Seiichirou sent a silent signal to Aresh with his eyes, and then followed Yua to a terrace overlooking Romany's capital.

He took a seat facing Yua, and a maid brought them tea.

"Kondou... What do you plan to do?" Yua asked him. "About Aresh..."

"I've already made my decision. You need to make your own," Seiichirou said bluntly.

For a moment, Yua looked as if she was about to choke up, but then she clenched her fists and simply hung her head.

"Right... I have to make my own choice..."

"You do. But...as was mentioned before, it may be possible to come back to this world after returning to Earth, even if it isn't one hundred percent guaranteed."

Traveling back and forth between worlds carried great risks, and there was no guarantee yet that it was even possible.

And beyond everything, it would cost money.

They needed people to draw up the magic circle and a vast amount of magical energy to activate it. The ore Ist had mentioned was scarce in quantity, and the price made Seiichirou's head spin. To make the crossing work, the sorcerers would also need training to up their success rate. The whole venture was comparable to space travel.

Although the Romany Kingdom was willing to wrangle the funds for a one-way ticket, a round trip wasn't so simple. Honestly, just returning Seiichirou and Yua to Earth would cost almost ten percent of the country's yearly tax. Seiichirou had heard that a space trip cost about two billion yen, which made the returning spell almost three times more expensive relative to the national budget. Seiichirou wanted to chip away at the costs as much as he could in the year that remained.

"I'll have a talk with Yurius."

Indeed, Yua's decision was a matter between her and Yurius.

Seiichirou intended to go straight back to the mansion after that chat. Just as he was leaving the palace, he crossed paths with an unusual figure.

"Why, if it isn't Seiichirou."

Seiichirou hadn't seen Aresh's older sister since they got back from Egorova.

"What are you doing here, Erene?" Seiichirou asked, wondering if something had happened with Egorova. Although she was the daughter of a marquess and the current wife of a count, Erene did not work at the palace.

"I got permission to enter the Sorcery Department since I'm participating in that research experiment," Erene answered breezily.

Apparently, she was serious about taking part in that whole thing. But still, Seiichirou had to wonder how she already had permission to enter the Sorcery Department when the project was still in its planning phase...but then he saw how Erene acted when she spotted the man arriving from behind Seiichirou.

"Hi there, honey!" she squealed, and he could practically see hearts in her eyes.

"Oh, Erene. You're already here?" the man responded in his usual tranquil tone.

"Qusta...," began Seiichirou.

"Hi there, Kondo. I hope my wife didn't give you much trouble the other day," Qusta said apologetically.

The garden variety middle manager in his thirties had a stunning beauty hanging off his arm.

Which reminded Seiichirou... Qusta *had* mentioned that he had a younger wife and that he was newly married. Not to mention that Erene had introduced herself as a lady of House Rein. That was Qusta's last name, wasn't it?

"Oh no... She's been an enormous help," said Seiichirou.

"But of course! Don't you have more to say, Seiichirou? Tell my darling husband how well I did."

Erene had in fact used her clout as a noble to their advantage, so Seiichirou thanked her again.

"And now I can help my darling with his work anytime." Erene swooned.

"Oh, right, Kondo, I should tell you," said Qusta. "Erene has more than enough knowledge to help out. She only lacks magical capacity."

Okay, now it all made sense. Milan had mentioned that Erene worked hard at her magic studies. Honestly, Seiichirou had been thinking that, much like Sigma, Erene would fit right in at the Sorcery Department even without magical power, so he welcomed her addition to the team. Her connections as a noblewoman were also bound to come in handy for securing more staff.

"I never imagined for a second that my dream would come true because of you." Erene took a deep breath. "I ought to apologize to you for my bullying."

"Your...bullying?" Seiichirou cocked his head, not quite grasping what she was saying.

According to her, she had said some disquieting things when she came to Aresh's mansion in his absence.

"There were objections when I first got together with my darling.

It took a terribly long time for us to be wed. But when Aresh told our parents about you, they were willing to welcome you with open arms. I was so frustrated, I just…"

But even then, she hadn't done anything particularly mean. All she did was tell Seiichirou things he would have heard later down the line. Seiichirou wondered if maybe she just had an intimidating face and she was actually a very nice person at heart.

I had no idea that their parents were so accepting of me…

That was news to him. Suppressing the blush that threatened to creep onto his face, Seiichirou said his goodbyes and left the scene.

Just as he came to the palace entrance, he spotted another familiar figure in black. He must have been waiting for Seiichirou.

"You don't have any work to do after this?" Seiichirou asked.

"I only had the meeting today, just like you," Aresh replied as they entered a carriage together.

"Are you still worried?"

They'd talked everything through last night, but Aresh was still unwilling to let Seiichirou out of his sight.

"Are you really sure…?"

"I told you everything last night, didn't I? Actually, no… I'm willing to talk with you anytime."

Facing each other directly, Seiichirou put his left hand over Aresh's left hand. Their silver rings clinked against each other.

"We were born in different lands. We grew up in entirely different worlds. Our core values and worldviews are too different for us to understand each other, but I'm sure we can meet in the middle as long as we talk it out."

And so they would face each other, talk to each other, and put their heads together.

That was what Seiichirou was thinking with a smile on his lips.

Aresh squinted as if he was looking at something blindly bright, and drew his arms around the man he loved.

∨∨∨

"All right, I'm counting on you, Shiraishi."

"Sure thing, Kondou! I'll make sure to deliver it to your parents in person!"

"No, you can just put a stamp on it and send it by post."

Dressed in the same high school uniform she was wearing when she first arrived, Yua took Seiichirou's letter during the ceremony.

In the end, she chose to return to her original world.

But she was not turning her back on this one.

"Yua..." Clad in a formal white outfit, Yurius called out Yua's name in a strangled whisper.

"Yurius."

Yua's expression, however, was bright and jubilant.

Right there in the middle of the Holy Maiden's returning ceremony, she ran up to Yurius and grasped his hands tightly.

"It's going to be okay. I swear I'll come back. When I grow up, I'll send a signal to this world. Wait for me until then, okay?"

Indeed. Yua's ultimate decision was to return, and then say her goodbyes to those around her once she had reached adulthood.

It was very much a "have your cake and eat it, too" kind of choice, but Seiichirou thought that she deserved it after being kidnapped as a minor. By "when I grow up," she was talking about turning twenty, the age of majority in Japan. This was now two years away. Being a high schooler when she left, she had a lot of catching up to do when it came to living in adult society, and she knew it. That was part of what she meant when she talked about "growing up" first.

Bringing her back to this world would cost the same as a fresh summoning. It would be a long while before Seiichirou could realize his plan of traveling back and forth, but he was an adult. He could put up with it.

Meanwhile, Yurius was twenty-two years old, which meant that he would be twenty-four in two more years. That was quite late to get married in this world. Two years was a precarious amount of time for a future king to stay unmarried, but that was his and Yua's problem to deal with. Seiichirou wished them well. He figured that Yurius would deal with the nobles' aggressive "advice" to get married with the help of the Second Royal Order's commander.

Since the Holy Maiden's returning ceremony required vast magical energy, the Sorcery Department, the Third Royal Order, and even members of the church were present. They'd managed to shave a fraction of the cost with the large store of magic stones they'd received from Egorova over the past year—which also explained why a small group of trustworthy Egorovan sorcerers had joined the ceremony to study it for future reference. The group included Lufina, who was an exchange student at Sigma's school.

"Stand back, Seiichirou," Aresh told him, to which he obliged. Although he had a barrier around him, getting hit with a vast amount of magic would render it moot.

Even as Seiichirou moved, Aresh kept a hand on his shoulder. He was pouting, too.

"Does it still bother you?" Seiichirou asked. Over the past year, they'd had many discussions, arguments, and reconciliations.

"I swear… I'll send you back one day."

"I know you will. I know it will be a long while yet, but…won't you come with me, when that day comes? To see my hometown?"

The man in black, known among the gentry as "the Ice Nobleman," had distinctive purple eyes that went wide at Seiichirou's comment.

Seiichirou could not help but snort at such an unguarded show of astonishment. "What's so surprising? I've been to your hometown and said hello to your parents, so why can't you do the same?"

"It's not so simple…"

"Heh. If you're talking about the budget, don't sweat it. I might not look it, but I'm quite good with money." Seiichirou was quite proud of how he had managed to trim the budget of the returning spell.

Seeing his partner looking so happy with himself, a broad smile came over Aresh's face.

"I figured that one out a long time ago."

They were talking about something still far in the future, and which might not even come to fruition at all. But when Seiichirou imagined what it would be like to show Aresh the sky, trees, and land of the world he had grown up in, he smiled.

The other world's books—and the original world's books—depended on the bean counter…

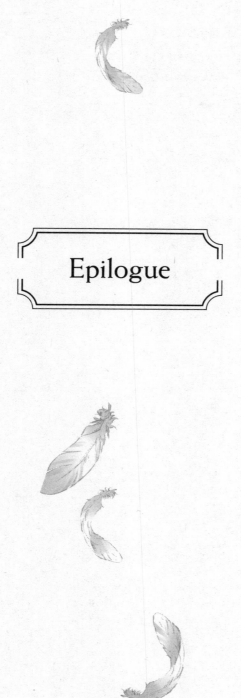

Epilogue

It was the Wood Season in Romany, when the flowers were in peak bloom.

Seiichirou was struggling to put the silver flower pin on his formal clothes when a knock sounded on his door.

"I'm coming in. You're still not ready?" Aresh strode in before Seiichirou could even answer the knock.

That was a little exasperating, but just for today, Seiichirou decided to keep his complaints to himself.

"I can't get this on properly..."

"You just stab it in."

"I can't bring myself to put a hole in such a nice outfit." Seiichirou huffed.

Aresh smoothly put the lapel pin in place on Seiichirou's chest. While he was at it, he kissed Seiichirou's pouting lips.

"Thank you," said Seiichirou.

"For what?"

"For putting on the lapel pin, obviously."

They laughed and linked hands. Their rings were on their left hands as always.

"I should've at least had a jewel embedded in the rings," Seiichirou said.

"Why?"

"An engagement ring is meant to cost three months' worth of

your salary. You can sell it if something happens to me. Sounds handy, right?"

"Bizarre, more like."

Conventional logic dictated that the man present the ring to the woman, but that was irrelevant in their case. If anything, Aresh seemed displeased about the "if something happens to me" part.

"It's a way for the man to show his value to his partner," Seiichirou said. "But, well, I got them as a pair, so they're more like wedding rings, I suppose."

He'd heard it was getting more common these days to get rings that served as both engagement and wedding rings.

That said, Seiichirou's idea of "these days" was from four years ago.

The two men arrived at the palace, both clad in navy blue formal outfits. Within the palace walls, everything was even more opulent than usual. There was a sort of restless energy to the attendants coming and going from the rooms.

"Mr. Seiichirou! You're here!" Siegvold, dressed in his priest garb, came running up to Seiichirou. Selio followed him, clad in a similar outfit. He was quite a bit taller now.

"I'm so glad you could make it, Priest Siegvold," Seiichirou said.

"Of course I would be here for this happy day. I'll be sure to fulfill my role as a priest of the Abran faith."

"Selio, I hope you can support Siegvold."

"You don't even need to tell me. I'll do the job perfectly!" Although he had gotten taller over these past two years, Selio was unchanged on the inside. He quickly looked away, his ears bright red.

"I'll be seeing you later, then," Seiichirou said.

"Yes, I'm sure we'll be crossing paths again soon."

They stopped at a room reserved only for special ceremonies. Unlike the room in the tower where Seiichirou and Yua were summoned, this room was situated on the highest floor. The light streaming in through the ceiling gave it a natural spotlight.

Within this grand and majestic atmosphere, Seiichirou felt out of place next to royalty and select nobility, though he stayed by Aresh's side nonetheless. A young couple entered the room and knelt before Priest Siegvold. It was Crown Prince Yurius...and Yua.

Both were in the white clothes of Romany royalty. Yurius was wearing a white cloak with fine gold embroidery. Seiichirou heard later that this was the royal family's ceremonial garb. Meanwhile, Yua's outfit looked plain at first glance—a slim white dress that went all the way up to her neck. Yet on closer inspection, the skirt she wore over it was embroidered with the same fine gold. Above all, the white lace veil that fell from her tied-up hair to her toes was magnificent to behold.

Priest Siegvold performed a song-like chant and held his hand out over the couple's heads. When a multi-colored light began to shine over them, murmurs rose from the crowd.

"Is something the matter?" Seiichirou whispered to Aresh, who told him that the colors of the lights signified God's blessing and the couple's future prospects.

In other words, the more colors at the ceremony, the more blessed they were. One certainly had to hand it to the Holy Maiden—she never disappointed.

"Oh, hey there, Sei," a familiar voice called out to him after the ceremony.

Seiichirou turned his gaze to Norbert, whose hair was even more impeccable than usual. He wasn't alone, either. Lars and Lufina were also standing there in traditional Egorovan clothing, and so was Sigma in a formal suit.

Although it was hard to tell from the blue and gold in Norbert's outfit, Seiichirou got the impression that there was a fair amount of white in there. Given that white was the color of royalty, he wondered if it was meant to signal his status, but it seemed very complicated and confusing, so he decided to ignore it.

"My thanks for the invitation," said Lars.

"Oh no, thank *you* for coming," Seiichirou responded humbly.

Lars extended his arm, and the two men shook hands.

Dressed in a deep red formal suit, he possessed the same doll-like beauty as always. Golden stitching ran its way down his arm and the right side of his chest. The color matched his buttons. The cloth hanging from his left shoulder fell loosely to the belt at his hips. This design was unique to Egorova.

"Long time no see, I must say. As much as I would love to meet up more frequently, I understand that we are both busy people," Lars said with a dazzling smile, although he refused to pull away from the handshake.

From what Seiichirou understood, Lars frequently delegated diplomatic duties to others now that the research on the relationship between magicules and magical capacity had finally gotten off the ground. This made sense given that he was the most prominent individual involved on the Egorovan side.

"I'd say a more hands-on approach suits you. You would be excellent at providing assistance at the scene rather than acting as an overseer." His expression and actions made it seem like he was laying it on rather thick, but things generally seemed to be going well on his end.

"Lay off already, Elder Brother." Lufina broke up the handshake since Lars didn't seem inclined to let go anytime soon and there was a man glaring daggers behind them.

She had grown up quite a lot herself in the intervening years. Her black hair was as neat and pretty as always. Today, she wore part of it as a braid and let the rest of it hang free. Instead of the one-piece dress she wore when they met in Egorova, she was donning a form-fitting dress for adult women, complete with a vivid embroidered pattern. The way the pattern ran from her nape to her hips was vaguely reminiscent of a kimono, although the shape of the dress was different.

The right sleeve billowed out, while the left sleeve only ran up to her elbow. The accessories were what really made her outfit stand out as a foreign dress, with their subtle gold and faint red colors paired with a beautiful, intricate design.

"It is unseemly of you to engage in illicit relations," she went on, addressing her brother.

"That's rich coming from you. You used to be so zealous about Ist, but now Sigma is all you talk about whenever you come home," Lars shot back teasingly.

"Hey!" Lufina turned bright red.

"What?" Next to her, Sigma went wide-eyed and blushed.

It seemed like there was something going on between them.

"Oh yes, that reminds me, how is Ist?" asked Seiichirou.

"Well, uh!" said Sigma, still sounding flustered. "After he got the results of the latest summoning, he holed himself up in the lab to start a new research project!"

As hardworking as he was, Ist wasn't suited for these kinds of social situations, so his absence was actually something of a relief.

"Don't be so sulky, Aresh."

Seiichirou and Aresh were alone. Aresh's displeasure remained so pronounced even after Lars and the others left that people went out of their way to avoid them. It was as if they had a barrier.

"They were all being *much* too chummy," said Aresh.

"It's good to network. Oh, look, Aresh, it's your favorite wine."

"Are you treating me like a child?"

"What kind of adult would push wine onto a child? Now cheer up. I'll go get you some."

"Like I said..."

As Seiichirou attempted to distract Aresh by approaching the wine on the table, a familiar blue cloak appeared before him.

"Oh, Prime Minister Camile."

Aresh stomped his way between Seiichirou and Camile before Seiichirou had even finished saying the man's name. Apparently, he'd held himself back somewhat around Lars because of his foreign prince privilege.

"Care to explain your guard dog's hostility on this auspicious occasion, Seiichirou?"

"Who knows? Don't ask me."

Aresh glared at Seiichirou as he stared off vacantly, prompting Camile to produce his distinctive dry chuckle.

He was wearing suitable clothes for the occasion along with his usual cloak to signal his administrative position.

"In any case, today has brought you one step closer to your goal," Camile said.

"The Romany Kingdom's goal, not my goal, I would say."

"Indeed. This is a day for the history books." When a maid astutely brought over some wine for the group, Camile took a glass and drained it. "Won't you take me with you when you visit your world? I'll pay the expense out of pocket, of course."

"I'm not sure about that…" Seiichirou glanced over his shoulder to see Aresh scowling mid-sip. He turned back to Camile with a smile. "I'll have to ask you to refrain from joining our honeymoon."

"Oh, *there* you are, Aresh! Get your behind over here already! It's starting!" Erene barked at Aresh when she spotted them in the garden after they left the hall.

She was wearing a gorgeous dark blue dress that matched her eyes. Standing next to her was Qusta, whose suit looked downright shabby next to hers. There was an affable smile on his face.

"You're late."

Orjef was there in his suit, too. Erene had probably chased him down as well.

The palace's orchestra was arranged in two rows, their instruments creating notes that drifted away into the blue sky. At the same time, something resembling pink flower petals danced in the air.

Past the orchestra, one could see Yurius and Yua in their

resplendent white wedding outfits, peering down at the garden from the balcony.

Their wedding ceremony had only just concluded.

Yua kept her promise. Two years after she returned to Earth, a descendant of the previous Holy Maiden received a divine revelation from the Abran god. Yua responded to the summoning spell, gracing this world once more with her presence. At twenty years of age, she had matured since her last stay, and yet she dove right into the twenty-four-year-old Yurius's arms.

And so at last the Romany Kingdom saw the marriage between its prince and the Holy Maiden.

"Shiraishi's very pretty," Seiichirou muttered, dazzled by the sight of Yurius and Yua waving from the balcony.

Clad in the white wedding dress of the royal family, the nervousness was now gone from Yua's demeanor—she was the very image of a happy bride. The couple wore matching rings on their left hands, which made for a deeply stirring sight. Although Romany had no tradition for engagement or wedding rings, the royal couple had them made after they saw Seiichirou and Aresh's pair.

Despite having no blood connection whatsoever to Yua, Seiichirou felt moved at the sight of Yua in a wedding dress. Her family would have loved to see this, he was convinced.

"There's that magic tool which preserves images as portraits, right?" he said to Aresh.

"Yes, their image will be recorded."

"I wonder if they'll give us a copy if we ask."

"And what would you do with that?"

"It's not for me. I'd want to give it to her family." Like how she had delivered Seiichirou's letter two years ago.

"If you'd like to have a ceremony, too…"

"No, I'm good. A part of me does like the idea of leaving a record, but…I can't say this sort of thing is up my alley."

Aresh couldn't help wanting to shelter and provide for

Seiichirou. He never changed, it seemed. But that was who Aresh was, and Seiichirou had no desire to criticize that.

"You know, Aresh, I'm a greedy man."

When Seiichirou stealthily took his hand, Aresh blinked for a moment in pure surprise.

"I want to have all of you."

Everyone at the wedding was entranced by the Holy Maiden in her dress, yet Aresh alone paid no heed to the bride as she smiled and waved. His purple eyes were fixed on just one person.

Seiichirou.

[backstage]
Norbert's Reports 3

I'm groaning as I hold my pen.

I can shift my entire body across the desk in my dorm room. I can look up, and I can look down. But my pen won't move.

Because there is nothing to write.

"How am I supposed to report on Sei? I only vaguely know what he's doing, and he's already reported it all to the prime minister anyway. What's the point of this whole monitoring thing when I don't even fully know what he's up to?"

The thing I'm racking my brain over is my regular status report about the guy who got summoned alongside the Holy Maiden from another world. King's orders. You see, the Romany Kingdom suffers from miasma once every century, and only the Holy Maiden can purify it. This time, the Holy Maiden came from another world or something, so they revived an ancient magic spell to summon her here, only to drag along this other random guy who had nothing to do with it. That's Sei.

Sei is an adult man who isn't very energetic. The higher-ups wanted to pretend the whole gaffe never happened by paying him a basic stipend to lounge about. But then, for some reason, he asked for a job. Even now, I still can't wrap my head around it. So they shrugged and threw him into the Funnel Department, which used to be the Accounting Department's nickname.

Nobody told him to do a thing, but he threw himself into work anyway and did all kinds of things to earn himself a good reputation, like fixing the kingdom's finances, proposing a way to stop the miasma without the Holy Maiden's purification, exposing corruption in the church, and making a school to train future employees. He gave me stuff to do as well, and my house's title even got promoted from viscount to count. I've got him to thank for that.

I was keeping an eye on Sei in case he had any hostility toward the royal family, but the opposite turned out to be true. I wouldn't be exaggerating if I called him the savior of Romany.

Not that Sei was putting in all that effort for the kingdom's sake—I bet he'd get pretty mad at me if I called him a savior. He was just trying to do his job efficiently. Well, to be precise, he had his own goal and was ticking off the steps to achieve it one by one. Sometimes he ended up spinning three or four plates at the same time. But anyway, that's not the problem here.

The problem is that the country no longer has a reason to make me spy on Sei, who is now my boss, but I still got a letter telling me to hurry up with the report.

You see, the king wants me to write him a letter. He calls it a report, but he basically just wants to hear from me. Because I'm his illegitimate son.

My mother was a low-ranked woman who worked in the palace, and when I was born, I was adopted into the Blanc family. Oh, I should mention that this isn't a huge scandal or anything. All the higher-up nobles know about it.

Me, I've thought of myself as Norbert Blanc for as long as I can remember. After I had my christening at six, the people I thought of as my parents told me about my background. Even then, I was like, "Uh, okay?" Nothing actually changed after that anyway. Every now and again I get called to formal ceremonies so I can learn my role as a retainer, and that's about it, so I kind of forget about my royal blood most of the time.

Things changed a little after I started keeping an eye on Sei, though. Before, the king and the prince (my half brother, basically) just watched me from afar at ceremonies and whatnot. Now I have more chances to see them and talk to them in person. That's all well and good, but the distance never really bothered me, and I get the impression that they're weirdly conscious of me. A part of me is like, "Um, why now, after all this time?" but if I say that, my adoptive dad will do an awkward chuckle and I'll feel like a kid going through his rebellious phase.

Anyway, that's why I'm writing this pointless report. Well, I would be if I didn't have crazy writer's block.

Sei's been juggling so many projects over these past ten months—I bet he can't take on *more* work. That's what my dumb brain assumed, at least.

Activity Report No. 34

Sei was appointed to guide the Egorovan guests on their upcoming visit. This sounds excessive for a person who already deals with a mountain of work. Apparently, he will be handling everything except for the technical magic explanations, which a member of the Sorcery Department will help him with.

I hope that you do not overburden him. Although his health has improved significantly, his constitution has never been the strongest, and the air of this world does not agree with him.

In the meantime, I have taken on his Accounting Department work.

After I wrote that down, I wondered if I sounded kind of accusatory, but oh well. I sent it off. I mean, we're talking about assigning a super important state matter to a guy who does three times the work of a normal person—*and* is frail to boot!

I mean, sure, Sei is brilliant and all. I can always rest easy when he's on the job. But can you really extend that to the whole kingdom of Romany? What are we even going to do if he goes away?

Wait. It just hit me.

"Oh, right... Sei's gonna leave someday..."

For sure he wants to go home. He was dragged here against his will, and he came up with a whole bunch of initiatives to establish a way back to his world. No duh. Who *wouldn't* want to go home in his shoes? Not to mention that this world's air doesn't even suit him. I can't imagine why he'd want to stick around.

I don't have the right to stop him.

"Huh? They want me to go to the dinner party?" Just when I was sinking my teeth into the work Sei left for me, I got a missive telling me to attend the welcoming party for the Egorovan delegation. "What about Father?"

"He's doing a mandatory inspection in the hinterlands."

"Where exactly?"

"A town called Agiral, to the northwest. It's an isolated community that hasn't had many dealings with the state. You know how it is."

I've heard of Agiral. The region was boxed in by mountains and was more of a village than a town. Not that I've been there myself.

"But what about my brother and sister?" I asked, but my adoptive mother just responded with a smile.

That's when I realized and thought *Oh, this again.*

I've been to many ceremonies throughout my nineteen years of existence. I've long since caught on to what they were about: making me serve as a retainer while teaching me about stuff "just in case" the worse came to worst. I sure hope that will never happen—I want Prince Yurius to have a nice long life. For both his sake and mine, I want him to be a great crown prince who doesn't just exist to chase after Her Holiness Yua.

Activity Report No. 35

I participated in the Egorova welcoming party.

The envoys all wore distinctively Egorovan-style clothing.

Although I merely watched them from afar, Lord Luciano walked over to the lowest seat at the end of the party and spoke to Qusta from the Sorcery Department. The young lord's guard almost immediately ushered him away, but I got the impression from the short exchange that Lord Luciano was displeased about Qusta being his guide.

On that note, I must profess my own displeasure about Sei occupying the lowest seat. Why does he deserve that when he is overseeing the entire tour? Sei said he had no issue because he has a meeting tomorrow, but the kingdom should acknowledge his achievements better, in my opinion.

I was worried about the food served at the party because his tolerance for magicules remains low, but fortunately, there was a special menu just for him. I am grateful for the consideration.

Sei was wearing an outfit at the party that made it way too obvious that Commander Indolark was staking his claim on him. I burst out laughing when I saw that—you should've seen Sei's face.

I'd asked my mother to prepare an outfit for Sei the last time there was a formal occasion. This time, Commander Indolark told me not to get involved, so I just waited to see what he would do for Sei. I've got to say, it was a riot. The color of his cuffs needed no explanation, and he was even wearing a mias lapel pin—the symbol of engagement or marriage. Once I got over my shock, I had to laugh.

It was made of super high-quality silver, and there was an amethyst in the middle referencing a certain somebody's eyes. Anyone who knows how intimate Sei and Commander Indolark are would guess at a glance that they're either engaged or married.

But judging from Sei's reaction…he didn't seem to know. It boggles my mind that he would wear such a luxurious item without knowing a thing, but then again, Commander Indolark prepared his outfit from head to toe. It felt like the commander had carved himself into Sei's very being.

Anyway, Commander Indolark has to be serious if he's sending an ignorant Sei off into a welcoming party for foreign envoys in *that* getup. I guess he really doesn't want Sei to go home.

There's only one person in this country who can implore Sei not to go home, and it's Commander Indolark. Between him and Sei, I don't know who I ought to support.

But anyway, my adoptive dad told me about the Egorovan delegation, but it turns out the third prince is leading the party. He's very talented from what I've heard, although his mother came from a viscount's house. Apparently, he was originally just meant to be a pawn to marry off for diplomatic relations, but he proved his mettle by working with the country's major industries. People said he deserved better than to be shipped out to another country when there was a faction backing him to be the next king. That's pretty darn impressive for a royal with a mother of low standing! Not that it is right of me to compare when I got adopted out to begin with.

I mean, Romany is fundamentally different because it's unified under the support of Crown Prince Yurius (which is another reason why I want him to get together with Her Holiness already), while Egorova seems to have a lot of infighting. Apparently it's a delicate issue, since the first prince is sickly and his mother comes from a count's house. Meanwhile, the second prince comes from a duke's family, which just makes things stickier. I hear the military backed him. On the other hand, Egorova derives its national identity from its technology, and it's the third prince who has the technicians in the palm of his hand… Complicated, right?

Honestly, I don't care much about foreign royal squabbles, but this was all drilled into me because of my role as a retainer. Their drama makes me appreciate how peaceful things are over here. We definitely owe some of the recent political stability and peace to Sei!

Anyway, I feel like I've seen that Luciano kid somewhere before, but where?

"Hey, Helmut, could you check this document for me?" I passed the document I made to Helmut, the director of the Accounting Department.

"Thanks, Norbert. You've been quick at your work lately."

"Huh? You think so?" I still can't hold a candle to Sei, but it feels nice to be praised.

Thanks to all the new staff, we can split a lot of work between multiple people. The guy in charge of it all juggles a lot of different stuff, but I want to help out with the Accounting Department and gather the paperwork about Egorova.

To be honest, the Accounting Department didn't used to be important, even though it operated inside the palace. I barely even thought about my job, once upon a time. Ours was famously called the Funnel Department and it really only existed for appearance's sake. So of course I never got a sense of purpose from it, and nobody expected anything of me, either. I never really thought of myself as having a role to play.

I didn't feel good about monitoring Sei when he first came. But when he kept pulling one surprise after another, I realized how fun it was to hang out with him. It was exhilarating, watching him spark a revolution. I didn't think the word "revolution" existed in my vocabulary.

Sei gave me this abacus thing and work to do. Somewhere along the way, I started thinking, "Hey, maybe I should do what he does?" and I took up a job teaching at the private school in the church. It's been fun learning to do things I couldn't do before, and I want the kids to experience that as well.

Activity Report No. 36

The members of the Egorovan delegation made a sudden visit to the church's private school. The relief house was only made aware *of this shortly before they arrived, which resulted in a great deal of internal chaos. I happened to be on teaching duty that day and was quite flustered myself. This was not because of the delegation, but because of Sei.*

Predictably, Sei gave me the harsh score of sixty-five points after he saw me at work. Nevertheless, his advice encouraged me to redouble my efforts.

I also gave my regards to Prince Lars that day. He appeared to know about me.

Although the Egorovans are staying for seven days, they have one rest day. Staying on one's feet for seven days straight would tire anyone out, I imagine. Plus, I bet they want at least a day where they can explore Romany on their own. Today is that day for them.

I thought Sei would come to the Accounting Department, but he never showed up. Apparently, he had a status report with the Prime Minister and a meeting with the guide from the Sorcery Department. Man, I wish he'd just take a break, but I get how important it is to keep track of things and plan for contingencies.

I figure he'll pull through, though. Commander Indolark is really thorough about managing Sei's health, and the Egorovans will only be sticking around for another three days. I was optimistic. So imagine my surprise when I heard the story from Vice Commander Rhoda.

"Commander Indolark went back to his family home?!"

"Keep your voice down!"

"But how? Since when? When?!"

"Oh, the day before yesterday."

So wait, he left Sei to the dogs for three whole days?! Last time the commander went away on a long trip, Sei buried himself in work and almost died! Okay, to be fair, the reason he almost died was because a heretic at the church was stirring up trouble, but his sickliness sure didn't help.

But the point is—why would Commander Indolark choose this busy time to leave Sei alone?! I got the answer later that day, when I read my adoptive father's letter.

Excuse me, Commander Indolark got a marriage offer from the Egorovan royal family?!

It makes no sense to me. The guy has such a one-track mind when it comes to Sei—I bet other people just look like rocks to him or something. So how would he get engaged to someone else? Besides, I thought he already declared to the world that he and Sei were getting married (even if it was one-sided on his part).

Father's letter went on to say that Egorova's fourth princess was the prospective partner. From what I imagine, she is in a precarious position. Maybe she is being married off to a different country because staying in Egorova is dangerous for her? It makes me wonder why they don't just adopt her into a retainer's family like they did with me, but I guess things aren't so simple for them.

Gee, I wish the royals could keep their family drama to themselves. Why do they have to throw their dirty laundry onto other nations?

Activity Report No. 37

Sei has actively continued working even when he has time off. I worry for his health.

It is my opinion that the state should offer him more support. He is involved in numerous important tasks related to our country, even while suffering from health problems due to his incompatibility with this world's atmosphere.

I asked Vice Commander Rhoda about Sei, and he said he has only glimpsed the guy from afar, though he did look tired. The kingdom really ought to be more considerate and give Sei regular health check-ups at the Medical Bureau. I can only hope that Commander Indolark will come home soon…

I prayed. I really did. But I never asked him to wake me up with a messenger bird at my dorm window at the crack of dawn.

"What took you so long?" the bird says in a deep voice when I drowsily open the window. Judging by the irritation in its tone, I can tell that it isn't a recording; the commander is speaking to me in real time.

I have to hand it to the guy who led the magically gifted Third Royal Order. I wonder if this is a waste of his abilities.

"Seiichirou ran away from home. Help me find him."

"Say what?!" What the heck is Sei doing?!

But wait, this tells me that Commander Indolark is back home now.

"Hey, shouldn't you be the one going after him?"

There is a long pause.

"He might run if I give chase, so I'm asking you."

"So, uh, did you guys have a fight?"

"……" No response.

What the heck? A lovers' quarrel, really? What a thing to wake someone up for so darn early in the morning. And hey, isn't that all the more reason for Commander Indolark to go after Sei himself? When I say as much aloud, the messenger bird gives this really skillful impression of a sulky frown.

"I think me being there will have the opposite effect."

"Aw, c'mon, how'd it wind up like that?" I ask, wondering how things could have gotten so bent out of shape after just one night with him home.

What he tells me has me clutching my head in pain.

So basically, Sei caught wind of the marriage proposal addressed to Commander Indolark, and when the commander didn't want to talk about it, they had a scuffle and Seiichirou ran out.

That's, like, the textbook definition of a lovers' quarrel. What are we even doing here?

"I have yet to reapply the barrier because of that. So be quick."

Uh, so why are lives at stake over a lovers' quarrel?

Anyway, there are only two places Sei would stay the night: the residence hall or *there*, so I rush outside before I can even do my hair. This would have been so much easier if Sei came to me first.

Just as I predicted, he's in the nap room at the Sorcery Department, which he had established himself. When I approach him, he calls me "Aresh's dog." What a low blow! I'd take his side any day over Commander Indolark's!

Listening to Sei's side of the story, it turns out that he isn't mad about Commander Indolark getting a marriage offer so much as the fact that he didn't communicate it. Which made me think...

"I see how it is... *He* thinks little of me, and so does everyone else."

"That's not true..."

There isn't a single person in Romany's royal palace who would underestimate Sei at this point, but I also know that isn't what he's getting at. Basically, what I am trying to say is...

"Yeah, Commander Indolark could have said more, but you're not being reasonable, either."

It really was a lovers' quarrel. All I can do is shrug and sigh over being tossed around by these two having a miscommunication.

Then Sei flicks me on the forehead. I really don't get him.

Activity Report No. 38

Commander Indolark has joined the Egorovan delegation as a bodyguard. He did not stay around long enough to manage Sei's condition. Despite finishing his guide duties, Sei returned to the Accounting Department, where he not only completed his work backlog but even applied himself to future tasks. I believe urgent support is necessary.

Activity Report No. 39

I will be going to Egorova.

It appeared to be an impulsive decision by Her Holiness Yua, yet apparently Sei had been making plans from the start.

I find my own presence on this journey incomprehensible. This was not the kind of support I meant. My capacity to help is limited, in my view.

Activity Report No. 40
  I write this report from inside my carriage.
  I believe that the carriage arranged by Her Holiness and Lady Erene of House Indolark is quite speedy. It is a new model, pulled along by four horses. Furthermore, we are proceeding at a considerable pace due to a reckless method proposed by Sei and implemented by Her Holiness, the assistant director of the Sorcery Department, and the vice commander of the Third Royal Order. As groundbreaking as this method may be, I cannot recommend it enthusiastically. I imagine Sei will submit the details when he returns, so I ask that you await his report.

And so I arrived in Egorova. It is my first time setting foot in another country as either a member of royalty or the nobility, but I have no time to get cold feet. I swear that mad dash shaved years off my life. God forbid a ruthless guy (read: Sei) ever join forces with a competent person. I learned my lesson: don't get involved if you know what's good for you.

I'm surprised that Luciano turned out to be Lufina, the third princess (I knew I'd seen her somewhere). But what really catches me off guard is how much the fourth princess's situation resembles mine—although in her case the royal family openly acknowledges her as one of their own. That explains why Prince Lars is so weirdly considerate toward me. I guess he sees me as a success story.

The silver-haired princess—Sofia, apparently—is sickly and low on magic, but Sei fixes that in an instant. Isn't he kinda *too* brilliant?

When did he come up with that whole plan? Isn't he doing a whole bunch of other work, too?

But anyway, he solves the problem, and Princess Sofia gets the opportunity to recuperate in Romany and contribute to a national project. So, basically, there is nothing to worry about anymore. I mean, she already has her older brother and sister, who went to such incredible lengths for her. Likewise, I had my mother, father, brother, and sister, who all cared about me even though we weren't related by blood. As long as somebody has that, they don't *really* need anything else.

So I say: "Not to worry. Long as she's got a family who loves her, she'll be just fine!"

Activity Report No. 41

Under Sei's proposal, Romany will take custody of Princess Sofia of Egorova. I am sure that there will be many details to process, but Lady Erene of House Indolark has volunteered her home for the stay. I believe that this will advance our diplomatic relations significantly.

Then, all of a sudden, a way for Sei to return to his original world appears. Apparently, the local specialties in Agiral, where Father made that agreement, will come in handy for completing the spell. Who would have thought that my family could pay Sei back for everything he's given us!

Sei's absence will be a big loss for the kingdom, and I'm going to feel lonely without him around, but it is Sei's decision to make. I made up my mind to support him no matter what he chose.

Activity Report No. 42

Sei will be remaining behind in Romany. To be precise, he chose both options: to stay and return.

It appears that a method to facilitate two-way travel has already been established. However, it is not simple to achieve due to its cost. Nevertheless, I would very much like to see the world Sei grew up in if the opportunity ever presents itself to me. I wonder what kind of world can produce a person so full of surprises.

Aresh's Homecoming

"Come in," Aresh answered the knock on the door.

Valtom the butler bowed and entered his lord's room.

"A letter has arrived from House Indolark."

Aresh's already surly face darkened further as he regarded the letter in Valtom's hand.

"From the main house?"

"No, from their mansion in the capital."

Aresh's expression cleared up slightly in relief. He took the letter and read it. The message was more or less along the lines of what he expected. Valtom must have anticipated it, too, because he told Aresh to call him whenever he was ready, and that the preparations were already done.

He also added: "Your actions this morning were somewhat immature."

Aresh did not need anyone to tell him this. Valtom was talking about how he had gone to work first thing in the morning, avoiding Seiichirou after their fight the night before. Perhaps he was also talking about how Aresh had locked himself in his room.

"I know," said Aresh, after a short silence.

"No, you do not. I speak of the lapel pin matter as well."

Aresh gritted his teeth. Few people dared to reproach him, a member of a marquess family and the current commander of the

Third Royal Order. One of those people was Valtom, who had served Aresh since his childhood.

"Young Master, if you will allow me to speak. I was overjoyed when you asked me to prepare Mr. Seiichirou's suit and lapel pin, for I thought the day had finally arrived. Milan and Pavel were of a similar mind. And then what happened? You sent Mr. Seiichirou to that dinner party without asking his opinion, and when he returned to you in confusion you started blaming him instead. Then finally, you sulked and shut yourself in your room. You are well past twenty now. Here I thought you were doing a fine job as a knight commander, but I seem to have been mistaken."

Aresh groaned. "I get it. Lay off already."

"I am pressing the issue because that is what your actions deserve. You have finally met someone with whom you wish to spend your life, and you wish for him to return the sentiment… Young Master, heed this advice from your elder. You will blunder if you rush into anything."

Valtom spoke sense, Aresh had to admit to himself as he sat in a carriage bound for the house he'd lived in until just a year ago. But Seiichirou would disappear if he did not hurry.

Because the journey was not terribly far, Aresh only calmed down right before the carriage reached its destination. When he stepped from the carriage, a familiar butler's face was already waiting for him at the entrance.

"Welcome home, Master Aresh."

The man opened the door with a respectful bow. Although it was not strong enough to qualify as "nostalgia," the familiarity of the mansion did bring back some memories. Yet Aresh had no time to wallow in emotions when an unexpected face came into view.

"Welcome back, Aresh."

"What are *you* doing here?" Aresh's frown deepened at the sight of his older sister Erene in the entrance hall. He thought she had moved out after getting married.

Although Erene was his closest sibling in terms of age, they didn't have much to do with each other these days. Partly, this was because gender differences meant that they occupied different stations in life, although Erene had always rushed to help him when they were children. Even now, she remained an indomitable figure.

"I came here because my husband is busy at work for the week. Anyway, Mother and Father are waiting for you. Put your things down and come to the reception room," she urged, leaving no room for him to get a word in edgewise.

Aresh put his luggage in his room, which was still exactly as it was when he'd left it, and headed for the reception room as he'd been told. A butler opened the door for him, and there he found Erene and a middle-aged couple sitting in the room. It was Marquess Indolark and his wife—Aresh's father and mother.

Having always been a capable and obedient child, Aresh had no recollection of being scolded by his parents. This strained atmosphere was a first for him. Seized by an unfamiliar tension, he did as he was told and took a seat—opposite his parents.

"You know why we called you, yes?" his father asked in a low voice.

Aresh did his best to keep his face blank as he responded.

The current Marquess Indolark was pushing sixty, which added up when Aresh considered the fact that he was the youngest child. A former knight, his impressive physique still retained its burliness, and his bearing exuded majesty.

"We heard the story from someone who attended the welcoming party the other day, and I must say we're surprised." The woman next to Marquess Indolark tilted her head in a girlish manner, as if she were a little bird. Her purple eyes, the same shade as Aresh's, conveyed dismay.

The marquess's wife came from a distinguished ducal lineage. Aresh had heard that his father was given permission to marry her as a reward for his military achievements. Although her appearance was beautiful, the girlishness she retained in her actions and mannerisms accentuated her charms. Yet she was certainly no young girl on the inside. She possessed all the wiles of a canny noblewoman, and her cutesy behavior actually was a trap to lower the other person's guard.

"Is it true, then, that the otherworlder was wearing your color and an accessory signifying betrothal?" she asked.

"Yes. I gifted those to him," Aresh responded in no uncertain terms. He'd never harbored any intentions of pulling the wool over his parents' eyes.

His mother brought her hands to her mouth in surprise. Even the duke, who normally showed very little emotion, was wide-eyed.

"We knew the otherworlder was under your care," said his mother. "You left the house because of him, yes?"

Indeed, it was so that he could properly keep an eye on what Seiichirou was doing and manage his health. "Yes," said Aresh.

"Yet unlike the Holy Maiden, I have heard that he has no abilities or social standing, and that he is a man of weary countenance. Is that also true?"

"It is not. Although Seiichirou—the otherworlder—does not possess special powers, and this world's atmosphere is ill-suited for his body, he is still an exceedingly capable man. He has rectified the kingdom's finances and devised countermeasures against the miasma."

"Goodness."

"I heard about that plan. Was that not Prime Minister Carvada and Count Blanc's doing?" said the marquess.

"Seiichirou was almost entirely behind the actual idea and planning. I should also add that he was the one who refined His Highness the Crown Prince and Her Holiness's idea for a private school. He is also involved in managing human resources within the palace."

The extent of Seiichirou's exploits was not public. Seiichirou himself did not want to stand out (because this would get in the way of efficiency). Others around him, including the prime minister, concealed his contributions as well.

Some of the wilier nobles were already dimly aware of this, however, and the marquess was not an exception.

"Yes... I think I did hear something along those lines..."

"So are you trying to say that you wish to marry this otherworlder for the sake of the kingdom?" his mother said.

For a moment, Aresh frowned as if he did not understand the question.

True, Aresh did first take notice of Seiichirou because he found it puzzling that an ordinary person who was unintentionally summoned to the kingdom would work in the palace for the kingdom's sake. But it turned out that Seiichirou had no lofty notion of serving the nation. He was just a workaholic.

"Well, no..." Seiichirou's compulsion made him press on even as his body deteriorated from the world's hostile atmosphere. He even relied on a life-threatening drug so that he could keep working, for pity's sake. When Aresh tried to stop him, Seiichirou complained as if *he* was the bad guy. And yet... "I was just...helping him out because it didn't feel right to let him out of my sight..."

He could not abide the thought of this unwitting victim of the kingdom's machinations perishing in this land. And so he—quite physically—connected their lives. After that, he could not bear to watch the otherworlder's body continue to weaken, but as he continued helping Seiichirou, he realized that he didn't like it when other people did the same. It did not take terribly long for him to figure out that this feeling was jealousy.

Even after Seiichirou slowly yet surely built up his magic tolerance, he would push his body past the brink. Aresh knew quite well that Seiichirou would not listen to anything he said, and he understood that the man derived fulfillment from work, so he resolved to support Seiichirou in whatever way he could.

This caught Seiichirou's attention in turn.

"My oh my!"

His mother's high-pitched voice rang out just then, making his thoughts screech to a halt.

The lady of the house was genuinely blushing like a young girl. Her cheeks were rosy red, and her eyes sparkled as she peered at him.

"Finally! It's finally happened for you! You've met your soul mate!"

"My...soul mate?"

"We never interfered, but your father and I always worried about how you never got emotional, even when you were very young. But now you've finally found somebody who stirs your heart! You cannot imagine my happiness!"

"Wait, you're actually allowing this, Mother?!" Erene stood up and shouted at their mother, who looked like she was about to break into song and dance at any second.

"What are you talking about? Aresh has found someone he truly loves, and that person returns his feelings. What is there to object to?"

"You weren't so lenient with me, remember?!"

Erene had harbored a crush on a sorcerer ever since her student days, but he never noticed her affections. Even when he finally reciprocated, his relatively lower status meant that it took quite some time before their union was acknowledged.

"We learned from your example," said their mother. "Of course we want happy marriages for our children, but what matters most is that you chose it for yourself. Also, Aresh has never been interested in anyone until now, so just him finding someone is delightful."

"I can't believe this!" Erene still seemed affronted.

For a while, she and their mother continued to argue, but then the marquess coughed and spoke to Aresh.

"But I am dismayed that we heard about this secondhand. Make sure you tell us before you take action."

"...Okay." Aresh nodded obediently. As both parents and nobles, it stood to reason that they would be unhappy about being blindsided by their child's betrothal. In truth, he and Seiichirou were not actually engaged, although sending Seiichirou to the dinner party with a mias flower accessory meant practically the same thing.

"Aresh." Their mother must have finished arguing with Erene, because she beckoned to him. When he approached her, she whispered softly into his ear: "Valtom told me the story."

Aresh gasped at this gentle utterance. So she knew that Seiichirou did not wear the lapel pin out of mutual knowledge and consent.

"You mustn't be so unscrupulous with your methods. A soul mate is not so easy to come by," she went on.

More surprises. Evidently, she supported Aresh's relationship, but this did remind him of his earlier unease.

He had tried to bind Seiichirou to him quickly so he would not return to his world. But this meant disregarding Seiichirou's thoughts and feelings. Part of the reason why Seiichirou threw himself into work was because he was a workaholic, but it was also so that he could secure a return route.

He wanted to go home.

Of course he did. Who wouldn't want to go home after being forcibly dragged to another world? Getting clout or a romantic partner wouldn't change that. Aresh wondered if his desire to tie Seiichirou to this world, heedless of the other man's feelings, was pure selfishness on his end.

Then he remembered—that Seiichirou smiled when Aresh invited him to his family's health resort once work settled down. The look on his face when Aresh proposed an idea with Seiichirou's thoughts and feelings completely in mind.

"But this is some sensitive timing." The marquess's sigh snapped Aresh out of his reverie.

"What do you mean?" Aresh asked.

It was then that he learned that a letter had arrived from the third prince of Egorova just the other day.

"He is asking whether you would be a suitable match for the fourth princess," his father said.

"The fourth princess...? I thought she was still of tender age."

Anyone who belonged to a marquess's house had the names of neighboring royalty and influential nobles drilled into them. The fourth princess was born out of wedlock only a few years ago.

"There are a lot of internal politics going on over there. It seems the plan is for her to take refuge in another country via marriage."

Being a knight commander from a prestigious family, Aresh was the ideal man for the job, apparently.

"The prince will be visiting the day after tomorrow, as a matter of fact. That's one of the reasons why I decided to call you here sooner rather than later. But given the circumstances, I suppose I'd better break the news of your engagement to him ahead of time," said the marquess, who seemed to dislike the idea of the prince going on a fool's errand.

Aresh raised a hand to stop him. "I might as well meet him. I'm not opposed to just having a chat."

"What?! But you're already—"

"You have a partner, Aresh!" his mother chimed in. "You shouldn't be sniffing out other options!"

This went without saying. Aresh was completely uninterested in being with anyone other than Seiichirou.

But there were so many things he had to do if he wanted to respect Seiichirou's feelings without letting go of him entirely. And part of that *could* be achieved if someone from Egorova gave him access.

"Don't worry. I will speak to him the day after tomorrow."

And that was how Aresh decided to meet with a prince of Egorova without asking Seiichirou—so that he could go to Egorova and find a way to travel between worlds.

Afterword

Thank you so much for picking up a copy of *The Other World's Books Depend on the Bean Counter*. I'm also grateful to anyone who came here after reading the web novel or manga adaptation.

I overthink the afterword every time. I keep trying to write something funny or witty, but it all comes out sloppy and rambly instead (looking back, the first volume's afterword was really dire). I've decided to do it properly this time.

This volume marks the end of the *Bean Counter* series.

Admittedly, there are still some loose ends. A part of me wanted to write side stories showing a glimpse of Sigma and the Holy Maiden's perspectives (the biggest go-getters in the story), but this tale is ultimately about Seiichirou and Aresh.

I started writing this story on a whim, and I certainly would not have made it this far without all my wonderful readers. It is entirely thanks to you that I was able to write three volumes about a frail white-collar worker with no powers to speak of and the knight who helps him.

Given the initial lack of romantic development between the two characters (although they do get physical, I suppose), you wouldn't think they had it in them to involve a whole bunch of people in a lovers' quarrel, eventually culminating in XXX (censored in case anyone reads the afterword before the story).

As I mentioned before, this story was supported by its readers. I would not have been able to come this far alone. I am really, truly grateful for all you have given me.

My health has not been the best lately, so I caused a lot of trouble for others when working on this volume, my editor particularly.

I must thank Kikka Ohashi, who made time in their busy schedule to draw the insert illustrations. I loved their take on Luciano's pretty boy appearance. And the cover...phew. I invite you all to remove the wraparound jacket after you finish reading the story. I am *so* grateful that even my tiniest wishes have been granted.

I'm stoked about the manga's positive reception as well. Kazuki Irodori brings such beautiful art and keen attention to detail to every chapter. I'm in awe. The manga is ongoing, so I really encourage you to pick it up. It even got an ad the other day, so now Seiichirou and Aresh have voices! The video is super well done—I hope you check it out.

Finally, I extend my deepest thanks to everyone involved in the publishing of this novel. Their hard work is the reason why this book is on shelves.

I hope we can meet again someday.

Respectfully yours, Yatsuki Wakatsu